Melissa Nathan was born and raised in Hertfordshire and now lives in north London. She is a journalist and has worked for a number of leading women's magazines. She is currently Deputy Features Editor for a national women's magazine.

Pride, Prejudice and Jasmin Field

Melissa Nathan

PIATKUS

For more information on
other books published by
Piatkus, visit our website at
www.piatkus.co.uk

First published in Great Britain in 2000 by
Judy Piatkus (Publishers) Ltd of
5 Windmill Street, London W1P 1HF
e-mail: info@piatkus.co.uk

A catalogue record for this book is available from the British Library

ISBN 0 7499 3116 7

Typeset in Bembo by Palimpsest Book Production Limited,
Polmont, Stirlingshire
Printed and bound in Great Britain by
Mackays of Chatham PLC, Chatham, Kent

To Andrew

Prologue

The television was on.

'ooh, look – it's whatsisname'
  'who?'
  'you know . . .'
  'which one?'
  'the one with the hair'
  'oh yeah – God, haven't seen him for years. What was he in? Years ago now?'
  'he was in that detective programme – what was it called?'
  'oh I know, with that woman'
  'what woman?'
  'you know the one with the um – oh – married to that actor'
  'what actor?'
  'big guy, funny eyes – oh god what was he in? That's going to really annoy me now'
  'I never knew they were married'
  'yeah (belch), pardon'

'I wish I could remember the name of that programme'
'what programme?'
'the one that bloke was in'
'what bloke?'
'you know, whatsisname'
'*who?*'
'DO YOU TWO MIND IF WE ACTUALLY *HEAR* THE PRO-
GRAMME AS WELL AS WATCH IT?'
'Sorry'
'Sorry'

Chapter 1

The tube train was stifling and packed. Jasmin Field – Jazz to her friends – couldn't read her book because someone's entire body was in her private space. Pinned to the door, she shut her eyes and imagined a cool breeze gently nudging a weeping willow as she swung lazily in her hammock. Somewhere in the distance a woodpigeon cooed and the smell of freshly cut grass wafted by. She smiled drowsily and hoped she wouldn't have to move a muscle ever again.

Then the man next to her farted and the moment was lost.

'It's Harry Noble!' shrieked someone suddenly and the squash eased as a mass of sticky bodies shot to where the words had come from. Jazz was grateful for the extra room. The train had been stuck in the station now for ten minutes – some poor bastard had fainted in the front carriage apparently. Jazz was certainly no Harry Noble groupie, but she was grateful to him because now at least she could move her book up into the right position and start reading again.

Then, as one, the entire carriage moved to the windows. Not a word was spoken, of course – this *was* the

London Underground – but a silent, almost mystic power of understanding bound everyone together. It's a common enough phenomenon when a mass of people all repress the same emotions – in this case, exhaustion, resentment and fascination – and it's one that happens every second of every day on the tube. But this time it was increased to the nth degree and you could almost hear it buzzing. Jazz looked up from her book and watched in wonder.

And then there he was.

Unbelievably, Harry Noble strode past them all, just a foot away, down West Hampstead Station's now empty platform. It was like being in a film. No one made a sound, they all just stared at him as he walked, elegant and tall, his neck straight, his eyes fixed ahead, to the exit. He *was* beautiful. Jazz was sure his lips were moving, as if he were talking to himself. He could have been on a desert island he was so wholly unaware of his audience. So *this* was the real reason the doors were still shut, surmised Jazz. No fainting passenger, just a famous one, who expected star treatment wherever he went. Suddenly, one young woman could hold back no longer – even if she was on the London Underground. She didn't care, dammit. She banged on her bit of the window and screamed, 'HARRY!' in a voice full of longing and heartache.

He didn't even turn his head. His eyes kept staring straight ahead, as if no one was there.

'HARRY!' came more voices, plaintive and hoarse.

Eventually, ever so slowly, he turned his majestic head and smiled a curt smile. And then everyone forgot their reserve. Now every carriage took its turn shouting, banging on windows and squealing as he passed them by. It was like a Mexican soundwave of passion and loss. It was quite moving, thought Jazz. And Harry Noble, of the illustrious Noble theatrical dynasty, heart-throb English actor who had gone to Hollywood and got an Oscar for his troubles, had the decency to look touched. He even winked at one girl who caught his dark, brooding eye.

And then he was gone.

There was silence for a moment and then, miracle of miracles, commuters actually started talking to each other.

'Oh my God, he's even more gorgeous in real life!'

'He winked at me! He winked at me!'

'I think I'm going to faint!'

'My daughter won't believe this!'

'He winked at me! Did you see him wink at me!'

Jazz marvelled that these people, who had unwittingly been kept in a stuffy, enclosed space for fifteen hellish minutes just so that one man could get out faster and easier than them, could make such fools of themselves. He's just a man, thought Jazz. A man who has to go to the toilet like them, who gets headaches, verrucas and wind.

Her smile widened as she wondered what these people would say if they knew she was actually about to *meet* the pompous twat. And with that thought, she returned to her book. Ten minutes later, the doors finally opened and the train haemorrhaged its dazed and sweaty passengers onto the platform.

Once out of the Underground, Jazz walked to the monstrous Gothic church at the end of a nearby road. She was meeting Mo, her flatmate, and Georgia, her elder sister, at the audition, and couldn't have moved fast in the hot, airless atmosphere engulfing north London if she'd wanted to. There was no sign of the famous Harry Noble. He must have been picked up by a limousine, she thought. Shame she hadn't been able to catch up with him – she'd have cadged a lift.

Much more of a shame, though, was the fact that she wasn't in the least bit nervous about doing this stupid audition. It would have made excellent copy for her column: she always wrote well about suffering from nerves. But she just couldn't work up a sweat about performing in front of the great Harry Noble, the director of what was intended to be the celebrity fundraising theatrical experience of the millennium – *Pride and Prejudice, An Adaptation*. She'd tried, but it was all too ridiculous. So there would be no self-deprecating humour about sweaty palms and a faltering voice. Damn. Not for the first time, Jazz cursed the fact that she could never write what wasn't true.

She was glad that she wasn't going to tomorrow's audition, which was for the steaming masses. Today's was for specially selected actors, writers and personalities as well as anyone lucky enough to be personally invited by one. As a journalist, Jazz fitted into the second category, and had chosen to invite her best friend and flatmate, Mo, to see if she could get herself a small part. Georgia, a budding actress whose career filled Jazz with sisterly pride, had also been invited along. Jazz wondered if tomorrow was purely a publicity stunt and today was the real thing. Would they really let complete unknowns work with the great Harry Noble? Seeing as they wouldn't let the great unwashed share an Underground platform with him, it seemed unlikely.

As she approached the church, Jazz could see about 100 people cordoned off outside it and she tried to ignore the thrill it gave her to force her way through and show her pass to the bouncers. The crowd didn't even look at her; they were too busy scrutinising the streets for signs of their idol.

Jazz opened the heavy door and was instantly assailed by a musty church smell. She walked down the darkened corridor and wondered if Mo and George were here yet. She hoped not – it would give her more time to watch everyone else.

She turned the corner and came face to face with a pair of glasses.

'Did we know you were coming?' asked the glasses. They were amazing. Big purple frames that almost covered their wearer's entire face. Tragically, not all of it.

'Sign your name and then go to the end of the corridor where you'll be given a script,' instructed the glasses – which, Jazz noticed, were in the company of a chunky metal brace on the top row of their wearer's teeth. Jazz blinked, fascinated. The woman looked as if she had suddenly woken up one day and thought, How can I make myself as unattractive as possible? and had come up with a damn fine answer.

Jazz signed quickly. At the end of the corridor was a trestle table peppered with piles of scripts, each one entitled *Pride and Prejudice, An Adaptation*. Jazz picked one up. She tried reading it but couldn't concentrate. She sat on one of the chairs by the wall and waited for more people to arrive. Some knew each other and there were various luvvie air kisses and much affected affection. She watched intrigued, trying to guess who was an actor and who was a fish out of water. It wasn't too difficult to make the distinction.

An actress entered. She wore a beautiful big brown fur-lined leather jacket and had a commanding presence. Her jet-black hair fell to angular shoulders, her long legs seemed to go on for ever and her eyes were like bullets. Jazz recognised her from a recent three-part thriller, in which she'd played a malicious killer. She was surprised to see that she actually looked even harder off-screen than on. The actress's name

7

was Sara something – Jazz couldn't quite recall. Jazz watched her pick up a script and read it intensely, while pacing the floor. She seemed to desperately want a part.

A group of impossibly attractive people entered the hall and one of the men among them stood out from the rest. Jazz knew him instantly – he was a household name. He was the actor William Whitby, famous for his role in the popular series *The Trials of Father Simon*. In it he played the eponymous Father Simon, a warm, loving priest who brought peace to a rough inner-city housing estate. He had sandy-coloured hair and a handsome, easy, round face, but the most attractive thing about him, Jazz decided, was that he chatted to nearly everyone in the room. He was obviously well-liked, and Jazz could see why. Although he made a lot of rather unnecessary body contact with people, he seemed sincere and likeable. He stood with his head inclined towards them, a hand gently touching their elbow while they spoke to him, or he nudged them before saying something that he followed with a big, loud, warm laugh. He seemed delightfully unaware of the effect he had on everyone he talked to. No wonder he made such a perfect priest, thought Jazz.

She found it almost impossible to tear her eyes away from the actors. How did they manage, so instinctively, to make themselves so interesting to watch? It was compelling viewing. She wanted to know everything about them, and yet oddly enjoyed this temporary stage of not knowing anyone well enough to be able to fix any significance to their actions. It was like watching a foreign film in glorious technicolour without the subtitles. She didn't want to miss a moment of it. Her eyes were everywhere. She kept trying to turn her attention to the wallflowers like herself, but couldn't do it. The butterflies were too entrancing.

A tall, blond man wandered in, looking keenly at everyone, reminding Jazz of a big golden Labrador looking for a stick. He had twinkly blue eyes and rosy cheeks. She couldn't remember what play or programme she'd seen him in, but she knew his face well. He sat down on a chair by the wall opposite her and quietly studied a script. To her surprise, the woman in the brown jacket went over and joined him. She noticed that they were intimate enough not to need to talk to each other. The woman in the jacket was then joined by a shorter, less stunning friend, who was in turn accompanied by a man whose face had had a fight with gravity and lost.

What made the whole exercise so enjoyable for Jazz, was that for the first time ever, she was able to watch people without them minding. Usually, when she people-watched, she had to do it subtly – with quick sideways glances – otherwise people started to stare back. But these actors seemed to expect her stares; in fact, some of them were happily giving Jazz her own private performance. She wondered whether, if she got up and left the room, they would, en masse, collapse in a silent, audience-less heap on the floor, waiting for the next observer to come in so that they could start again. Naturally, not one of them was wasting any time looking at *her* unknown face.

Eventually, she tore her eyes away from them and looked towards the door. There she saw a face that made her innards shrink. It certainly wasn't an unpleasant face; in fact, Jazz could still see its charms, although now they left her cold. It was a smiling, unctuous face that she could now barely tolerate. Yet at the same time, by some obstinacy she didn't understand, she couldn't take her eyes off it. It was incongruously feminine, with pale skin and full red lips and cheeks, topped with a crop of dark hair, slicked forward into the newest French style with thick Brylcreem. Of course the mouth was upturned into a forced smile, but those eyes she knew so well were darting here and there; it was only a matter of time before they alighted on her. Still she couldn't look away. All too soon, the bright eyes met hers and Jazz only detected a nano-second of consideration before they were filled with careful warmth.

'Jasmin Field, I might have guessed you'd be here,' said Gilbert Valentine, ex-colleague and now self-important theatre journalist for a small, exclusive, self-important theatre magazine. Gilbert, she knew, always liked to think of himself as a superior sort of journalist – and, indeed, as a superior sort of person – but it was common knowledge that he used his privileged position, one that enabled him to get into previews and cast parties, to supplement a spin-off career as the tabloids' primary source of luvvie gossip. He didn't do it for the money, although the money was good; he did it because it gave him the kind of fame he craved. To be famous within the most desperate circle of fame-hunters was quite an achievement.

Gilbert Valentine was dangerous. When he had first entered the theatrical world, he had, chameleon-like, adopted a camp manner to endear him to his victims. He had never been able to shake it since. Gilbert was the only 100% straight man who minced like a true thespian. And like his manner, nothing about him could be trusted. He was the sort of journalist who gave journalists a bad name, and he put all actors in a no-win situation. If they didn't invite him to their parties, he got the gossip on them anyway, through fellow-actors anxious to get on his right side. So actors were forced to treat him as a friend, which for many of them was the most successful performance of their lifetime. However, it wasn't really difficult to butter Gilbert up. All one needed to do was flatter his writing. Gilbert's Achilles' heel was his genuine insecurity about the quality of his work. He was the sort of man who couldn't wait until his obituary was published and all the quality newspapers would beat their chests for never utilising his genius themselves. It didn't occur to him that his obituary was already written and filed under *T* for *Tosser*.

'I didn't know you were an actor *manqué*!' he oozed patronisingly, as if Jazz's presence at the auditions was somehow more revealing than his. He came over and sat down next to her.

Jazz always found herself in the unhappy position of wanting to say to Gilbert, 'Likewise', but knowing that it would only belittle her. It was incredibly frustrating.

Instead she smiled and said simply, 'Well, now you know everything.'

'Oh, hardly everything,' he simpered. 'How are things at your lovely little women's mag?'

Jazz decided not to mention the trivial fact that *Hoorah!* her 'little women's mag' had roughly three-quarters of a million more readers than his. Instead, she took a big breath and answered composedly, 'Lovely thanks.'

'Oh good, good,' he smarmed.

'And how are things in the artistic world of theatre journalism?'

Gilbert sighed heavily, rubbed his eyes with his podgy, pale hands and just remembered in time not to brush them through his Brylcreemed hair. Jazz began to worry that he might be auditioning for the part of Darcy.

'*Extremely* harrowing. Nobody appreciates the work we do. But,' he admitted bravely, 'I love it. Couldn't be without it.'

'Of course you couldn't.'

'Yes, you know me so well.'

11

Jazz nodded sadly.

He patted her hand. She moved it to scratch a suddenly itchy cheek.

'So tell me, what part do you want?' he asked.

Jazz laughed. 'Oh, I'm just here for the experience.'

'Aha!' exclaimed Gilbert, pointing an accusing finger at her. 'You're using it for copy in your column! "Working with Harry Noble." Like it! Well done, that girl! I did exactly that for a piece last year when they opened up auditions to the public for *Where's My Other Leg?* at the Frog and Whippet. It was a *very, very* funny piece. *Very* funny.'

Jazz impressed herself by managing a smile. She knew she didn't need to ask Gilbert why *he* was here. Just sitting in this church hall he had surrounded himself with people who were scared of him and could make him money at the same time. And she knew that deep down he had always wanted to be an actor, like so many arts journalists before him, and doubtless many after him.

'Of course,' said Gilbert silkily, 'you do realise I almost know Harry Noble personally.'

Jazz raised her eyebrows questioningly and Gilbert needed no more prompting.

'Well, you know that his aunt, Dame Alexandra Marmeduke,' here Gilbert cast his eyes downwards as if she were dead, or a saint or something, 'is the patron of our magazine? Without her, my life would have no purpose. No other publication, as you well know, has quite the same reverence for the theatre as we.' Jazz winced. 'I owe her my livelihood and therefore my life. She's a spectacular woman. And her 1930s' Ophelia . . .' he closed his eyes as he savoured the memory '. . . was an all-time great. No one has *ever* surpassed it,' he whispered in hushed reverence.

12

Jazz nodded, wondering if that was the version where Ophelia wore a wig that looked like a dead octopus.

'But of course,' continued Gilbert, when he had quite recovered, 'she and her nephew' – he paused for effect – 'Do Not Speak.'

Jazz's eyes lit up. Inside information! 'How come?' she asked.

'Didn't you know?' said Gilbert, delighted. Strictly speaking, he was aware that he shouldn't impart such a valuable piece of gossip to a fellow journalist without consulting terms first, but the temptation to impress Jazz proved irresistible. And anyway, it had always frustrated him that he could never actually make any money on this one – he couldn't risk Dame Alexandra finding out that he had been the source of such information. But, one day, who knew? He could receive payment of another kind from Jazz . . .

'Well, strictly *entre nous,*' he began, as he always did when about to sell a gem to a hack, 'they had a furious family row years and years ago. That part's common knowledge within the theatrical world, but nobody – and I mean Nobody – knows the details quite like myself. Not many have had to visit Dame Marmeduke's Devon cottage. If I didn't work for that *wonderful* woman, I'd have sold this for a fortune, my dear. A *fortune.*'

Jazz started to grin mischievously and her eyes twinkled. She'd never heard this one.

Gilbert was just about to launch into the story when, to Jazz's extreme frustration, he sat back and stared at her, much in the same way one would eye a painting.

'You know, it's an absolute living, breathing *joy* to see you again,' he said, emphasising each word as if someone, somewhere, was writing down everything he said. 'You look *ravishing*.'

Just when she thought she was going to have to get up and run out screaming, Jazz caught sight of her smiling sister George, coming towards her. She introduced George to Gilbert, hoping that somehow she could get him back to spreading malicious gossip and away from 'joy', 'ravishing' and, indeed, breathing.

'Ah yes, the *working* actress,' cooed Gilbert, standing up and kissing George on both cheeks. He was obviously impressed by what he saw, although he did manage to say the word 'working' as though it was an insult.

Jazz explained to her sister how she knew Gilbert and hoped that George would have forgotten the many midnight conversations she had bored her with over her crush on him at her first job on a local paper. She also hoped George would vanish until her work here was done. Gilbert, luckily, adamantly refused to move from Jazz's side, leaving a polite George no choice but to sit down next to him, rather than edge past him to the free seat on her other side. Gilbert seemed to have no idea that he was in any way unwanted company for George. Instead he made lots of comments to the purpose of being a thorn between two roses, a comment he felt sure would delight Jazz.

Jazz winked at George and worked on Gilbert.

'So,' she said, forcing herself to look him in the eye, 'it would be worth a fortune, would it, this piece of gossip?'

Gilbert smiled. It was rather charming having Jasmin Field's attention. Made him feel rather warm, rather nostalgic. He decided he didn't want to let go of it just yet.

He pretended to look at her afresh. 'You know, I can't believe it's been so long,' he said, shaking his head at her.

'You should have called me. We could have done lunch.' A pause. 'Or something.'

With a fixed smile on her face, Jazz turned to the church door while racking her brains for a way to get the subject back to Harry Noble and his aunt. She knew that it probably wasn't ever going to be usable in her magazine, but she couldn't quell her natural journalistic instinct to try and get to the bottom of this. She loved to know more about people than they supposed she knew.

Just then, she saw her flatmate Mo walking towards her, looking unusually sullen. It was only when Mo got nearer that Jazz could see that it was, in fact, terror written all over her face, and not moroseness.

'Hi,' grimaced Mo, when she reached Jazz. She didn't notice Gilbert, who had in any case turned his attention to George. Mo squeezed herself past Gilbert and George and sat down heavily next to Jazz. She looked awful. After a long, deep sigh, she turned to Jazz.

'You haven't got a Portaloo on you, by any chance?'

'I knew I'd forgotten something,' smiled Jazz. 'You'll be fine. Just pretend you're teaching.'

'Oh – and that doesn't terrify me?'

Mo got up immediately and went to find the toilet. Jazz started to read the script, intrigued to see how *Pride and Prejudice* had been transformed into a play. The Jane Austen classic had been her all-time favourite book as a schoolgirl, and the young heroine, Elizabeth Bennet, was, without doubt, one of her favourite fictional heroines. Like many a sensitive, intelligent teenage girl, she had spent countless oppressive afternoons in a stuffy English classroom, dimly aware that a teacher was explaining Austen's use of plot, while fantasising that she was Lizzy Bennet – feisty, pretty, proud and poor.

They just don't write 'em like that any more, she thought to herself wistfully as she read the scene.

The excerpt chosen for the auditions was the explosive scene in which the hero, Mr Darcy, stuns Elizabeth by proposing to her for the first time. Jazz read it through and started to feel her heart pound against her ribcage: it was very well-written.

'It's a classic tale of intrigue, money and notorious family pride,' said a voice next to her. Jazz tried to look up, but couldn't tear herself away from her script.

'I said it's a classic tale of intrigue, money and notorious family pride. And it's yours for one smile.'

Gilbert was back online.

With an effort, Jazz looked up and gave him her best 'I'm listening' smile. It worked.

He inched closer. 'There was this *massive* Marmeduke and Noble family row years and years ago. Aunt Alexandra wanted our Harry to leave home and live with *her* instead of his parents when he was a child.'

Jazz frowned. 'Why?'

Gilbert paused. It was the first time he'd ever considered this to be an unusual thing for an aunt to do. Eventually, he shrugged. 'Because she's barking. Wealthy luvvies, you know,' he enlarged, gaining in confidence enough to start philosophising about something he knew nothing about, 'do bizarre things like that.'

Jazz nodded briefly.

'Anyway,' said Gilbert, 'she offered to pay for the best tuition in the country, give him everything money could buy – *everything* that his parents couldn't give him.'

Jazz was beginning to enjoy this.

'Wow,' she said quietly.

'Yes,' smiled Gilbert, 'it's good, isn't it? You see, Alexandra had made her fortune as an actress and she'd always hated the fact that her little sister, Katherine – Harry's mother – had given up her career to become Wife and Mother. Alexandra was an early feminist. Told you she was barking.' He corrected himself. 'Wonderful, of course,' he said quickly, 'but eccentric, shall we say.'

Jazz's teeth began to grind.

'And she resented Harry's father Sebastian even more for being an excellent actor,' continued Gilbert, in full flow, 'but one who was never in anything that made him or his family any money. Alexandra felt he should have provided better for her baby sister – accepted TV ads as well as RSC roles, that sort of thing – but Sebastian would never stoop to it. So, she thought they were irresponsible parents and she'd do a much better job of bringing up their child.'

'What made her so amazingly arrogant?' asked Jazz, fascinated.

'Well,' sighed Gilbert sympathetically, 'she was almost fifteen years older than Katherine and had rather mothered her during her childhood. Katherine had always idolised her older sister, and had gone into acting to be like her. Alexandra couldn't quite get used to the fact that little Katie could give it all up – and hence, give up idolising *her* – for a mere man. Took it as a big rejection. Never forgave Sebastian – never.'

He paused dramatically.

'Minto, anyone?' came a voice from behind Jazz.

Jazz turned to Mo and shook her head impatiently. Mo was nervous, she knew the signs. Frequent trips to the loo, witless interruptions and offers of Mintos. She should try and calm her down, but Gilbert's story was getting good. She loved a good yarn.

When Gilbert had her attention again, he explained: 'Adopting little Harry would have been a way for Alexandra to recapture control of Katherine's life, you see. She was a complete control freak – still is.'

'And did it work?' asked Jazz.

'Nope. Sadly, it had exactly the opposite result. It sounded the death knell for Alexandra and Katherine's relationship.'

Jazz nodded. That made sense.

By the time Mo had returned from another trip to the toilet, Jazz was so engrossed in Gilbert's story that the distant sound of female screams from outside the church made no impact on her.

Harry Noble had arrived.

By the time she'd noticed the hush and looked up, Harry Noble had already walked past her and was on his way to a big black door leading to the audition room. Every head in the room was turned towards him. Jazz didn't get much of a chance to watch him go, but she caught a quick glimpse and it was enough for her to spot the same manner of striding past his fans, the same jeans, the same jacket. It made her feel she knew him somehow. He put his hand on the door handle, turned round to the room and spoke in a deep, clear, velvety voice.

'The first two in five minutes,' he said. And with that he was gone.

There was silence for a moment and then everyone started talking at once.

'I think I need the loo again,' said Mo.

Chapter 2

'Who's that girl with Georgia Field?' asked the actress in the leather jacket, Sara Hayes, to her new bosom friend Maxine.

Maxine looked over. 'Which one?'

'The pretty one. Next to Georgia.'

'I don't know,' said Maxine. 'The other two can't be actors. Unless they're character actors.'

They smirked.

'Do you think she's Georgia Field's sister?'

'The one who's a journalist? I think she may be. They've got the same nose.'

'Ye-es,' said Sara thoughtfully. 'Although she just doesn't have It like Georgia does. Maybe if she were blonde . . . She'd vanish in a snowstorm, she's so pale. And she's fatter than Georgia.'

'Oh, she's not that bad,' said Maxine. 'She's just curvy. Some men like tits and arse.'

'Yes,' said Sara, 'but they're all over sixty.'

Maxine smiled. 'She's got fuller lips than Georgia.'

'Mmm,' nodded Sara. 'Very eighties.'

Happily unaware that she was being scrutinised by the actress and her friend, Jazz was busy observing their smiling, blond companion. His large blue eyes, which were admittedly flitting around a fair bit, seemed to alight on George rather often. And while there, she saw in them that dazed expression she so often noticed in men watching her sister. It was like a friendly rabbit caught in the headlights. She liked him, she decided instantly.

Every time two more people had gone inside to audition, Mo had told herself that she'd go in next. Every time they had come out, her body had told her not to be so rash. Jazz finally forced her in with the threat of making her do the washing-up for a month.

Seven minutes later she re-emerged, a pack of unfinished Mintos still visible in her tightly clenched fist.

'That man is a bastard,' she said coldly. 'I'm going home.'

Gilbert started to stand up slowly, as if to stretch his legs.

'Suppose I'd better give it a whirl,' he said with a grin. 'So to speak.'

'So that's it then?' asked Jazz, keen to find out as much of Gilbert's story as possible. 'A simple family feud?'

Gilbert sat down again.

'Oh no, it gets much better,' he said. Jazz noticed that every time Gilbert started up the story again, he got closer to her. Any more interruptions and he'd be sitting on her lap.

'Give them their due,' he went on, 'Harry's folks actually let him – their only son – make the choice. Told him that his aunt was rich and could give him more than they ever could, blah blah blah. They were big on children being treated like small adults –' here he stopped to interrupt himself. 'Whole bloody lot of them are barking, if you ask me.'

Jazz unclenched her jaw, which had gone numb.

'Upshot was young Harry refused her offer. Not just refused it but, unbeknown to his parents, he wrote her a stinking letter, as only a twelve-year-old boy can. Well, you can imagine the effect *that* had,' he said proudly.

Jazz couldn't. Gilbert elaborated for her.

'An eccentric, hypersensitive, control-freak luvvie being told by a twelve-year-old brat that she's a fat old cow.'

Jazz gasped. How *did* Gilbert get this kind of information? From the fat old cow's mouth?

'Well,' said Gilbert with a finishing flourish, 'that was it for the Marmeduke and Noble entente cordiale. Fin*ale*, as we say in the trade.'

Jazz nodded slowly. So! she thought to herself. The adored Harry Noble had one very bitter enemy.

'With no encore,' added Gilbert.

Jazz nodded again.

'Curtain.'

'Yes, I see,' said Jazz firmly, realising that nodding was not doing the trick.

Then the audition door opened and in a moment, Gilbert was gone.

Jazz tried to lean back and unwind, but she couldn't get rid of the tension in her body caused by spending some of her quality time with a moron.

George went in next. She came out twenty-five minutes later with a big grin on her face.

'That was amazing. He's going to be a brilliant director,' she beamed. 'Tough, though. God, I hope I get a part.' And with a quick glance over at the blond rabbit in the headlights, to check that he was still looking, she sat down next to Jazz to dissect the audition.

Jazz's stomach was starting to feel as tense as the rest of her body, but she was determined to stay until the end. It would give her more to write about.

After Gilbert had come out of his audition, he had spent some time chatting to all the hopefuls he knew and loved. Quite a while later, he came to say goodbye to Jazz.

'How did your audition go?' she asked, with a healthy vested interest.

'Oh, you know,' said Gilbert, affecting indifference, though looking rather shaken, 'I'm only doing it for the work possibilities. Couldn't miss an opportunity like this.'

'Are you a spy for Dame Alexandra?' gasped Jazz.

'Hush, my dear,' said Gilbert, suddenly nervous. 'Good Lord no. If *she* knew I was here, I'd be out of a job in no time. Oh no,' and a slow smile appeared on his lips, 'she has no idea, lives in her little cottage, happily filling her scrapbooks and feeding Revenge and Sweet.'

'Eh?' said Jazz, her eyes wide.

Gilbert sat down next to her again, unable to hide a grin. This time he was so close that his thigh was pressed against hers, and his mouth was so near that if Jazz turned round too quickly they would, in some parts of the world, be technically married. She decided the best policy was to freeze rigid and keep her eyes down.

'That's the best part of the whole story,' he whispered urgently, his breath ice cold on her neck. 'The part that nobody else knows but me. Alexandra hasn't spoken to the Noble family for twenty years. And she has fifty scrapbooks of cuttings on them all, starting with the infamous letter from twelve-year-old Harry. She won't let anyone mention their name in her presence and has called her two Persian cats Revenge and Sweet.'

22

To Jazz's relief, Gilbert inched away so that he could register her shock and awe.

'*Twenty* years,' he repeated. '*Fifty* scrapbooks. *Fifty*.'

Ooh, thought Jazz. That was almost worth having to sit through. Cats and scrapbooks — spooky. However, if she didn't get up soon, she would lose sensation in the leg Gilbert was practically sitting on.

'Right, well. I suppose I'd better go in soon,' she said and leapt up away from him. 'Just going for a walk, get rid of my nerves. Bye then.' It didn't work. Gilbert sprang up to give her a big, wet kiss very near her lips. '*Ciao*, honey. Break a divine leg.'

She watched him walk away and sat straight back down to finally give her script a proper read. Eventually she and George were the only ones left, except for Purple Glasses, who was by now tidying the scripts.

George was finally ready to leave. 'I must go — I'm seeing Simon tonight,' she said, working up to a smile.

Jazz looked at her sister. 'What, Action Man? Swivel hips, roving eye, no genitals?'

'I wish you wouldn't call him that, Jazz.'

'Sorry. How about Fuckwit?'

'Jazz. That's not funny.'

'I know,' sighed Jazz loudly. 'Sorry. I'm just nervous,' she lied. She'd rather eat her own heart than hurt George intentionally.

George didn't reply. Jazz studied her sister. Tragic, she thought sadly. Congenitally unable to enjoy life without a boyfriend.

They both stood up and smiled the short, wistful smile they used when they disagreed about something. As George walked out, Jazz walked silently to the audition door. It was ajar. She was about to knock to remind them she was still there, but for some reason decided not to.

The soft sound of conversation came from inside.

Matt Jenkins, the producer, a short man in a bulky anorak and sneakers, had joined Harry halfway through the auditions and Sara Hayes had never come out since her audition. Her staccato laughter had punctuated the intervals between each victim.

'Dross of the highest order,' boomed Harry's voice. 'The only cast this lot could play is a plaster cast.'

'Really?' Sara's voice, genuinely hurt.

'Come on, Harry, it can't be that bad.' Matt's voice.

'It's worse. I've seen better acting from sitcom sets. The nearest thing we've got to Darcy is a five-foot-four actuary – unless I succumb and give it to that poisonous hack they call a theatre critic – and not a single Lizzy in sight.' He threw his pencil on to his desk. 'It would damage my reputation to be seen at the same *nightclub* as most of these people, let alone direct them in a play.'

Jazz shut her eyes tight and committed everything he'd said to memory. This was too good not to use one day.

'Think of what this charity work would do for your reputation, Harry. Something like this is sure to make you the golden boy in Hollywood, as well as our tabloids, for *ever*. Hollywood *loves* London actors at the moment. Put that together with fundraising and they'll want to make you President.'

'I don't want to be President, Matt.'

Matt wasn't listening. 'It's just a shame their golden boy Tim Shanks couldn't take a break off filming to be Darcy. Everyone loves him. We'd have had them queuing as far as the Finchley Road if we'd got *him*. We'd have bloody cured

24

cancer with that! But if you play your cards right, Harry, we could get the nearest thing: someone everyone hates. Poison Pen Peters has more enemies than he has blackheads. People will be *longing* to see him fail – they'll come in their droves. And, as a nice little bonus, Harry my boy, if you give him Darcy, you need never worry about a first night again in your life. It couldn't be better.'

During the pause that followed this impassioned speech, Jazz found herself thanking her lucky stars that Matt and Harry hadn't been referring to Gilbert when they mentioned the word 'hack', but of course, were talking about the most feared man in theatre, critic Brian Peters.

'Anyway,' continued Matt, after he'd let all that sink in, 'you haven't seen everyone yet.'

'Who else is there?' sighed Harry.

A pause indicated that the three of them had caught sight of Jazz, who was by now standing just outside the door, facing away from them. She froze and tried to pretend she was invisible, which seemed easy with her eyes half-closed. They had no idea she could hear every word they were saying.

After a moment, the voices started up again.

'More of an Ugly Sister than a Lizzy Bennet,' said Harry laconically, at which Sara burst out into a loud and delighted laugh. 'I wouldn't give her a lift in my car, let alone a part in my play,' he went on, warming to his theme. Laughing again, Sara shushed him so loudly that for a moment Jazz thought the Thameslink had entered the church.

Jazz opened her eyes wide and found herself staring at a noticeboard with some Psalms pinned up next to an advert for a charity cake sale.

Too stunned to move, too angry to breathe, she was still

there when Matt Jenkins opened the door wide and stood grinning at her.

He was still wearing his anorak. He was about one inch shorter than Jazz, with thin, tufty hair, small, blinking eyes, no neck and a long, thin nose that twitched nervously. He looked like a Womble.

'I'm afraid I'll have to be your Darcy,' he said, his earlier confident tone now somewhat diminished.

'Oh,' she said, and followed him in. If he can do Darcy, she seethed silently, I can do Lizzy. Hell, if he can do Darcy, I can do *Elvis*. Her spirits rallied.

The room was the size of a small shopping mall. She strode up to the desk where Harry was perched, with his back to her, looking out at the view of rooftops. She crossed her arms and waited for him to turn round, her breathing shallow from the sudden shock of discovering what he thought of her. Sara was staring at her with an infuriatingly knowing smile. Infuriatingly, Jazz knew why. Eventually, with a monumental sigh, Harry turned round.

'Name?' he asked, without looking up at Jazz.

'Jasmin Field,' she managed.

He scraped his chair back noisily, lowered himself into it with effort, and wrote down her name. Then he stopped and looked at what he'd written.

'Georgia's sister?'

'Yes, that's right,' said Jazz, barely controlling her fury. 'The ugly one.'

Sara pretended not to be able to hold back a stifled guffaw, but to Jazz's increasing anger, Harry didn't even look up as he fiddled with his papers. He obviously hadn't even heard her.

Jazz's nerves and anger zoomed into adrenalin mode. Her

26

heart was thumping so hard she thought it might leap on to the table.

'Right,' said Harry, in a thoroughly bored tone, as if he was reading a shopping list. 'Lizzy doesn't realise Darcy is in love with her, she's surprised when he appears at the door—'

'Yes, I know the story,' cut in Jazz.

Harry paused.

'Right. Off you go then.' He crossed his arms, leaned back and scrutinised her properly for the first time. Jazz preferred it when he was ignoring her.

She took a deep breath, turned her back on him as rudely as she could and walked to the end of the room, telling herself this would all be over in ten minutes and then she could buy herself a chocolate bar the size of a house. With her back still to the desk, she closed her eyes for a second and imagined herself in an Empire-style dress. Unconsciously, her shoulders dropped and her chin lifted. She turned round slowly, walked back to the middle of the room, and with as much confidence as she could muster, she sat herself down with one swift movement that managed to make her look inches taller.

Matt Jenkins rushed into the room – quite an alarming sight with his flat feet. Lizzy was all astonishment.

Matt Jenkins paced the room, the toggles of his anorak flapping wildly and his elbow jerking out at right angles from his body due to an unfortunate nervous tic. Lizzy sat stiffly on the chair, staring in quiet bewilderment at him. Was this for real?

Matt Jenkins paced back and forth, toggle in mouth, stopped, read his script, twitched and then eventually asked her to allow him to tell her how much he admired her and loved her. Then he insulted her family and took the toggle out of his mouth. Lizzy's dark eyes widened as she tried to hide her mortification. If she'd have had scissors on her, she'd have cut off his toggle and fed it to him. Matt Jenkins insulted her personally, sneezed and apologised. Lizzy looked horrified as he wiped his nose on his anorak sleeve. Matt Jenkins' neck went rigid as he told her he loved her profoundly, asked her to put him out of his misery and consent to be his wife, picked his ear and looked at it.

Lizzy's face was utter disbelief.

Slowly and stonily she collected herself and answered Matt Jenkins, explaining that she had done nothing to excite these feelings and could not accept them. Once or twice, her voice failed her as the humiliation of the situation overcame her.

Matt Jenkins nodded firmly, twitched, jerked his head disconcertingly, then turned two pages over at once. He said, 'whoops,' wiped his sweaty brow and then demanded to know why he had got such a rude answer.

Lizzy, her voice growing in strength with her confidence and anger, assured him quietly but firmly that there were two reasons. One, he had been instrumental in breaking the heart of a much-beloved sister and two, he had ruined the life of a certain Mr Wickham.

Matt Jenkins started shifting his weight from left foot to right and noted that she took a great interest in that man. He peered closer at his script, took a deep breath and read that perhaps he should have pretended *not* to have been in any doubt about proposing to someone whose family's position was so much further below his own. His left shoulder hunched suddenly to his ear in a spasmodic twitch of tension. Then in a split second, his right elbow shot out to his side and back again.

Lizzy fixed him with a steely eye and clenched her teeth,

sharpening her cheekbones even more. She explained clearly, and with a quiet force, that far from preventing her from accepting his hand, that had only made it easier for her to care less about hurting him. In a voice like iron wrapped in velvet, she used this perfect opportunity to vent her hurt feelings and told him that from the very first time she had met him she had found him unpleasant. He was the last man she could *ever* want to marry. Her voice broke and her eyes shone with injured pride as she went on to tell him he was arrogant, rude and self-satisfied, and that even if he had acted in a more gentlemanly-like manner, her answer would have always been the same.

Relieved beyond belief that they had reached the end, Matt Jenkins said 'Rightie ho,' beamed at Harry, tapped his watch and scarpered from the imaginary stage.

Lizzy, stunned, angered, confused and exhausted, stood up to start pacing but realised she felt too weak. As Matt Jenkins did a scene-hogging Scoobydoo-tiptoe to the front corner of the room, Lizzy sat down heavily again, put a hand to her heaving chest, closed her eyes, let a tear fall down her cheek and an unexpected sob escape.

The sound of her sniffing filled the audition room.

Slowly Jazz took a tissue out of her pocket and blew her nose loudly.

Eventually Harry spoke. 'Have we got your phone number?' he asked quietly.

Jazz looked up at him. He was staring intently at her. 'No,' she said dully. 'I wasn't asked to give it.'

'That's all right, we'll get it off your sister.'

She waited for a while, and looked at Matt Jenkins. He smiled back and winked at her. Then his shoulder twitched again and his elbow shot out from his body, leaving his hand on his waist. No one took any notice. Good God, thought Jazz, alarmed. Any minute now, he's going to break into *Riverdance*.

She was surprised at how exhausted she felt. Harry was still scribbling but Jazz decided she'd had enough. She didn't care if he was planning to try and direct her like he had George, she was ready to go home.

'Bye then,' she said to Matt.

'Ta-ra,' he said jovially, his nose now the only part of him that was moving out of context. 'You were rather good.'

Jazz thanked him, knowing she was not enough of an actress to return the compliment. She looked at Harry. He was still writing. She walked out, humming determinedly, without glancing at Sara Hayes.

Chapter 3

'Anyway, thanks for the mango, George,' said Mo and they all started chortling weakly. Jazz could still taste toffee at the back of her teeth and Mo had just eaten most of a packet of chocolate eclair sweets. George, who had polished off the marshmallows, joined in guiltily.

They all looked at the unpeeled mango that Georgia had brought round. It lay on the coffee-table, surrounded by lots of brightly coloured sweet wrappers. They just couldn't be bothered to peel it.

'A mango is like a man,' decided Mo.

'Why?' asked George.

'Because it's too much effort to open up and has a heart of stone.'

Jazz smiled. 'You forgot "And it tastes like shit to swallow and it's always you who has to wipe up afterwards".'

Mo snorted the remains of the last eclair up her nose.

'I love mangos,' smiled George happily.

They all turned to watch the mute TV for a moment.

The flat in West Hampstead belonged to Mo. It was bright, cosy and well-worn. She'd bought it five years ago, just before the latest boom, when her mother had died and left her a substantial amount of money.

Jazz loved living there. She could be in the heaving metropolis of central London in fifteen minutes and in Brighton in half an hour on the Thameslink. And she could be with Mo when she needed good company or stay in her room with its sofa and heaving book shelves when she needed space. What's more, George lived five minutes away in the next road. Jazz was delighted with her home.

George pulled her face away from the TV screen.

'Did you see that gorgeous blond bloke at the auditions?' she asked.

Mo shook her head. 'Nope. I was too busy wondering when, how and where I was going to be sick.'

Jazz knew exactly who George was talking about. Maybe Action Man was on his way out, she thought hopefully. She turned her gaze away from a tap-dancing tube of toothpaste and a happy set of sparkling white teeth doing a Busby Berkeley number. It wasn't easy. She looked at her sister.

'Why don't you chuck Simon?' she suggested bravely.

George grimaced. 'I'm too scared.'

'Of what?'

'I don't want to hurt him.'

Jazz wasn't sure if that was an answer or a new thought. She suspected the latter.

'How many bastards have hurt you?' demanded Mo.

'Exactly,' said George. 'I'll know how awful he'll feel.'

'George,' interrupted Jazz. 'How long have you been going out with him?'

'Three and a half months.'

Only Jazz's sympathy for her sister could have stopped her from laughing out loud.

'Chuck him, girl,' she said firmly but kindly. 'I know he'll probably never find anyone as lovely again, but he *will* get over it.'

George's large white-blue eyes looked at the carpet. 'I'll wait until he chucks me,' she said quietly.

Mo and Jazz erupted.

'Chuck him!' they both shouted.

'OK!' shouted George back, shutting them up.

She pulled her long legs under her little bottom, as if making herself smaller would somehow improve things. Jazz watched her. Her naturally fair hair suited her highlights so well and her skin went a stunning honey colour after just one sun-bed session every six weeks. She had no hips to speak of, a pretty bust, a concave stomach and the rest of her was golden skin and delicate bones. Perfection. Very occasionally when Jazz looked at her, for a split-second it was like looking at her reflection, only in technicolour and on a thinner, taller scale. Jazz's hair was much darker than her sister's and her figure more rounded. Whereas George had the kind of tall, androgynous body that the media and fashion world adored, Jazz had what was known as The Winslet Body – that is, a body that the media and fashion world trumpeted as obese but that men seemed to like well enough. Jazz also had their father's translucently pale skin and his deep chestnut eyes. She often wondered wistfully if, had she been born with George's vivid colouring, she'd also see the world in bright primary colours. But as for envying George's figure, Jazz wouldn't have known how to. That was one thing Martha – mother to George, Jazz and their younger sister, Josie – had taught her girls. With her splendid bosom, gloriously rounded bottom and shapely ankles, Martha had given each one of her very different daughters a priceless gift – the gift of loving their

33

bodies. By example alone (and some very choice words at sensitive, adolescent times), she had taught them how to celebrate their own shape. She'd left it up to the world around them to present it as something to be ashamed of.

They all stared at the telly in silence, Jazz wondering how she could open up the conversation again. But within seconds her concentration was diverted by the images on the screen.

George sat up and pointed. 'Oh look – it's Andrew! I was in *Lysistrata* with him in Cardiff!'

'Have you had him?' asked Mo.

George smiled a confessional smile. Jazz shook her head in amazement. Was no actor safe?

Before yesterday's audition, all Jazz and Mo had wanted to know about the Gala charity play was the address of the audition and the measurement of Harry Noble's inside leg. Now they had both, they wanted more information.

'It's a one-off, one-night play in aid of breast cancer research, to be performed at the King George Theatre in the West End,' explained George, in an excited rush. 'Part of a massive theatrical bonanza-type thingy. The *Pride and Prejudice* part is semi-professional, with a complete range in the cast from unknowns to working actors, journalists, novelists and artists. Then the next night there'll be a pantomime with soap stars and on the last night they'll be doing *It's A Knockout* with all the country's news presenters. They say they're going to get Jeremy Paxman in a Daffy Duck outfit. So our bit is the only bit that's serious acting. But what makes it so different from all the other charities is that the *audience* will be full of celebrities and the *cast* will contain some ordinary working people for a change. Get the celebs to actually pay the money this time – that's the twist. They'll edit the highlights for a TV programme and the cameras will be on the audience as much as – if not more than – the stage.' George ignored Mo's gasp of terror. 'And the way to get such a star-studded audience was to ask Harry Noble to direct. Every actor wants to see his work. It's a massive coup. Apparently they managed to get him because his great-aunt died of the disease.'

'And his Great British Public want to see him doing something good,' added Jazz. She told them how she had heard the producer, Matt Jenkins, telling Harry that this would enhance his reputation in Hollywood and the tabloids.

'Are you going to put that in your piece?' asked Mo eagerly.

Jazz shook her head. Much as she detested Harry's hypocrisy, that wasn't her style. She was a journalist and columnist for the popular women's weekly *Hoorah! The women's magazine with a difference.* She didn't waste her time writing celebrity gossip, although that didn't stop her being fascinated by it.

Jazz had the perfect personality for a columnist. Where George was ready to give everyone the benefit of the doubt, Jazz was happy to give them the benefit of her wisdom. She was highly judgmental of everything and everyone. She could spot bluff at a hundred paces. She couldn't help it, it was like a sixth sense. But most importantly for a columnist, Jazz was very emotional and easily riled. Her weekly tirades were a unique blend of heartwarming tales about her perfect family and home life, mixed with apoplectic opinions about society's foibles. Her columns were highly popular with the readers. She felt fairly sure she had a future, with or without *Hoorah!* It was just a case of waiting to be snapped up by a broadsheet and never having to do a proper day's work again.

'Is Harry Noble always going to be that terrifying?' asked Mo.

'No more than your average pretentious, egocentric actor,' grinned Jazz at George. Jazz had interviewed so many celebs over the years that she wasn't remotely in awe of them any more. Apart from the odd one or two who showed a genuine interest in the stranger to whom they were pouring out their one-dimensional hearts, she had found that most of them were self-obsessed and pathetic. But she'd never interviewed anyone nearly as famous as Harry Noble; he was way out of her league. He was A-list, while she had only ever done strictly B- and C-list actors. And of course, he was a member of the famous Noble dynasty – a whole family of celebrated Shakespearean actors and part of England's heritage. Harry though, had been the first Noble to break into Hollywood.

Jazz had been impressed by every performance he'd done; even the cameo role he'd performed in a tacky American sitcom had had class. And he had shone at the Oscars. She thought he was a truly wonderful actor. And she'd been delighted to discover that in real life, he was every bit as abominable as she'd expected.

The next morning, Jazz sat at her computer in *Hoorah!*'s features department, her eyes unfocused and her mind free-wheeling. She'd finished *'I married my poodle!'* in only two hours and was trying desperately to think of a way into this week's column.

Miranda, the junior researcher, was tapping away furiously at her wretched keyboard and Mark was pretending to be John Humphreys over the phone to a woman who had eloped with her husband's son by his first marriage. He had now asked her the same question four times. She imagined the woman was probably close to tears at the other end.

Maddie Allbrook, their boss, was reading her horoscope.

'Ooooh,' she said excitedly. 'I'm going on a long journey. Maybe that's my summer holiday?'

'Crikey, how do they do that?' said Jazz, shaking her head. 'Genius.'

Maddie pouted happily. It was impossible to upset her; God knows, Jazz had tried over the years. Maddie had creamy white skin and long, wavy black hair. She was petite and always wore little mini-skirts. She loved her job, her colleagues, her life. If she had been a house, she'd have been a little country cottage, complete with beams, log fires and creeping clematis up the front wall.

Mark slammed the phone down.

'Hopeless. Fucking hopeless,' he shouted dramatically. Maddie and Jazz looked at him as he wiped his hand over his eyes and over his head. 'Woman had a brain the size of a split pea,' he went on. 'I've gotta get out of this place.' And with that he strode out of the room, off for a fag no doubt.

Mark had long since stopped intriguing Jazz. By now, she had him pretty well sussed. With his saucer-shaped, dazzlingly blue eyes, angular cheekbones and high forehead, he had obviously been a beautiful baby and child. Which explained why he compensated by being a total dickhead to work with. He used every macho trick in the book to hide the fact that he was actually a rather sweet bloke. He had worn his thick curly, golden hair – the sort of hair any self-respecting woman would have grown as long as possible and nurtured with loving care – cropped close to his head for as long as she'd known him. If he knew that it actually made him look more vulnerable, he would no doubt have grown it. And he moved his body – which, she guessed, had only shot up and broadened in his late teens, long after the insecurity had set in – with a studied aggression.

Jazz's desk was opposite Maddie's; Mark sat in the far corner of the room facing them both. There was an empty desk opposite Miranda, but Mark had astutely chosen not to sit there when he joined almost a year ago. Jazz could see why. Miranda was about as interesting as varicose veins, although not quite as attractive. Over the past few months Jazz had begun to get the oddest feeling that she was being watched whenever things went quiet in Mark's corner. And his bolshie outbursts had grown more and more unpredictable. She hoped to God he wasn't starting to fancy her. She tried not to think about it. Just like she tried not to think about the depths to which her principles had sunk.

When she'd started at *Hoorah!* it had been one of a dying breed, a magazine that was interested in the higher qualities of life; relationships that lasted instead of those that collapsed spectacularly, people who were an inspiration, not an example. Unfortunately the readers were leaving in their thousands. 'Nice' just wasn't a seller any more. People wanted short, they wanted snappy, they wanted dirt. Agatha Miller was brought in as the new Editor and she changed everything. *Hoorah!* became *Hoorah! the women's magazine with a difference* – the difference being that it had readers. The writing style went downmarket, the morals stooped, the storylines stooped lower still and the circulation hit the roof. Jazz found herself working on a trashy women's magazine instead of the last remaining decent one.

Agatha had brought with her a few colleagues from her previous magazine and Mark was one of them. Thankfully though, Agatha had liked Jazz's column and hadn't wanted it changed too much. Just a few more exclamation marks – known in the business as screamers – put in here and there to alert readers to the fact that they had just read a joke. Each screamer cut Jazz like a knife, but she was grateful that her column hadn't been axed completely.

'Oh look, another one bites the dust,' said Maddie happily. She read out the first few paragraphs in the tabloid she was holding about another highly regarded columnist's descent into infamy. His skeletons had finally struggled out of the cupboard after years of being locked away in the dark. It was always the same. After this gleeful character assassination, no one would ever read his criticisms of others, his comments on the world and his observations of human nature, without thinking, You're a fine one to talk. However brilliant he was. And this one *was* brilliant.

Jazz was eternally grateful that her personal life was so straightforward. She had a family that would make the Waltons look like the Kennedys, and a track record that was neat and uncomplicated. She knew it had to stay that way. You couldn't be respected as one of society's critics if you stepped off the straight and narrow yourself. Society loved to hate a hypocrite. Especially a famous one.

She sighed a deep sigh. She just couldn't start her column. The longer it took to get going, the worse the column was. Why couldn't she focus her mind?

There was a squeal from the corner of the open-plan office, followed by some raucous laughter.

'Listen to this, it's priceless . . .'

It was Sandra, the agony aunt, reading another of her letters out to the eager office. Usually Jazz would tune in, but with a monumental effort she stared at her screen. Focus, focus, focus. She spread her fingers out on the keyboard as if about

39

to plunge into a piano concerto . . . and stared hard at the blank screen. She started her favourite daydream puzzler, wondering which Baldwin brother she'd most like to get stuck in a lift with.

Her machine bleeped. Excellent, an e-mail.

She scanned her messages. The one at the top said **Stop Press**. She double-clicked it.

> AARRGGH!! I've worked out how to use the e-mail. I'm so excited, I can't write any more.
>   Write back NOW. My address is Maureen-Harris @loughborough.co.uk. But if you ever call me Maureen to my face you're a dead woman.
> Mo.

Excellent! It had only taken one year. Mo must be using the one staff computer. Maybe one of her four-year-olds had showed her how it worked. She started tapping.

> Gold star!! Ten out of ten!! Etc!!
> Jazz.
> PS. What's for dinner?

Then she tried to concentrate. Another bleep on her computer. Bloody hell. She double-clicked.

> AARRGGH!! I've worked out how to use the e-mail. I'm so excited, I can't write any more.
>   Write back NOW. My address is Maureen-Harris @loughborough.co.uk. But if you ever call me Maureen you're a dead woman.
> Mo.

Oh dear. She'd write back and then she'd start her work.

> Mo hon, you just sent me the same message twice.
> You've managed to do what some people can never
> do. Be boring on e-mail.
> Love, Jazz.

Another bleep. Mo again.

> I know I sent it twice. I didn't think you were listening
> the first time.
>   PS. It's your turn to cook tonight. I cooked last
> month.

Jazz smiled. Thank God for modern technology.

Maddie had finished reading the papers. She was now standing up, sorting through her filing tray.

'Mark, your *100 Things You Didn't Know About Wicked Willy* piece is outstanding.'

Jazz saw Mark grin widely, his eyes warm with pleasure. 'Cheers, babe.' He winked at her.

'No, Mark,' said Maddie. 'It's *outstanding*. It's late.'

'Oh. Yeah. Well, you see, there's a bloody good reason for that.'

'Yes?'

'Bloody good . . .'

Maddie and Jazz watched him try and get out of this one.

Jazz's phone rang. 'Bloody hell, I can't get a thing done,' she muttered before picking it up.

'I'm going to do it,' said a voice that sounded as if it was in a mangle.

'Do what?'

41

'Chuck Simon, like you told me,' said George almost inaudibly.

'Jesus,' whispered Jazz in awe. 'When? Where?' For the first time she realised that a single George was as unknown territory to Jazz as it was to George herself.

'Do you think that blond bloke at the audition really liked me?' asked George.

'I'm sorry, I fail to see the significance,' said Jazz in her favourite pompous tone.

'Never mind,' answered George. 'Will you come round tonight? We can talk tactics.'

'Of course,' said Jazz sincerely. She just stopped herself from saying, 'It will be my pleasure.'

'Thanks,' whispered George.

'We'll be nasty about Simon together,' promised Jazz. 'It'll be fun.'

'There isn't anything nasty to say about him,' said George pathetically, remembering his broad shoulders and forgetting his broad rump.

'Oh, I'm sure we'll find something,' said Jazz. 'I seem to remember he only has one eyebrow. I always meant to ask you if it goes all the way round his head.'

Jazz could hear her sister smile. 'See you tonight,' she said.

Jazz put the phone down and started her piece. Title – *Taking Control*. She finished it forty minutes later, and then read the dailies.

Chapter 4

The doorbell rang at number 5, Winchester Road, Hampstead and Sara Hayes took a last look at herself in the gilt-framed mirror.

The doorbell rang again and she went to answer the front door. She smiled at her welcome guests.

'Hello, popsie,' she said to Maxine and the two gave each other air kisses. The affection bordering on gratitude that Sara felt for her new confidante, Maxine, was as much to do with the fact that she was married, as it was to do with the fact that she was unquestionably less attractive than her. Next to Maxine, Sara looked even more stunning. Happily, Maxine's fondness for Sara was based on her friend's amazing good looks and daring single lifestyle. Next to Sara, Maxine didn't feel so married and dull. Nothing bonds some women together more than their differences.

'Charles!' exclaimed Sara as warmly as she could to Maxine's husband, whose shoulders sloped at such a sharp angle she wondered that his blazer didn't fall off.

Expensive wine was handed over and surprised delight expressed. Then they all went into the lounge, where the

43

lights were dimmed and some carefully selected dinner jazz was playing quietly in the background.

'Are Harry and Jack here yet?' asked Maxine, as she sank into the soft, deep plum-coloured sofas and looked round appreciatively at the large room.

'No, they're keeping us waiting, naughty boys,' winked Sara affectionately and poured out two gin and tonics.

She couldn't help but be excited. It had been two weeks since the audition and Harry was bound to reveal what parts he had given her and Maxine. She was on tenterhooks to know. She was in danger of being typecast as a bitch, which as every actor knows, is good for the short term, but if you had real ambitions, like Sara, it had to stop. This would be a golden opportunity for her to be seen to work for charity, and it could also be the chance she'd been waiting for, for over ten years, to finally work with Harry Noble. She had been desperate to work with him ever since her brother Jack had made friends with him at RADA.

Maxine cared only slightly less passionately about getting a part in the play. She used to be an actress too before she had become big in celebrity fundraising. Her little black book now had more names in it than *Who's Who*. But it would be nice for her to get a bit of exposure again, just like the good old days, when she and Charles Caruthers-Brown had met.

Charles had first seen Maxine in the chorus of a West End production of *Forty-Second Street*, and he'd been so bowled over by her that he'd sent her an enormous bouquet of red roses backstage that night. After that, he had come and seen every performance for a fortnight until she had agreed to go out with him.

It certainly wasn't love at first sight for Maxine. Charles courted her very cautiously, and eventually, after seven

44

months, a holiday in the Bahamas on his private yacht and a diamond necklace with matching tiara, she fell head over heels in love with him. After they married, her career had taken a back seat while they did up their London home and their country home, and she'd been only too happy to get involved in some high-profile fundraising work. She was to be involved in the fundraising aspect of this production too, but had auditioned with the hope of getting back into the limelight – and of adding the great Harry Noble to her little black book. In fact, she couldn't quite believe that she was going to be in the same room as him tonight. Neither could Charles. Even he was a bit tense.

The doorbell rang again and the men arrived.

Everyone stood up and said, 'Ah,' as they came into the lounge. Jack Hayes's smiling face appeared round the doorframe first, followed almost immediately by his tall, slender frame. He ambled in, all jollity and eagerness to please. His cheeks were as rosy as ever and his eyes shone with warmth and interest. He was a tall man, but next to Harry, he looked slight, and beside Harry's crow-black hair, his blondness looked almost silly.

The genuine pleasure that Jack exhibited at being there would have eased the tension somewhat, had it not been for Harry's seeming indifference. Jack greeted them all warmly, kissing his sister and her friend on the cheeks and shaking Charles's hand vigorously. Harry stood in the corner and nodded his greetings to them, without a smile. Everyone was delighted by him. He made no reference to having met Maxine or Charles at the auditions and, as general conversation began, he let Jack do all the talking, preferring instead to study the various ornaments in the room. Sara grew more and more irritated with her brother. Why wouldn't he shut up, so that Harry could talk? After twenty tense minutes, the hired butler came in and announced that dinner was served.

The dining room was vast and decked out in rich red and gold with sumptuous velvet curtains swept up at the sides of the sash windows. A suit of armour occupied the corner of the room, somewhat unnerving those with sensitive dispositions. Sara had arranged the place cards so that she was sitting opposite Harry. Maxine and Charles were facing each other and Jack was at the head.

As they ate the gazpacho soup, Sara could wait no longer.

'The last time we were all in the same room, Mr Noble, we were all desperate for your approval,' she said, with pretence at a coy smile. She had insisted on calling Harry *Mr Noble* ever since he'd won the Oscar. He had never expressed displeasure at it, so she had kept it up whenever she was trying to be more intimate with him.

'Oh yes,' said Maxine, affecting surprise at the subject. 'Can you put us out of our misery and tell us if any of us made the grade?'

She and Sara laughed in amazement at the idea and Jack joined in willingly. Charles was now preoccupied with his soup. The food had taken away what nerves he had felt at the thought of meeting Harry Noble. Harry Noble was just a man but soup was soup. Even if it was cold.

'Oh, you can assure yourselves I approved heartily of you all,' said Harry, and continued to eat.

Sara tried again.

'Did any of us spring to mind when you cast the part of . . . say . . . Elizabeth Bennet?'

Harry kept on drinking his soup.

'Perhaps that girl – now what was her name?' Sara laughed gently, 'You called her the Ugly Sis—'

Harry interrupted. 'Jasmin Field.'

'Yes, that's right – I think she's Georgia Field's sister,' said Maxine.

Jack looked up.

'Oh yes,' pretended Sara. 'She was petrified, poor thing, I felt mortified for her. Mind you, she made a sterling effort, I thought, didn't you?'

Harry put his spoon down and wiped his mouth with his well-pressed serviette.

'Yes, sterling,' he said, placing his serviette on the table. 'So sterling that she is our Elizabeth Bennet.'

There was a stunned silence.

'Marvellous!' said Jack genuinely.

'*Elizabeth Bennet?*' gasped Sara. '*Lizzy?*' she tried, hoping that she might have misheard.

'Yes,' said Harry simply. 'Delicious soup, by the way.'

Sara struggled to keep her voice composed. 'I must say I am most surprised,' she managed. 'After all, when you first saw her you called her an Ugly Sister. Aren't you at all concerned that that's what the audience will think too?'

'No.'

'Surely you can't have a short, busty, *ugly* Lizzy Bennet? It will spoil everything.'

'When I first saw her,' corrected Harry, 'she was standing in the shadow. I couldn't see her face properly from there. Especially her eyes.'

'Her eyes? What have they got to do with anything?' demanded Sara, her own eyes shrinking in anger.

'You didn't notice them?' asked Harry.

'No, I did not,' shot back Sara. 'But I did see that she is far less attractive than her sister, Georgia.'

'Mmm, I agree,' conceded Harry. 'Convincing the audience that she is a real beauty will definitely be the biggest challenge I've ever had. But I've given the part of Jane Bennet to her real sister, Georgia Field, which should add authenticity.'

'Excellent!' said Jack, even more genuinely.

'*What?*' cried Sara.

'Well, as you just said,' explained Harry calmly, 'Georgia Field is more instantly attractive than her sister and as you recall, Jane Bennet was the reputed beauty of the family.'

'They were *all* reputed beauties.'

'Well I can assure you that all of Jane's sisters are very pretty girls, and when we tog them up in their dresses, they'll all look just the job.'

Sara controlled her anger but she seethed into her soup.

Harry didn't feel it necessary to add that Jasmin Field's acting had a raw vitality and depth that he couldn't wait to work on.

Sara stood up, took his plate before the waitress had time to do so, and walked out of the room.

Maxine wondered if it would be tactless to ask if she'd got a part. Charles belched loudly. Jack looked round the room and beamed happily at them all.

Meanwhile in the kitchen, Sara stood leaning on the marble-topped counter. She ignored the cook when asked whether she wanted the crêpe suzettes cooked on the mobile stove in the dining room or the kitchen. She was too busy hatching a plot.

Chapter 5

Jazz hopped off the bus in East Finchley and walked briskly along the road towards her parents' house. As she drew near, she could see Josie, her younger sister, and her brother-in-law, Michael, getting out of their car. Ben, their twenty-two-month-old, was holding Josie's hand. He'd only been walking for a few months and it still gave Jazz a jolt of excitement to see him upright on his two fat legs. He was wearing a nappy the size of a small suitcase. Josie had known Michael since her college days and Jazz had long since got over the shock of her baby sister becoming an old married woman three years before.

Jazz ran up to greet them.

Josie hugged Jazz absent-mindedly while locking the car door and checking she hadn't left any vital toys in the car. She looked very tired. Michael was carrying all Ben's paraphernalia. He had temporarily placed the multicoloured furry teddy bear on his head, while steadying his grip on various other bits and pieces, and Jazz managed not to laugh as he greeted her with his usual intense expression. Jazz picked Ben up and he just about stayed still long enough for her to give him a very loud kiss. He giggled and said her name, filling her with pride.

As she put him down, she spotted Simon's shiny red MX5 parked in her parents' drive. So George still hadn't done the dirty deed, even after a whole evening of helpful hints, courtesy of herself. And that would mean that the entire family tea would take place under his cold eye. Damn.

The door opened wide. 'Darlings! Come in, come in!' Martha, their mother greeted them. She hugged them all fiercely, her bosom making contact first. 'Everything's ready, you must be famished.' Martha always assumed that none of her children ate in between their visits to her.

In the lounge sat George and Simon with the nominal head of the family, Jeffrey. Jeffrey was delighted to see his other daughters. He'd been stuck talking to Simon about rugby, a sport he detested, while George had stared vacantly into the middle distance. Everyone shot up, grateful for the intrusion and there were noisy greetings all round.

Tea was an informal, loud affair. Jazz waited for a lull to tell the family about the impression she'd made on the famous Harry Noble. She had to wait a while.

'He called you *what*?' asked Jeffrey, outraged.

'The *Ugly* Sister,' grinned Jazz, enjoying the reaction it received. She wished now that it had been a stronger insult to have got her more of a dramatic response. She also wished Simon wasn't there, because she knew he would assume that secretly she had been greatly offended by the slight. Which she found greatly offensive.

'Has he seen Josie?' asked Martha.

'Oh, cheers, Mum,' said Josie.

'I can't believe that,' said George, shaking her head. 'Are you sure you heard right, Jazz?'

50

'Yes, George. Just because he's won an Oscar doesn't mean he has to be a nice person,' said Jazz gently.

'I should think it probably means quite the opposite,' added Jeffrey.

There was a pause in the conversation when Josie spoke.

'We've got an announcement to make,' she smiled weakly.

Everyone gasped. She didn't need to say much more.

'I'm pregnant,' she said.

Martha and George screamed, Jeffrey hugged Michael and Jazz felt a curious mixture of envy, joy and sympathy.

Josie was only one month gone, so they were all sworn to secrecy.

'So I don't want to read about it in any magazine,' smiled Josie, wagging her finger at Jazz.

'Hey no worries, we work four months ahead,' grinned Jazz.

'I mean it, Jazz. Tempting fate and all that. I've been much more sick with this one. And we all know how bad I was with Benjy. It wasn't planned, you see.'

'Of course. You can trust me.' Jazz remembered how Josie had had to stay off work and in bed for six weeks before Ben had been born, due to complications. And how Martha had exhausted herself visiting her daughter in hospital and cooking hot evening meals for Michael every day.

Harry Noble's comment was forgotten and the conversation shifted wholeheartedly into baby mode. Then they caught up on the gossip about the rest of the family, they argued over whose turn it was to phone Great-Aunt Sylvie and they admonished Martha for making enough food for a football team. Until she started getting upset and then they all tucked into second helpings. And all the while, Jazz was aware of Simon sitting there with a very slight, fixed smile on his handsome face, not understanding any of the conversation and not caring enough to pretend that he did.

It was only when Jazz was saying goodnight to her father that the subject of Harry Noble came up again. 'Harry Noble may be a great actor,' he said softly, as he kissed her, 'but he needs his eyes testing.' Jazz wished he hadn't said that. For some reason it made her feel the slight much more.

George gave Jazz a lift home in her beloved VW Beatle. Thankfully, Simon had had to leave early, so they'd come in separate cars.

'I hope it's a girl,' George confided, as she put the key in the ignition.

'Really?' smiled Jazz, dreamily. 'How selfish.'

'Selfish? What do you mean?'

Jazz took a deep breath. 'I mean, you hope that Josie will give birth to someone who will spend up to a quarter of her adult life having painful periods, who will be susceptible to all sorts of complex eating disorders and self-confidence problems because society will be obsessed with her physical appearance; someone who will have less chance of getting the same respect and money in the workplace as her male colleagues; who will be treated as thick if she's pretty and pitied if she's plain, who will spend more time than her partner doing household chores even though they work the same hours – that is, if he doesn't beat her or abuse her mentally,' she took another deep breath, 'and someone who will have to go through the untold agony of labour if she wants to have a child and will then be pilloried by society and said child for being a mother – and all so that you can bond with your niece over chocolate and lipstick.' Jazz turned to George with a smug smile. 'I call that selfish.'

George had heard it all before.

'Yup, and you hope it's a girl, too.'

Jazz nodded. 'Mmm, tragic isn't it?'

Five minutes into the journey George could hold the question in no longer. 'So what did you think of that blond bloke at the auditions?'

'Shame on you, you hussy. And Simon only just out of sight.'

George sighed.

'I thought you could eat him for dinner,' said Jazz. 'I hope you'll both be very happy.'

George was delighted. 'He's *so* cute, isn't he? I'll die if I don't get a part.' She started humming.

'What if you get a part and he doesn't?' said Jazz. 'Who'll die then?'

'I'll die then too,' said George definitely. She continued humming.

'Right you are,' said Jazz, watching the road contentedly.

As Jazz ran up the stairs into her flat, she could hear George's car drive off down the road. Mo's light was off, so Jazz went straight into her room and started getting undressed. When the phone rang she rushed to get it with her toothbrush still in her mouth.

'Hello?' she whispered

'You're Lizzy!' came a breathless squeal down the phone.

'What?'

'You're Lizzy, I'm Jane and rehearsals start next Monday. I've just picked up the message on my answerphone. You're *Lizzy*!' repeated an overjoyed George. 'I'm Jane. Rehearsals start next Monday. I've just pick—'

'Yes I heard what you said,' said Jazz. 'Bloody hell.' Excitement welled up inside her. 'Are you sure?'

George was hyperventilating.

'It was Sandie, Harry's PA,' she gasped. 'She said I was Jane Bennet and please could I phone my sister, Jasmin Field – that's you – and let her know she's got the part of Lizzy Bennet. *Lizzy Bennet*, Jazz. Oh, and Mo's got a part too. I think she's Charlotte Lucas.'

There was silence.

'Jazz? Are you there?'

'Yes. Yes, I'm here.'

'Well, what do you think?'

She smiled slowly. 'I think Harry Noble is remarkably shrewd for someone with bad eyesight,' she smiled.

Chapter 6

Jazz stopped in her tracks. Mo was standing in the kitchen wearing a fresh white tracksuit and gleaming trainers. She looked like a short fat ghost with a perm.

'I'm going to get fit and slim and beautiful,' announced Mo. 'I'm on a diet as of today and I'm on my way to join the gym. Wish me luck.'

Jazz was staggered. If Mo had said, 'I'm going to marry a Mormon and help look after his five wives,' she couldn't have been more stunned.

'Why?' was all she could manage to utter.

Mo picked up her gym kit and brushed past her.

Jazz followed her into the hall. 'But you've – you've always said looks don't matter and women only diet for men and life is obsessed with the superficial, and that's why so many people are starving,' she gabbled desperately.

'Yes, I know,' said Mo, 'but then I thought, Hey, wouldn't it be fun to be sexy?'

'Mo!' Jazz slammed her hand down on her kit. She couldn't think of one cogent argument that would stop her friend. 'Who am I going to eat chocolate with?' she ended up saying weakly.

Mo slowly peeled Jazz's hand off.

'See you later, there's a whole gym waiting for me,' she said, and then she stopped. 'We can go together some time, if you like.'

Jazz's face showed such unadulterated horror at the idea that Mo simply turned and walked to the door.

'Life's too short!' shouted Jazz angrily.

Mo yelled back, 'So am I!' and slammed the door.

Jazz looked down at her body. Sure, she could probably do with losing a pound or two here and there. But then she could also learn some Greek or go Flamenco dancing. Or have a hot bath, listening to a play on the radio. Or, more importantly, watch telly.

She went into the lounge and turned on the box before she could notice how quiet the flat was. It was the ads. Skinny women (who were paid to be skinny) eating chocolate. Skinny women (who lived on apples and water) holding products and smiling. Skinny women (with bulimia) laughing into the eyes of adoring men. Skinny women (who were just born that way) confiding about washing powder. Skinny women (who were nicknamed Pinlegs at school) talking about Weight Watchers.

Jazz turned off the telly and went to run a hot bath and have a look at her script which had been posted to her that morning.

At the first read-through of the play, Jazz was already growing fond of the musty smell of the church. As she sat herself down in the circle of chairs in the centre of the hall and settled back to watch everyone come in, it dawned on her for the first time how much more the actors had to lose in this production than anyone else. She was only just beginning to realise how high-profile this affair was going to be. The audience would not only be full of celebs but also stacked to the rafters with casting agents, national theatre directors, top fringe theatre directors, journalists and critics. It could make or break the actors. It was massive. But from a funding point of view, it needed to attract more than just luvvies. The organisers needed all the publicity they could get, in order to persuade the punters to tune in and get out their chequebooks. Which probably explained why two key journalists had been chosen for the main parts, thought Jazz suddenly, as well as giving the tabloid darling, Gilbert Valentine, a look-in. With Gilbert's regular titbits of gossip from the play, her columns about the rehearsals and critic Brian Peters' forthcoming acting début, Jo Bloggs would easily be herded into a frenzy of excitement about the whole enterprise, turning it into the viewing experience of the year. There would hardly be anything for the press officers to do.

As for worrying about her performance, Jazz just couldn't work herself up to it. What did she care if some bored critic lambasted her? She could always lambast his syntax in her next column. She had never professed publicly to being able to act, and if there was one thing she had never judged in her columns, it was actors' ability or otherwise. But for Brian Peters it was quite a different matter. He was going to have a lot to prove in his one-off reincarnation as one of the most romantic fictional heroes in English literature. Jazz smiled. This was going to be fun.

Mo had come straight from work and George would be coming straight from doing a play on Radio 4. Jazz didn't think she'd tell Mo that she was the only person there not involved in the arts. She'd only end up in the toilet throughout the entire rehearsal interrupting herself with offers of Mintos.

She barely noticed that Sara Hayes and her friend Maxine were there, but she instantly recognised their friendly, blond companion – George's next conquest – who seemed to recognise her and greeted her with a warm smile. She didn't know anyone else. There were lots of ridiculously handsome people taking their seats and hiding their nerves behind self-conscious airs of indifference or weariness. Jazz watched them all keenly.

Mo came and sat next to her. As the seats filled up, Jazz realised that William Whitby wasn't there. How could he not have been given a part? He was so . . . watchable. Just as her stomach was deflating with disappointment, the door opened and there he was. Maybe it was because she was so obviously aware of him, maybe it was because there was a spare seat next to her and their eyes had met as soon as he had walked in, she didn't know why, but he saw her, grinned and came to sit down next to her.

'Hi,' he smiled, proffering his hand to be shaken 'I'm Wills.' Jazz nodded. It would have looked stupid to pretend she didn't know his name. His openness of expression and large, brown eyes that crinkled at the edges when he smiled, were even more endearing in the flesh than on television. Jazz almost had to stop herself from bear-hugging him.

'Hi,' said Jazz, shaking his hand vigorously and grinning like a moron. 'Jazz.'

'Short for?' he questioned.

'Men over six foot four. My only restriction.' Dear God, had she really said that?

He chuckled. 'Who are you playing?'

'Lizzy,' she said, wondering if her pupils were dilating so much that her eyes were now just two black holes.

His grin widened and he touched her arm affectionately.

'Hey wow, congratulations,' he said. 'You must be really good.'

Impossibly, she warmed to him even more.

'Must I?' she said as coyly as she could. 'Who are you playing?'

'Terribly Wicked Wickham,' he said wickedly.

'Ooh, how exciting,' she said, noticing that he had several freckles on his nose and golden flecks in his eyes.

'Yes, it'll be a laugh,' he agreed. 'And from a professional point of view, it's a great opportunity to play a baddie. I don't want to be typecast as a priest for ever, you know.' A heart-blisteringly wide smile, 'Of course, you realise we'll have to learn how to flirt with each other.'

With considerable self-control, Jazz managed not to cheer. Maybe this acting business was going to be more enjoyable than she'd anticipated.

Just then, she became aware of a blurred image behind William's head and, with some effort, drew her eyes towards it. It was a beaming Gilbert.

'Jasmin!' he exclaimed. 'You made it, I knew you would!' He kissed her smack on the mouth. She was too shocked to move. Thankfully there wasn't a seat next to her and with an affectionate squeeze of her shoulder, Gilbert had to go and sit somewhere else. As she watched him go, she wondered idly what part he could possibly have got.

Wills turned back to Jazz. 'That's Gilbert Valentine, Theatre Hack, isn't it?' he whispered to her.

'No,' whispered Jazz back. 'It's Gilbert Valentine, Pathetic

Twat. We used to work together.' She wondered why life was never perfect.

Wills meanwhile, was laughing with delight.

The atmosphere cooled as soon as Harry Noble entered the room. He walked over to where the chairs were stacked, his eyes fixing on no one. He picked up a chair and stood silently behind two people in the circle. Without a word being said to either of them, they made room for him. Jazz was so preoccupied watching the remarkable reaction Harry seemed to create on everyone that she scarcely noticed the quiet, red-headed young woman who had come in with him. Silently the woman – or girl – found herself a seat at the back.

Eventually Harry honoured his cast by looking briefly at them.

'Hello people,' he said quietly, and Jazz marvelled at how he could fill those two short words with such considered condescension. Everyone inched closer and Harry took off his black leather jacket exposing a loose, black V-neck jumper and faded black jeans. He leaned back lazily in his chair, fully aware that everyone was watching him avidly. Jazz observed in wonder as the entire room eyed his body, greedily taking in the curve of his Adam's apple and the enticing peek of olive-brown collarbone, his languidly elegant torso, broad shoulders, long, flat stomach and perfect thighs.

Harry was almost sunbathing in the warmth of everyone's stare. Then without eyeing any of his new cast, he delivered a speech that Jazz thought he must have had written for him by some out-of-work ham playwright – a speech called 'Director Drivel'. He hardly bothered to move his body as he spoke, and his voice was so cold and quiet that people were leaning forward to catch every little gem. Jazz was transfixed, amazed that someone with such screen presence could be such an atmosphere vacuum in real life. It was as if he only gave of himself when he thought it was worth it, and he certainly didn't rate his present audience.

'Some of you have never acted before,' he droned on. 'Some of you may think you have. But all of you will discover new meanings of the word if you listen to me.' He now looked deliberately at them; some of the women blushed under his steady gaze. 'And trust in me. Let me be your guide.' Jazz gazed round at his audience. They would let him drill their molars if he so desired. They were eating out of the palm of his hand.

Incredible. She'd never seen anything like it before. Slowly, she tore her eyes away from his entranced followers and looked back at him. She was more than surprised to find that he was looking straight at her. She became aware that everyone else was now looking at her and realised that he had just asked her a question.

She smiled half-heartedly. 'Sorry, I – I . . . wasn't listening.'

He tilted his sculpted face at her with an expression she couldn't yet read.

'An excellent start, Miss Field,' he said calmly, hardly moving his perfect lips.

There was a slight laugh from the audience.

Jazz felt her cheeks warm.

'I just asked our starring lady, our *Elizabeth Bennet* (crescendo) to stand up and introduce herself.'

Jesus Christ.

She stood up.

'Hi,' (cough), 'my name is Jasmin Field. I'm a journalist. So don't piss me off. Ha ha. And um – well, I can't really act. Ha ha.' No one laughed.

She didn't know what else to say. Harry's almost inaudible voice cut the atmosphere like an ice-pick.

'I don't work with people who can't act, Miss Field.'

Oh pur-lease, she thought. Get *out* of your bottom, it's dark in there.

'Good job this is voluntary then,' she smiled sweetly.

There was an uncomfortable pause.

'Money has nothing to do with an excellent performance, Miss Field.' He smiled wrily at the rest of the cast. 'Although I don't expect a journalist to understand that.' They broke into relieved laughter, grateful that he had shared a joke with them. Out of the corner of her eye, Jazz could see Gilbert attempting the look of an offended genius.

Harry started looking around the room for his next victim.

'Oh, you'd be surprised,' Jazz said a bit too loudly. 'We journalists understand lots of things. Particularly,' she pretended to pluck words out of the air, and finished softly with 'pomp and affectation.'

The room held its breath, but Harry merely looked back at her. 'Oh dear,' he said in an infuriatingly measured tone. 'Miss Field, we might as well sort this out once and for all. For the short period of your life that you leave behind the tacky world of women's magazines and work with me, I will turn you into a good actress. However painful that experience may be for both of us.'

Jazz bristled. 'I never leave behind my "tacky world", as you put it, Mr Noble – it follows me, I'm afraid. Much in the same way that a bit-part in a "tacky" American sitcom would follow a classic actor.'

A couple of people coughed nervously.

'Well, there you're very much mistaken, Miss Field,'

said Harry, leaning forward and allowing his voice more inflection. 'I don't allow anything to follow anyone when they act with me. I want you, Miss Field, completely and utterly naked.' A fractional smile. 'I'm speaking emotionally, of course.' Jazz grimaced. 'And that's your first lesson.' He threw her a hard smile that landed, with a dull thud, in her gut. 'Learning the difference between pomp and affectation and substance and integrity we'll have to leave to another day.'

And with that he turned swiftly to his next victim. Somehow Jazz found her seat again without falling flat on her bottom. The fact that everyone had now stopped watching her did nothing to lessen her sense of embarrassment. She hated him. In fact, she was so shaken by the public humiliation that it was several moments before she began to look forward to describing it in her column.

It was Mr Darcy's turn next. Jazz had at first been delighted to discover that Harry had succumbed to Matt's advice and given the part of the greatest romantic hero to the acerbic critic, Brian Peters. But within moments, her delight turned to serious concern. Poison Pen Peters' prose, albeit cruel, was always elegant, well-honed and majestic. His 'voice' was an aesthetic joy, something every reader was in awe of due to its obvious natural superiority, whether or not they agreed with its content. As a writer, he would have made a perfect Mr Darcy. As an actor, however, he would have made a perfect ferret. It appeared to Jazz, as she studied Brian Peters for the first time, that testosterone had passed him by. His shoulders were narrower than hers, his voice higher, and his long, slim head made him look as if he was still recovering from a forceps delivery. How could such magnificent prose come from such an unimpressive person?

By now, everyone else knew the sort of interrogation they

would receive from their director and had time to think of something half-witty to say for their own introductions. They were all suitably banal and benign. Sara Hayes had won the part of Miss Bingley – Mr Bingley's sister and doomed admirer of Mr Darcy – which almost managed to cheer Jazz up. How wonderfully typecast, she thought, with glee, watching the woman preen herself. Better still, Sara's friend Maxine was Mrs Hurst – her sister – and the man chosen to play Mrs Hurst's husband was Maxine's own porcine husband. Charles Caruthers-Brown's look of utter indifference to the proceedings suited his new role down to the ground.

The tall fair man who was still impersonating a stunned rabbit whenever he looked at George turned out to be called Jack – he was playing Mr Bingley, troubled suitor to George's Jane. Would life imitate art here also? wondered Jazz to herself. Is the Pope Catholic? she answered herself happily. She was even quite excited to see that Gilbert had won the part of Mr Collins, the insufferable, social-climbing curate. Despite herself, Jazz began to feel some respect for Harry Noble's casting ability.

The part of Lizzy's mother, Mrs Bennet, had gone to a large woman with heavy-lidded warm eyes, cropped black hair and beautifully smooth skin. Mr Bennet was to be played by a character actor Jazz had seen in many period productions on the television. He had always had minor roles and she had never given him more than a cursory glance. She had certainly never attributed any great meaning to anything he'd said, yet now she saw him in the flesh, with his tired, ruddy skin, his desperately grave expression and deep, mellow voice, she realised that while she had been ogling handsome lead actors, she had been wantonly ignoring many actors' lifetimes' achievements just because they had less pleasing features. She felt profound sympathy for the man who was doomed to always have the smaller, instantly forgettable parts just because his nose was too bulbous, his eyes too close together and his mouth too far over to the left. Her sympathy for him didn't last long though. She watched him for a while. He was unexpectedly self-obsessed and so blusteringly affected that she started to admire his lifetime's work of modest, humble characters afresh. He was obviously a far better performer than she had ever given him credit for.

Lizzy's three younger sisters were to be played by young fairly well-known personalities – one a novelist whose debut novel *Monarchy, My Arse* had had rave reviews, another a young photographer who had exhibited twice to rapturous reviews, and the other almost an 'It' girl – cable TV presenter, party-goer. Even they were quite obviously flustered in the company of Harry Noble. So Jazz had been right. The second day of auditions *had* just been a publicity stunt. There was no one here who was a complete unknown. Apart, perhaps, from Mo and from Maxine's other half, Charles.

Just looking round the room at all the hopeful, determined faces was enough to convince Jazz that she had made the right decision never to try acting as a profession. She'd toyed with the idea for a week or two at the age of eighteen, but realised that she'd rather scrutinise the world than emotionally strip in front of it.

She was relieved to find out that her new friend Wills didn't think less of her after her *tête à tête* with Mr Noble. In fact, it was rather the opposite.

As soon as Harry and Jazz had finished their spar, Wills had turned round to her. 'May I be the first to congratulate you,' he murmured. 'You have answered back the great Harry Noble.'

'Is he always this pretentious?' she asked.

Wills tried not to laugh out loud. 'Believe me, you'll get used to the bastard.'

Jazz snorted. 'What, like I got used to PMT?'

At this he did laugh out loud. A great, manly bellow of a laugh. Jazz couldn't help but join in. She was hooked. Nothing was as attractive to her as a man laughing at one of her jokes. Except a crowd of men laughing at a string of her jokes.

'Probably,' he said finally. 'Perhaps that's why women seem to get on better with him than men.'

'Most women,' reminded Jazz, 'only want one thing.'

She looked over at Jack and George, already deep in conversation. When she glanced back at Wills, she actually blushed to find he had stopped laughing and was studying her.

Chapter 7

The first rehearsal had been just a read-through of the play. Jazz thoroughly enjoyed it. The adaptation had been very cleverly done – there was even a hint at a final snog with Darcy and Elizabeth, which didn't feel too anachronistic. However, every time Jazz looked at her Darcy, she felt seriously concerned. She certainly wouldn't be resorting to method acting with Brian Peters.

As soon as she and Mo were back in the flat, Jazz made a tape-recording of her part with long pauses for the other parts. Harry wanted everyone to be off scripts within a fortnight. She vowed to play the tape at every single opportunity. It took her three exhausting hours to make it.

Afterwards she and Mo met up in the lounge for their usual late-night tipple. Thank goodness Mo hadn't yet realised that her diet might be affected by alcohol. They were discussing George.

'There goes Action Man out the window,' sighed Jazz, feeling almost nostalgic.

'Oh? Why?'

'Haven't you been watching George at rehearsals? Talking

to the blond guy with NEXT stamped on his forehead. The bloke called Jack who's playing – wait for it – her lover.'

'Really? I didn't think she liked him.'

'Oh come on, she was practically salivating all over him.'

'Actually, I thought she wanted me to come over and save her at one point,' said Mo. 'Good thing I couldn't be bothered.'

'Are you mad? She all but sketched him her favourite wedding dress design.'

Mo frowned heavily. 'The tall guy with the pink cheeks?'

'Yes, the one whose lap she had to be hoovered off at the end of the rehearsal.'

'Nope. Can't see it myself,' said Mo and finished off her Baileys.

'Has your diet stopped blood getting to your brain?' asked Jazz in wonder. 'George was giving signals so big she was practically using semaphore.'

'Bollocks!' scoffed Mo. '*You* may be able to understand George's body language, but to the rest of us, she's as unreadable as a – a – Thomas Hardy novel.'

Jazz stared at Mo in disbelief. Mo continued, determined to put this subject to rest for the evening: 'Look. I'm very fond of your sister – you know I am, but . . .'

Jazz didn't want to hear any more. Didn't Mo know the rules? Only Jazz could criticise George.

'. . . But between you and me, I haven't got a clue what's going on inside her pretty little head. As for her *flirting* with anyone,' Mo snorted, 'I don't know what the hell you're talking about.'

'Well, that's because you haven't been feeding your brain for the past month,' scoffed Jazz. 'Your brain cells are slipping out of your ears, I can see them. I keep treading on them in the bathroom.'

'You're just jealous.'

'Jealous of what?'

'My new sleek body.'

Jazz was shocked. 'Are you calling me fat?'

'Yes, Big Bum.'

'Well, I'd rather have a big bum than a white tracksuit any day.'

'You'd look crap in a white tracksuit.'

'Of course I would. Everyone would. Everyone does.'

'You're just chicken.'

'Chicken of what? Looking like Littlewoods Man?'

'No, of coming to the gym.'

'I am not. I could beat you at step-a-crap anyday.'

'Bet you couldn't.'

'Bet I could.'

'Done!' yelled Mo, delighted.

Shit. How the hell did that happen?

'Are there any steps that go down?' Jazz asked feebly. 'Into a cafe?'

The next day she got a phone call in the office. It was Josie, her younger sister, she of the perfect marriage. Could Jazz babysit on Thursday evening please, because she and Michael needed to go out somewhere. Of course, Jazz would be delighted. The rest of the day was spent writing about her sister, she of the perfect marriage, who still went out with her husband, on their own, mid-week, six years after they'd met, three years after their wedding and two years after their firstborn had entered the world. It takes dedication, hard work, tolerance and a sense of humour, but marriages can still remain romantic, long after the glorious honeymoon is over, typed Jazz, and *Jazz Judges* . . . was over for another week. The Harry Noble character assassination could wait till next week, she had bigger fish to fry.

That evening Jazz arrived home to a depressing flat. Things just weren't the same since Mo had gone fit on her. She had joined the rest of the mad world and had stopped looking outward on life and was instead looking only at herself. As Jazz stared at the empty lounge, she mused that as far as Mo was now concerned, anything further than her nose was now out of focus and everything nearer than her nose i.e. the rest of her body, was blown up a size too big. She'd lost all sense of proportion.

Since Mo's changed life, Jazz had started looking more critically at her own body. Perhaps she could be less curvy. But then, she would be less her. No. She was damned if she was ever going to be at war with her body. She *loved* her body. It kept her alive. She used her strong legs and nimble feet to walk into the kitchen. She used her dextrous hands to put the kettle on. She used her graceful arms to open a cupboard and her agile fingers to niftily open a chocolate bar. She used her sensuous mouth to taste her favourite food. She used her joyous taste buds to experience pleasure and her contented mind to think of something that made her laugh while she was eating.

How could she hate her body? It was magnificent. It was a miracle. It was *her*.

Chapter 8

The room was dark and warm. The only sound was of everyone's breathing and Harry Noble's deep, mellow voice, which seemed to float through the heavy air. Jazz was aware that he could bring out different depths of his voice for different words. It was a language in itself.

'You're feeling sleepier and sleepier and sleepier,' he lulled. 'Your limbs are like lead and your head is floating on a cloud. You're in a garden. Somewhere in the distance you can hear a dog barking. You are sitting in your favourite part of the garden, enjoying the feel of the sun on your face.'

Despite herself, Jazz was relaxing – on a floral hammock wearing a matching summer dress.

'Now I'm going to go round asking you nice, simple questions that you must answer without a pause. Any pause and it will be ruined.'

Lying on the floor, Jazz started drifting off. Her Doc Martens made her feet so blissfully heavy, Harry's voice seemed to be inside her head.

'What's your first memory, Jasmin?'

Why did he always start with her?

She spoke quietly so as not to wake herself too much out of her trance. 'I'm not sure whether this is from my memory or from a snapshot I once saw,' she told him, keeping her breaths deep and slow. 'I'm in the garden shed in my pram and I'm crying because I want to come in.'

'You must have been very young.' Harry's voice was inside her head.

She half-smiled. 'About fifteen.'

Drowsy laughter went round the room.

There was a big sigh from Harry and then a very different voice. 'Ha Ha, Ms Field.'

'Yes, I must have been very young,' said Jazz quickly, realising she had spoilt the whole ambience.

His voice was now coming from her level. It was as if there were only the two of them in the room.

'What scares you most about dying?'

Bizarrely, Jazz felt a quick welling up of emotion.

'Not being able to talk about it afterwards.'

'Who to?'

Slight pause.

'You paused,' said Harry impatiently.

'I have to think. These are big questions.'

Harry hid a smile.

'Mo. George. Dad. Mum.'

'Did you have a happy childhood?'

Tiny pause.

'Most of the time.'

'What made you unhappy?'

How was this going to make her acting better?

'Is this really necess—'

'Yes,' said Harry wearily. 'If you can't be honest now, how can you be honest on stage?'

'I'm hardly being honest on stage – I'm reading a script. I hate to be the one to break it to you but I think the audience knows that.' It was so much easier arguing with him with her eyes shut.

She could almost feel him frowning at her, without having to see him. Isn't this emotionally naked enough, she thought? Lying with my eyes shut being watched by you while you ask me stupid questions?

There was a long pause. What was he doing?

She opened her eyes and fixed him with a questioning gaze. He was sitting next to her, elbow on knee, hand in hair, frowning intently at her face. She rested herself on her elbows and frowned intently back.

'Would it save time if I just sent you my autobiography?' she asked.

'I didn't know you'd written one,' he said.

'I haven't yet.' She lay down again.

She thought he'd gone and so started a slow, secret smile.

'Why are you so scared to let go?' he almost whispered from next to her. Then he jumped up and walked quickly to the other side of the room.

Wazzock, thought Jazz.

The truth was that no sooner had Harry told everyone that he had given himself his biggest challenge yet in casting an unattractive Lizzy Bennet than he began to realise that he had in fact made life very easy for himself. When he'd first set eyes on Jasmin Field, he had marvelled that her sister could have all the lucky genes while she had none. Then during her impressive audition piece he had realised that while Jasmin didn't have her sister's easy prettiness, she could be beautiful. Then at that first rehearsal, when she had proved to be such a concentrated pain in the backside, he had begun to notice

73

just how well cast she was. Her face was indeed rendered uncommonly intelligent by the beautiful expression of her dark eyes. If eyes are the window of the soul, Harry found Jazz's soul compelling.

But she was such a bloody challenge. She was so emotionally retentive — what was she scared of? If only he could tap into her depths, he was sure she could be a fine actress. And he was determined to, both for his reputation, and for his own growing interest in her. She could be a stunning Elizabeth Bennet. Yep, the more he looked at Jasmin Field — and he found himself looking longer and longer — the more he was struck by his uncanny knack for casting. Was there no end to his talents?

He walked slowly to the other end of the hall.

'What makes you unhappy?' He was walking round, looking for a likely candidate. 'Sara?'

Sara's voice was ever so husky at that angle.

'Poverty. People dying alone unloved. Homeless people make me weep. War. Famine—'

'Jasmin?'

Oh, not again. Was this punishment for snorting?

'Um. Finishing a bar of chocolate.'

Because her eyes were shut, she couldn't see how a full smile warmed Harry's chiselled features. 'You see, Sara,' he said, 'there's no point in playing this if you're not going to be honest. At least when Jasmin gives up, she does it honestly.'

Oh good, thought Jazz. I need an enemy.

The 'game' continued for forty minutes. People were saying staggeringly honest things about themselves, most of which Jazz had no desire to know. The whole thing, she was convinced, was to feed Harry's need to feel in control. Yet couldn't he see that most of the cast were only saying

74

things to impress him? On the other hand though, it had been fascinating to discover that Mo wished she had been able to cry about her mother's death, but was unable to – except in her dreams. Jazz thought she knew everything about Mo.

She had noticed that Wills got particularly short shrift from Harry. In fact, Harry never asked him one question and Wills didn't seem surprised by it at all. He seemed happy enough to be ignored. But why should Harry ignore him? Jealous probably, she answered herself confidently, vaguely aware that that didn't make much sense.

One hour later, Lizzy, Jane, Kitty, Lydia, Mary and Mr and Mrs Bennet were reading through Scene One.

For the first half an hour, the mood was so buoyant that no joke was too small for a hearty laugh from all. Mrs Bennet in particular was very hyped. She kept telling awful anecdotes that began with, 'That reminds me,' and ended with punchlines so weak that Jazz had to stop herself from saying, 'So what happened next?' and were filled with such total irrelevance to what had preceeded their telling that Jazz wondered whether the woman was in fact deaf. It wasn't long before she found it wearing to be with so many over-excited adults in one room.

'You know, that reminds me,' chuckled Mrs Bennet, *à propos* of nothing, 'of a very amusing story.' And with that, she interrupted herself by starting to laugh silently and shake her head, as though she didn't trust herself to tell the said tale.

Harry interrupted. 'Right people, let's try again from "While Mary is adjusting her ideas . . .", shall we?' Mrs Bennet didn't seem to mind at all, chuckling happily to herself and shaking her head as if it was just as well she'd been stopped. It seemed Jazz was the only one who even noticed Harry's rudeness.

Three hours later they were still doing the opening scene. It was approaching midnight. Jazz was tired, hungry and utterly bored. As she sat in the middle of the room, surrounded by the others, waiting for Harry to stop reading the script and tell the actress playing the part of Kitty what to do next, Jazz's stomach growled so loudly it actually frightened her. There was an embarrassed silence.

'I am officially starving,' said Jazz solemnly. 'Please call Comic Relief.'

The others laughed and added meaningful little quips like 'me too'. Harry didn't seem to hear any of this, he was too absorbed by the script.

'What do you *mean* by those words, Kitty?' he asked instead.

Kitty looked at the script as though if she looked hard enough the words would appear. She was so terrified of saying the wrong thing that she said nothing at all.

'Does *anyone* know?' said Harry painfully.

Jazz knew she might as well answer before he asked her anyway. 'She means "It's nearly midnight, you'd better let us go home now if you want us to ever come to another rehearsal".'

Harry looked at his watch.

'Jesus! Yes, of course,' he said quietly, as if only addressing himself. It apparently didn't matter to him that other people might find it late, only that it was late for him. He rubbed his eyes. 'Right then,' he clapped his hands. 'See you all Wednesday. Good work.' And he picked up his coat and walked out. He didn't even notice Purple Glasses who had been waiting for them all to leave so she could lock up.

Jazz and George dawdled getting on their coats and chatted outside the church door.

'That was absolutely knackering,' yawned Jazz.

'I know, he's brilliant.'

'Is he? Wills doesn't think so.'

'Wills?'

'William Whitby. He's playing Wickham.'

'Oh him. Well, he's not an Oscar-winner, is he?'

'No, but he's got a very nice arse.'

'Oh, and Harry hasn't, I suppose?'

'No, Harry has. There's no denying that. It's just one of my principles not to get involved with a man who talks out of it.'

'Want a lift home?'

'No, I need the fresh air, I'm completely shagged.'

'Well, phone me when you get home then.'

'Yes, Mum.'

The night air was deliciously fresh. Jazz loved being up when most people weren't – it was the closest she felt to nature, especially in West Hampstead.

'Want a lift?'

She looked over to the car at the end of the road. It was a clapped-out old MG with its roof down and Harry sitting in it. Despite the appealing picture, Jazz felt no urge to go any nearer. How long had he been sitting there? Had he heard anything they'd said? Did he think she needed a pep-talk already?

'No, thanks. I need the air.'

'You never know what's out there,' he said gravely. 'Could be dangerous.'

'No less dangerous than getting into the car of a strange man, I shouldn't wonder.'

'You think I'm strange do you, Ms Field?'

Jazz mulled this over. 'Well, put it this way,' she said. 'I'm still making you out, Mr Noble.'

'Well, have a lift,' he said with a touch of impatience, leaning across to the passenger door and opening it wide, 'and you'll get some extra material for your work.'

She managed a smile. 'I think I've done enough work for today, don't you?'

Instead of answering the question, Harry simply said, rather dramatically Jazz thought, 'I won't bite, Ms Field,' as he started to put his key in the ignition.

Jazz walked up to him slowly.

'Look, since you like honesty without any pauses, here goes. I would prefer to walk through the midnight streets of West Hampstead on my own than have a lift in your car.' She shut the car door and smiled at him. 'Thanks all the same.'

And she strolled into the sweet night air.

Chapter 9

Sara had arranged to meet her brother for lunch in an exquisitely smart, bijou Hampstead restaurant that was sufficiently
off the beaten track to be exclusive. Jack never said no to
meeting her – he hated her guilt-trips – and she had overheard
that he and Harry had planned to get together that afternoon.
She knew that Jack would turn up with Harry, which was
why she'd chosen this restaurant. Anywhere else and the
afternoon would have been spoilt by people stopping to ask
Harry for his autograph. They did it everywhere, even in
Hampstead, where they really should know better. But in this
restaurant, the waiters were even more condescending than
their many visiting celebrities, and no one would ever lower
themselves to ask for autographs. Even from Harry Noble.
Naturally Maxine had been invited as well and Charles would,
of course, be paying.

'And how fares our Ugly Sister?' asked Sara, as they were
all being given their menus.

Harry scanned the hors d'oeuvres.

She tried again. 'Are you enjoying your biggest challenge
since RADA or is it proving too much, even for you?'

Eventually Harry put down the menu.

'On the contrary, I hope I have enough humility to admit when I was wrong.'

Sara could hardly contain her relief and excitement.

'What are you going to do? Where are you going to get another Lizzy Bennet at this late hour? How will you break it to the poor girl?'

'No, I don't mean that at all,' said Harry stiffly. 'I mean exactly the opposite. She was the perfect choice. I couldn't have cast a more ideal Lizzy Bennet.'

'Nor a more gorgeous Jane Bennet,' beamed Jack, putting his menu down and rubbing his hands together. 'I'm going to have the steak, I think.'

'Ah yes, but Jane Bennet was never in doubt,' said Harry to Jack.

Sara tried to pull the conversation back on track.

'In what way is the Ugly Sister your perfect choice? Do tell, I'm fascinated,' she said, a careful lightness to her tone.

Harry thought about it for a while.

'Everything about her,' he said simply. 'Her temperament, her acting, her figure, her face, her eyes. She's perfect.'

Sara found herself staring at the menu without taking any of it in. She discovered she'd lost her appetite. Damnation. She loved their foie gras.

After the waiter took their orders, Jack started waxing lyrical about George. A thought crossed Harry's mind.

'I do hope you're not going to do your old trick of falling in love with your leading lady and then breaking it all off the day before opening night.'

Jack laughed, but said nothing.

'I won't stand for any of that, you know. Not in my production,' said Harry, sipping red wine. 'I'll never forget when your Beatrice tried to punch your lights out in the final scene of *Much Ado*. We could have renamed that production *Much Ado About Quite A Lot, Actually*.'

Jack smiled at the memory. He couldn't even remember the name of the actress now.

'There's nothing worse than getting involved with an actress while you're in the same play as her,' lectured Harry. 'Ruins your focus.'

Jack looked uncomfortable. 'Life's about more than focus, old chap.'

'Not if you want to be great,' clipped Harry. 'Relationships with actresses are doomed. Biggest mistake an actor can make. Drains him of energy. He'll either be unhappy or unsuccessful.' He gulped down his wine. 'Unless of course, she's merely an advert actress. Though why anyone would want one of them is beyond me. Better not to let women in your life at all. Unfocuses you,' he repeated himself grumpily. 'Present company excluded, of course,' he said as an afterthought.

Sara wondered desperately if that included marriage. Jack picked at his bread and looked around the restaurant.

'Wine's splendid,' said Charles, belching loudly.

The honeymoon period was well and truly over and Jazz now knew who in the cast she hated, who she found amusing, who she thought ridiculous, and who she liked. Purple Glasses fitted into all the first three categories. Even Jazz was surprised at how much Purple Glasses managed to irritate her. In the beginning, Jazz had maintained a cool but polite distance. But there was always some pretext Purple Glasses found for bossing Jazz around, and pretty soon Jazz could hardly look her in the eye without either laughing in her face or being downright rude. The ruder she became, the more Purple Glasses seemed to seek her out.

'You left your fan on the wrong chair again,' said Purple Glasses after a particularly long and difficult rehearsal, a note of triumph in her voice.

'How will I ever live with myself?' answered Jazz, in as bitter a tone as she could muster.

Purple Glasses ignored her and studied her notes. 'You're meant to leave it on the chair Upstage Right, not Downstage Left. How many times do I have to tell you?'

'Since you ask, you've told me quite enough times, thanks.'

'Well, it doesn't seem to make any difference, does it?' said Purple Glasses as if she was telling a small child to stop picking its nose in public.

'Not in the great scheme of things, Fiona, no. It doesn't make any difference at all where I leave a poxy fan.'

Purple Glasses stared at her and then stalked off.

Jazz also didn't like Sara Hayes, but she couldn't quite put her finger on exactly what annoyed her so much about the woman. There was of course, her obvious insincerity; that was entertaining, but it was more than that. From the first moment of seeing her in the audition room, it had been obvious to Jazz that Sara's one aim in life was to catch Harry Noble. Everyone else was happy merely to catch a glimpse of the man, Sara was determined to catch the man himself. Jazz didn't know women like her still existed. Jazz was used to women going out and getting their man, but Sara wanted to turn Harry into a man who would want to go out and get her. It was like watching living socio-history at work. What made it more entertaining to watch was that Harry was oblivious to Sara's charms. It made wonderful viewing. Jazz supposed that was why Sara hated her so much; because she was playing

Lizzy Bennet she was taking up most of Harry's time. If only Sara knew, thought Jazz with a smile, how little she thought of the great man. The friction between Sara and herself was beginning to add a certain piquancy to the rehearsals that Jazz was almost enjoying.

'I do like your method of acting,' Sara whispered to her, while they were watching Bingley and Darcy rehearse one afternoon. 'It's so refreshing.'

Jazz smiled graciously, and did a very good impression of a genuine thank you, pretending not to understand. It was worth the effort, as she saw Sara's eyes shrink in annoyance. She then watched Sara in awe as Harry slowly paced across the room to Sara's right, and Sara, sensing his presence there, moved her head away from Jazz towards him with such concentrated grace that it fell so as to accentuate her beautiful jawline just as he turned to face them. Amazing, thought Jazz. Her timing was so precise it looked as if the two of them were in a choreographed dance. But then, to her great amusement, Jazz saw Harry look straight through Sara to focus, in familiar frustration, on her.

That was it! thought Jazz. The thing that had been annoying her since she'd first met Sara – it had suddenly clicked! It was that every movement – however minuscule – was completely controlled. Did this woman ever do anything spontaneous? Not a flutter of her eyelashes, not a fractional glint in her eye or a twitch of her perfect mouth was natural. No wonder her acting always seemed so stilted – how could she act natural when she didn't know what natural was? Jazz started wondering if Sara only ever farted in her sleep.

To hide her smirk at that thought, she looked away from Harry to Brian. And there her smirk froze on her lips. The more she watched Brian the more obvious it became

83

to her that casting him as Darcy had been a complete mental aberration on Harry's part. It didn't matter how many first-night jitters this would save Harry in the future, the man acted like a stick. Harry was having terrible trouble getting Brian to even frown properly, let alone deliver his lines with conviction. What Harry didn't realise was that Brian, the critic feared by all, was absolutely terrified of him and the more Harry shouted, the more constipated Brian looked. It would have been amusing if it wasn't so worrying.

Jazz had never before even considered that every tiny movement on stage had to be choreographed by the director. And now that she had seen Brian on stage, she marvelled that in most plays, the actors didn't regularly collide with each other.

At one point while rehearsing a scene with her on the tiny stage at the end of the church hall, Brian had stood at her side, staring into the audience (which consisted of Harry and a few of the other actors who would be needed later in the scene), and addressed a whole speech to her, without looking at her once. Jazz had started a slow frown at Brian, then turned to look at Harry, pointed at Brian, then herself, and mouthed very slowly, 'Is he talking to *me*?' while Brian spoke. There were various titters from the audience but Harry wasn't amused. Instead he interrupted poor Brian mid-speech with a scornful, 'What are you doing, Brian?'

Brian froze. 'I – I –'

'Lizzy is standing *next* to you,' said Harry as if to a retarded chimpanzee. Brian turned and looked at Jazz blankly. She grinned at him and did a little wave. Brian didn't wave back. God, everyone was in such a bad mood, she thought. Wasn't this supposed to be fun?

'Move to your right, Brian.' Harry's voice was full of cold fury.

Brian was so terrified that he moved to his left, blocking Jazz entirely. She started giggling and waved to Harry from behind Brian.

Harry was unimpressed.

'YOUR RIGHT!' he bellowed. Brian leapt to his right, revealing a beaming Jazz behind him.

'Hello again,' said Jazz. 'Who turned the lights out?' She was having a brilliant time.

Eventually, after Harry had tried every trick in the book to get Brian to move to the right place at the right time – to no avail – he finally instructed him to stand stock still throughout the entire scene. It would have been what Darcy would have done anyway, Harry concluded.

Watching Jack Hayes rehearse, on the other hand, was a pure delight. His movements, his voice and his expression were now to Jazz utterly Bingley. And he could switch it on in seconds. He could also repeat the same line hundreds of times without showing the slightest bit of impatience or fatigue. And every time Harry gave him some other idea or movement to add to his words, he seemed sincerely grateful. She had to admit it – Harry Noble knew what he was doing. With just a change of tone or slight twist of the body, he could transform Jack's performance beyond recognition, adding layers of meaning to the simplest of words. She began to see what Harry had meant by the word 'honesty' when describing good acting. It was as if Jack wasn't acting at all, but speaking from his heart. Jazz wondered why the actor wasn't more famous. She mentioned this to Sara one day, while they were both sitting next to each other on stage, waiting for Brian and Jack to be blocked by Harry.

'Oh, he's a genius,' replied Sara in a stage-whisper. 'It runs in the family, you know,' she added, with a self-mocking smile that didn't suit her and a faraway look that did.

Flabbergasted, Jazz discovered that they were brother and sister. 'But he hasn't got the drive that Harry has,' sighed Sara. 'It's a tragedy. That's why he'll never be great, like Harry. They were at RADA together.' She was off on her favourite subject. 'That's how Harry and I met. I was still at college then, but that's when I decided my future. I would be an actress.'

Jazz knew that being an actress wasn't the only part of her future Sara had decided on when she met Harry. As far as she was concerned, they would make the perfect pair.

'They're quite simply blood brothers,' Sara went on. 'Jack would lay down his life for Harry. And Harry guides Jack completely.'

Jazz was intrigued by Sara's definition of blood relationships.

Possibly the nicest thing about Jack though, was that he was quite obviously head over heels in love with her sister. At every possible opportunity during rehearsals he would find his way to George's side and the two would talk as if no one else was in the room. To be honest, Jazz couldn't work out whether their roles as lovers had added to their mutual attraction, but nevertheless, it was fascinating to watch them at work. Jazz always enjoyed observing sexual chemistry between two people, but when it was between her sister and someone that Jazz liked, it gave her a particularly warm glow. Whenever he looked at George, Jack's eyes looked like they had little lightbulbs behind them, they were so bright. Every now and then, when George looked briefly away to offer him a glimpse of her face from a different angle, Jazz noticed that he would quickly blink, slightly self-consciously, and clear his throat. Then when George looked back, his eyes shone straight at her and his smile widened. Every now and then he would lightly touch her arm or her back, and she would either smile disarmingly sweetly or she would not, just to ensure that he didn't get cocky. And then she would lean forward or tilt her head towards him, so that he had to try and hide the fact that he was now forcing his attention on her face and away from her smooth, honey-coloured bustline. Until she flicked her hair back or pretended to look at the floor for a moment, giving him just enough time to take it in. She was a master at her unspoken art, marvelled Jazz, stopping herself from giving her sister a well-deserved ovation.

'This is *it*, Jazz,' George said as she dropped Jazz home after rehearsal number three. 'I've finally met Mr Right. Jack is everything I've ever been looking for. Have you noticed how white his teeth are when he smiles? He's going to be famous one day, I know it.'

'Hmmm,' replied Jazz, explicitly. 'What about Action Man?'

George went quiet. Jazz wasn't going to let her get away with that.

'Are you just going to pretend he doesn't exist or do the decent thing and give him the elbow?'

'I'll do the decent thing,' said George quietly. 'As soon as Jack does something *in*decent.'

'You are incorrigible. Spare a thought for those of us living a happy single existence.'

'You won't be single for long. I've seen the way Wills looks at you.'

Jazz was taken aback. She'd certainly been enjoying rehearsals that little bit more whenever Wills was there. It wasn't as if

87

they flirted with each other, they just had a lot in common. A shared disdain for Harry Noble, for one thing. It seemed they were the only two who felt the same about him. No one else seemed to realise that his rudeness would be unacceptable if he weren't so bloody famous. Yes, he was a good director – not that Jazz knew much about directing. But she did know about people, and Harry Noble was a nightmare. As far as Jazz was concerned there was no excuse for it. Oscar or no Oscar. Dynasty or no dynasty. Adonis or no Adonis.

And then during rehearsal number four, she had a scintillating conversation with Wills about the side of Harry Noble that no one sees.

It happened when they were having a coffee break together. The morning had been exhausting. Harry had been trying to get Brian to be more arrogant in his first scene. Jazz had been astonished by how rude he was to his cast. She even pitied the obnoxious critic.

'For God's sake, Brian,' shouted Harry, pulling his hands through his hair. 'You're an obscenely wealthy, devastatingly handsome, ridiculously eligible man. Not a nervous supply teacher.'

Brian went puce with embarrassment.

'For Christ's sake, man, stand tall,' and Harry walloped him on the back and almost punched him in the stomach. 'Darcy has no concept that anything he does is wrong. He is rude, arrogant and condescending. Watch me.'

Jazz and Wills exchanged some eloquent eye-contact and Jazz was surprised by the intensity of a short, sharp ripple of excitement at this recognition that Wills shared her secret opinion of Harry. Their director was blissfully unaware that he shared all of Darcy's worst personality traits. And unlike everyone else, only she and Wills were shrewd enough to look beyond his fame and money to see him for what he really was.

They watched in astonishment as Harry manhandled Brian out of his space and stood in for him. And then in an instant, he transformed himself into Darcy. He swelled his chest out and with the slightest change in his expression, showed utter distaste for all around him. Despite herself, Jazz was impressed. How could Harry not see that he himself was perfect for the part?

As Harry unhurriedly moved his eyes around the room, disdain oozing from every pore, he gave a running commentary of his thoughts in a clipped, upper-class accent. It was, as Gilbert would have said, a living, breathing Fitzwilliam Darcy.

'How utterly *vile* they all are.' (Jazz had never realised the word 'vile' could be so descriptive.) 'With their vulgar clothes and their dizz*gust*ing habits. I shall have to ask Brown to draw me a bath when I get home.' (Everyone laughed.) Harry looked at Jazz who was in place as Lizzy on a chair by a makeshift table. His eyes bore into her. 'Tolerable,' he clipped, visibly sizing her up, staring rudely at every bit of her anatomy as if she were a pig up for auction. 'But certainly not enough to tempt the likes of *me*.'

Jazz looked back at him, furious, humiliated. She found herself thinking 'Thank Christ for that.'

Staring at Jazz's expression of disgust for perhaps a little bit longer than was necessary, Harry dropped the act.

'Perfect, Jasmin,' he said quietly. 'Perfect.'

Jazz stared him out. 'I wasn't acting,' she replied, just as quietly, and turned her face away.

For a moment Harry didn't seem to know what to say. 'Well, you should have been,' he said finally. 'This isn't a free show,' and he slowly walked back to his place.

Once there, he clapped his hands loudly, making everyone jump. 'Now try again man, and don't waste any more of my time.'

Brian stood up slowly, looking as happy as if he was about to be burnt at the stake.

His performance was no better but Harry didn't seem to mind as much this time. In fact, he didn't even seem to be watching this time. He called a break immediately afterwards.

Wills, it turned out, had forgotten to bring any food or coffee, and Jazz was only too happy to share some of her flasked coffee with him and a precious Hobnob or two. *That's how much I like him,* she thought to herself.

Harry was sitting in solitary splendour, as ever, one hand through ruffled hair, a pencil in the other, eyes in the distance. The director never lowered himself to actually mix with his cast. Only Sara and Jack Hayes, Matt and sometimes Purple Glasses (who always carried her clipboard and spoke too loudly at him in a failed attempt to cover her nerves) went up and talked to him, and Jazz was convinced that a silent fame hierarchy was at work. There was no one there on the same level of fame as Harry, so he couldn't be seen to make the first move and talk to anyone. Jazz wondered briefly if he ever got lonely.

Just now, Sara was approaching him. Jazz and Wills loved to eavesdrop on this daily exchange while they pretended to do the crossword together – it was a ritual that happened every time Harry sat down. This afternoon it was particularly interesting.

It started as usual with Sara smiling at Harry with what she thought was her prettiest, most innocent-looking smile.

Harry raised his chin to show he was all ears.

Sara then sighed a very loud, girlish sigh, sat down next to him and asked him how it was all going.

'Fine,' Harry told her. Then: 'How can I help?'

Wills and Jazz both smirked at his curt reply, their eyes focusing on the Down clues.

'Well actually,' said Sara, as if it was painful to bring up the subject, 'since you ask, I wouldn't mind your professional opinion.' Then she lowered her voice as if it was all very sensitive. Jazz and Wills had to really concentrate hard to catch this. 'Between you and me, I'm finding it rather hard in the scene with – with – oh, whatshername?'

'Jasmin.'

Sara tinkled a laugh. 'Yes, that's right – Jasmin. How did you guess? Oh dear,' she laughed, 'I'll never remember that funny name.'

Harry said nothing and she was forced to keep going.

'I'm just finding that I can't get enough emotion in my reactions to her and I think it might be because . . .' Sara fought hard to find the right words '. . . there isn't enough emotion coming from her.'

Wills' shoulders were beginning to shake. Jazz grinned, but couldn't help feeling angered and hurt by Sara's cunning performance that would have made even Miss Bingley proud.

Harry still said nothing.

'I know she's your protégée, Mr Noble, and I don't want to—'

'We'll work on the emotion again after the break,' said Harry. 'Maybe I need to have a rehearsal with Jasmin alone. Thank you for bringing it to my attention.'

And with that, he started to pore over the script, leaving Sara no option but to leave him alone, wishing she hadn't said anything. Wills pretended that Jazz had said something funny and the two of them laughed loudly. Eventually they looked back over to Harry. He was now gazing thoughtfully at his fingernails.

'If only his Oscar-winning public could see him now,' hissed Jazz.

'Oh, I'm sure they'd love him all the more for it,' Wills said gently. 'He can do no wrong.'

'Yes, I've noticed that. But do I detect some bitterness in your voice?' Jazz had meant it as a joke, but Wills was serious.

He stared at Harry as he spoke. 'It's because of him that I didn't get the part of Maurice in *It's Nearly Over*.'

Jazz was stunned. 'How? Why? How do you know?'

'Harry knew Howard Fleaback, the producer, from working on *Heart of An Englishman*, and Howard asked Harry what he thought of me because they considered me perfect for the part. I'd already auditioned for another film that never saw the light of day. It turned out that Harry told him I was immature, self-obsessed and unfocused as an actor. He also said I had a drink problem.'

Jazz gasped.

Wills continued, 'My agent knows Howard and when I didn't get the part, she phoned him up and asked why. He said he'd been told on the best authority that I wasn't cut out for Hollywood. When pressed, he explained it more fully.'

Jazz couldn't believe her ears. She needed to be sure. 'So Harry ruined any chance you may have of a Hollywood career?' she asked incredulously.

'Yup.' Wills drained his coffee cup and dripped the dregs on the church floor.

'Why on earth would anyone do something so mean-spirited? Especially someone who's made it themselves?'

'Oh, no actor ever makes it for good,' replied Wills. 'That's the cruelty of the profession. You can win an Oscar one year and be *passé* the next. Even Harry Noble. And remember, for him there's more to lose because all his family are so well-respected in the business.' Wills shrugged and made an effort to look as if he didn't really care. 'Harry and I go back a long way. We were in a very bad production of *Waiting for Godot* together years ago and he detested me then. Made no bones about it. I've never got another job with that director either.' He paused. 'The great Harry Noble just doesn't like me and that carries a lot of weight in this profession.'

But something didn't fit for Jazz. 'So why did he give you this part?'

Wills laughed good-naturedly. 'I have absolutely no idea. Maybe he wanted me to see him now he's an Oscar winner. Maybe he gets a kick out of directing me, a lowly TV actor when he's a Hollywood star, when we were once on the same level. Who knows the way his mind works?'

He looked across at her, his eyes open just a little bit too wide and his smile just a little too forced. 'Anyway, I might never have made it in Hollywood. Who knows? Maybe Harry Noble saved my pride.'

His brave humility hurt her more than the story. How dare Harry Noble get away with something like that! And to think he was so universally respected!

'Have you ever told him you know what he did?'

Wills shook his head. 'What would be the point? It would make me look as immature and self-obsessed as he said I was. No. It's enough that I know.'

Boiling with anger at the injustice of it all, Jazz looked over at Harry. He was staring right at her.

She turned away immediately.

93

Chapter 10

It was Ben's second birthday party and the family was huddled in Josie and Michael's tiny lounge. Simon had been invited and Jazz didn't know who she was more furious with that he was still on the scene, him or George. She decided it was him.

Letting him sit uncomfortably on his own, she cornered George and related the amazing story Wills had told her about Harry.

George was adamant. 'I don't believe it, I just don't believe it.'

Jazz was exasperated. 'Just because he's the great Harry Noble doesn't mean he's not human, you know.'

But George was stubborn. 'That's not human, that's evil. And anyway, he'd already won his Oscar, so what possible motive could he have for damning Wills' reputation?'

'Jealousy? Small-mindedness? Arrogance? Haven't you often said actors are the most petty people on earth?'

'Not all of them,' said George loyally. She and Jack were going out for a lunch 'rehearsal' the next day. Which meant she had to finish with Simon tonight. It was enough to stop her eating any birthday cake.

'Face it, George,' said Jazz. 'Harry's a supremely arrogant bastard and he's done a fine actor out of a brilliant career.'

'You don't know that, Jazz.'

'Yes I do, I heard it from the horse's mouth,' she said, taking another bite of her cake. 'One with exceptional flanks.'

Mo walked over. She was the only person not eating any food.

'Aren't you eating, Mo?' asked Jazz.

'No thanks,' she beamed. 'I ate before I came.'

'You're looking fabulous,' said George. Mo had lost a stone in just a month. Jazz seemed to be the only one who preferred her before.

'Not as fabulous as this cake though,' said Jazz, biting into the rich chocolate and mocha cake Josie had baked. Another of her weekly columns was forming in her head. Josie had had a successful high-flying career before she became a mother, now had a busy social life and, like most of her friends, bought convenience foods, but when it came to her child's birthday cake, she was expected to make it from scratch. Ben was only two, but already Josie felt that a shop-bought cake would mean Mummy didn't love him enough. Where do they pick up these things? she wondered. She looked over at her sister. Josie was laughing politely at Great-Aunt Sylvia's joke. You'd never guess Josie was pregnant again.

Jazz and George followed her into the kitchen with piles of dirty dishes. All the men were sitting in the lounge easing the uncomfortable feeling of having eaten too much, while the women were in the kitchen, tidying up from tea, trying to take their minds off not having eaten as much as they would have liked.

Jazz had long stopped complaining about the men not offering to help with all the work on these occasions. But it still enraged her that she knew her brother-in-law's kitchen better than he did. She had served him meals in his own home ever since he and Josie had first married. Oddly enough, he had never served her in her home. The very idea seemed preposterous.

'You OK?' she asked Josie lightly, picking up a tea-towel, while Martha and George presided over the sink, talking loudly.

Josie just laughed bitterly as she stood on tiptoe and put all the crockery into the cupboards that were built too high for her.

'Come round for dinner one night,' pleaded Jazz for the hundredth time. She'd stopped taking Josie's rejections personally. 'Without Ben or Michael. Like the good old days.'

'I can't. Ben won't go to sleep unless I'm there and once he's off, Michael wants his dinner and I'm too pooped to do anything.' Josie said gently, 'When will you realise the good old days don't exist any more?'

Jazz felt blind fury at her stupid brother-in-law. She wanted to slap her sister and tell her to stop being so pathetic. Instead she just said, 'Has Michael's life changed at all since he's become a father?'

Josie took this calmly. 'Sometimes he gets up in the night,' she said quietly. 'And he's very good at weekends. He's knackered too, you know. He's been working very hard since his promotion.'

Jazz looked at her kid sister and felt a wave of longing for the old Josie she knew and loved. She vowed for the trillionth time never to marry.

Mo joined them in the kitchen. She clapped her hands loudly and then rubbed them together.

'Right, what can I do to help?'

'Eat cake,' shouted Jazz, and threw her a tea-towel.

'Never again,' Mo swore. 'I feel wonderful.'

Martha turned round. 'Mo? Is that you? I thought it was your shadow.' She was genuinely concerned.

'Thanks, Mrs F,' grinned Mo.

Martha ignored Mo's mistake and turned back to discuss Jeffrey's latest arthritis treatment with George while Josie was called into the lounge because Ben had hurt himself. He'd screamed even more when his daddy had tried to help.

'I've booked us in for a class tomorrow,' said Mo to Jazz.

'Pardon?'

'Step aerobics. You'll love it. Then we'll have a steam room and a sauna.'

Jazz just stared at Mo. 'You hate me, don't you?'

Mo just smiled smugly.

How should George chuck Simon? For the first time in her life, with her thirtieth birthday drifting away from her at a startling speed, Georgia Field was about to chuck a perfectly good man. Well, a man with all his limbs intact anyway. How to do it, though? And what if Jack proved to be a non-starter?

George had thought about this long and hard. She had considered phoning Simon at his office and telling him they 'Had To Talk', but decided against it because that was so melodramatic. She was going to take the bull by the horns and do it now. In the car on the way home from the tea-party.

Now.

She got into the passenger seat of his car, her heart thumping. She stared straight ahead into the drizzle as he reversed out, put on his shades and turned on his multi-layered CD shuffle function. She didn't know why he bothered with that, every single CD in it was one by Phil Collins anyway. Surely that was reason enough to chuck the man?

They drove in silence for a while. She just didn't know how to start the conversation. What if he got so angry that he drove them into an oncoming car so as not to lose her to anyone else? What if he shouted at her? What if he talked her out of it? But then one thought gave her courage. She pictured Jack's smiling, intent face.

She gave a small cough.

No reaction. He was mouthing the words to 'Mama', his all-time favourite Phil Collins track and tapping – out of time – on the leather steering wheel. Before she realised it, he was parking in West Hampstead. And now he would ask her if she'd be able to supply him in the caffeine area. She always hated it when he did that.

He turned the engine off, took off his shades, smiled at her and rested his hand on the wheel.

'Fancy furnishing me in the caffeine area?' he asked with a wink.

'Uh huh,' she said weakly and they got out of the car.

George flicked on the lights and Simon immediately plonked himself down in the middle of the three-seater couch. With a big sigh he picked up the paper lying on the coffee table, and turned it to the sports page. Suddenly George realised she hated him.

'We have to talk,' she said.

He didn't take his eyes off the paper.

'Sure, shoot,' he said.

Oh good God, did he really have to use sporting metaphors? Well, here was a googly for him.

'Um,' she said softly. 'Um . . .'

He looked up and smiled at her expectantly, his eyebrows raised, as if she was a blithering fool. She blinked at him like a blithering fool.

'Are you all right?' he asked.

Her ashen face answered him eloquently and for the first time he got a bit concerned. He'd seen that look before.

'Are you about to chuck me or are you dying of some mysterious disease?' he asked in mock seriousness. It was early days in the relationship and he wasn't sure yet which piece of news would hit him worse.

George's jaw dropped. 'I'm *not* dying of some mysterious disease,' she managed to say pointedly.

There! She'd said it! It wasn't so difficult after all!

'Right,' nodded Simon slowly. That hadn't worked out quite so well as he'd hoped.

There was a pause.

Now it was out in the open, George felt the black cloud that had been hovering over her head for the past month dissolve and disappear. She was suffused with a sense of goodwill to all men, including Simon.

'Coffee?' she asked sincerely.

Simon stared at her. 'Have you just chucked me?' he answered ungenerously.

Oh dear. She thought they'd cleared all that up. She tried again.

'Well, I *don't* have a terminal illness,' she said pathetically.

Simon frowned and sat forward on the couch.

'Are you *chucking* me?' he repeated.

99

George swallowed.

'Well . . .'

No sound came out.

'I think it's a simple question, don't you?'

'Yes – I . . .' she came to a halt.

'Yes . . . you think it's a simple question or yes, you are chucking me?'

'Yes . . . I think it's a simple question,' mumbled George, growing uncomfortably hot and finding her feet rooted to the spot.

'So you're *not* chucking me?'

George could only nod weakly.

'What does *that* mean? Yes you're *not* chucking me or yes you *are* chucking me?' Simon was vaguely aware that he was making a prat of himself.

'Yes I *am* chucking you,' she whispered, her eyes down. Really, she hadn't expected him to make it so difficult.

There was an uncomfortable pause.

Simon put the paper down and looked round her flat. Nothing much had changed. Except he was single again. Shit.

'Right, so that's that then.'

He got up suddenly from the couch. George flinched, which seemed to disgust him.

'My God, what do you think I'm going to do?' he asked. 'Hit you?' And then he added under his breath, 'Wouldn't waste my time.'

George thought she was going to be sick. Please, just leave, she thought.

Simon tried to laugh carelessly. 'You'll be all right,' he said, pretending to be fine about it. 'Go and see a soppy girlie film and eat chocolate cake – that's what you girls do, isn't it?'

George tried to smile. Maybe she'd been wrong about him. He seemed to understand her so well.

He stood up to go. 'And I'll just get rat-arsed and pick up some bird in a nightclub. Bye, doll.' And he gave her one last wink and slammed her front door so hard, she thought it would fall off its hinges.

She heard him stamp downstairs. Then silence.

She was free!

Her head felt light. Her stomach relaxed. Her flat was her own again. No more Phil Collins! No more afternoons watching rugby!

She looked round the empty room. And then rushed to the bathroom where she just made it in time before she was sick.

The lunchtime rehearsal the next day between Jack and George turned into an afternoon movie which turned into an evening meal which turned into a nightcap at George's flat which turned into a very passionate night together.

The next afternoon, when they finally got up, they wandered into West Hampstead for some food. They found Mo and Jazz in George's favourite café. Jack seemed genuinely delighted to see them both there and the four of them fell into easy banter. Jazz was overjoyed to see her George so happy. And Jack seemed totally besotted with her, as was right and proper. The very air around them sizzled. She hoped to God that he treated her right. Not everyone realised how fragile George was.

Eventually Jazz had to tear herself away.

'A step class? Whatever for?' demanded George.

'To repent for all my sins,' answered Jazz. 'Mo's turned into a fitness freak. She's unbearable, she's—'

'Thin,' interrupted Mo merrily.

'Save me?' implored Jazz.

But George looked far too happy to bother saving anyone today.

Jazz picked up her gym kit. She hadn't worn her trainers since she had played netball with her old schoolfriends eight years ago. She had borrowed Mo's kit – a skimpy pair of gym shorts and a leotard that split her up the middle. Mo was kitted out in yellow and white Lycra.

An hour and a half later, Jazz was lying on a mat in a position she never thought she'd be in until she gave birth, flexing muscles she didn't know she had.

The step class had been the longest hour of her life. Sweat dripped into her ears and stung her eyes as she lay drenched on the mat.

She hated the aerobics instructor. She'd bounded in, all teeth and tits, with a bottom like two tennis balls wrapped in cellophane and asked them all indecipherable questions, while fiddling with the earpiece round her head.

'Iny anjuries? Beck problems? Inyone prignant? Iny priblems?'

Jazz was too busy staring at her own legs in the mirror to answer, 'I think I'm in the wrong class, is this Oriental Karma?' She'd never realised until this moment just how white she was. She was so white she was blue. Every time she caught sight of herself in the mirror she thought there was a lighthouse in the room.

Then the aerobics instructor put on Pinkie and Perkie's *70's Classics* and started marching on the spot.

Oh right, this is easy, thought Jazz, and started to march. After a few moments, she realised this might be a little more difficult than she thought. Somehow, the instructor looked decidedly cool marching on the spot, while Jazz was doing exactly the same movement and yet looked like a complete arse.

Suddenly, with no warning, the instructor yelled: 'Ligs apart, stumech flut, bottom een, knees ovur fit, RELAX!'

Jazz had just got the position when the entire room bounded off to the right. The woman on her left bumped into her and didn't apologise. It dawned on Jazz that those instructions had just been the way to stand correctly. This was the real thing.

The steps Ingrid the Instructor inflicted on them were so complicated and the instructions so inaudible over the noise that Jazz had spent most of the hour looking like she was a contestant on *The Generation Game*. To Jazz's untrained ears, the instructor was speaking a different language. Thank God there had been a man there. He made her look positively sophisticated. Why had he come? It couldn't be worth humiliating himself so much just to get a look at tight buns in Lycra, surely? Then again, thought Jazz bitterly, he *was* a man.

Every time Ingrid shouted, 'SWAP LIGS!' Jazz wanted to shout, 'Bagsie yours.' Every time she bellowed 'RELAX!' Jazz looked for the couch. It was hell. Never again.

'Give yourselves a big round of applause,' shouted Ingrid at the end, as Jazz stood, fixed to the ground, panting heavily, wondering if they still burnt witches. Mo came over to her.

'Wow!' she said, looking at Jazz's beetroot face. 'I think you've burst a blood vessel in your head.'

'Don't talk to me – ' breathed Jazz ' – ever again.'

They trudged heavily up to the changing rooms where Jazz took a long shower and then, when she felt barely human again, joined Mo's pink, moist body in the steam room. It was how she imagined heaven would be. All steam and heat. She didn't like the sauna as much but at least in here, without the steam, they could talk. The heat and the silence were wonderful.

'So what are you going to do with this new body of yours?' asked Jazz dreamily.

'Get happy. Get laid. Get a promotion. Dunno.'

Jazz didn't say anything. Sweat was slowly building up on the gentle curve of her stomach.

Mo sighed loudly and put one sweaty arm above her head. 'Jazz, I'm not an idealist like you—'

Jazz interrupted. 'Me – an idealist? Where did you get that from? I'm as cynical as they come. Anyone will tell you that.' She turned over slowly and let the sweat drip down the dip in her back.

'And anyone will tell you that a cynic is a disillusioned idealist,' countered Mo. 'I don't care if the "personal" is the "political", I don't care if I'm setting a bad example to my "sisters". I just want a man. Sorry, Jazz, but that's the way it is.'

'But why diet for it?' asked Jazz gently. 'Don't you want a man who will accept you as you are?' She swung one foot lazily in the air.

Mo got angry. 'I can't *find* any man who will accept me as I am. Can't you get that into your thick head? They're shallow, superficial scum. And I want one.'

Jazz decided she had to get out of the sauna. It was too hot.

Chapter 11

The first of many cast parties was due and rehearsals were well under way when Jazz realised that it wasn't her imagination, Harry Noble *did* keep staring at her. And not just when she was acting. During every break, when she was usually either relaxing with Mo or Wills or trying to escape Gilbert, she could feel Harry's eyes boring into her. It made her feel constantly on trial. She was sure he was just waiting for her to do something stupid, like trip over her shoelaces or giggle at the wrong time or something. Was this his way of intimidating her?

Instead, Jazz would make a point of having a riot with Mo and George to show him that it was much more fun with the plebs than with the top set.

But one time, when Jazz was sitting with Mo and George, she'd felt so annoyed by Harry's surveillance that she'd turned and stared rudely back. It had taken all her self-control not to stick her tongue out at him like a four-year-old. To her extreme frustration, he took this as encouragement and came straight over and joined the threesome. It was unprecedented. The entire room turned to watch.

'Are you checking up on us, Mr Noble?' asked Jazz, looking up at him. Annoyingly, Mo made room for him on the chair next to her and gave him an encouraging smile. Without smiling back, he moved it to face Jazz so the four of them were in an untidy square.

'What would I be checking up on? You're allowed your breaks,' he shrugged, before crossing one beautifully long leg over the other and settling into his usual staring trick.

Feeling responsible for his coming over and spoiling the chat, Jazz started talking in an effort to entertain the girls.

'Well, you can be assured that we're all too exhausted by your rehearsals to have any energy to rebel against your firm leadership,' she said. 'I'm completely pooped. My feet are absolutely killing me.'

There was a pause.

'Perhaps you'd appreciate a lift home then?' asked Harry seriously.

Buggery bollocks. He must assume she'd said that to get an offer of a lift. But she was determined not to accept a lift from him.

'Mo'll give me a lift home, I live with her,' she answered shortly.

'No I can't,' answered Mo. 'Unless you want to go via Sainsbury's and the gym.'

'Well, George only lives a road away.'

George blushed and looked over to Jack. 'I'm – I'm going straight off somewhere else. Sorry, Jazz.'

Jasmin was stuck.

'Well,' said Harry. 'Looks like I'm your knight in shining armour.'

Jazz snorted unattractively. 'Do I look like I need saving?' she demanded.

'Hardly,' clipped Harry. 'It was a turn of phrase. It wasn't intended to insult you.'

Jazz felt momentarily embarrassed. 'Thanks,' she forced. 'OK.'

Harry simply nodded and walked away.

Jazz tore into the girls. 'Traitors!' she hissed.

The girls didn't understand.

'I don't want a lift with him, I hate him—'

'For God's sake don't overreact, Jazz, it's only a lift,' said Mo. 'From the most dishy man on the planet.'

'Most arrogant man on the planet, you mean.'

Mo looked at her. 'What is going on?' she asked. 'Possibly the most famous and respected – and gorgeous – actor of his generation is asking for some prime time with you alone. And you're a journalist. Where's your sense of professionalism?'

Jazz looked at her hands in her lap. The girls were right. She should see this as research.

'More importantly, where's your sense of *taste*?' smiled George. 'He's amazing. I'd get in his car any day, arrogant or not.'

'Yeah, and I'd pay the petrol,' agreed Mo.

'God, listen to you two,' said Jazz. 'Anyone would think your brains turned to jelly in the presence of a man. Does the word emancipation mean anything to you? Women burnt their bras for you, you know.'

'Why?' asked George, nonplussed. 'Were they planning to wear backless dresses?'

'If anyone burnt my Wonderbra, I'd boil their heads,' said Mo.

Jazz put her head in her hands.

The rest of the rehearsal was spoilt for her. Every time she thought about the lift home a knot formed in her stomach.

107

She detested that man, and to have to spend any time alone with him was too long. Also, it meant that she wouldn't be able to hang around chatting to Wills. She wanted to spit. At the end of the rehearsal, she was even ruder to Purple Glasses than usual.

'I didn't see you wearing your shawl in Act Four, Scene Two,' said Purple Glasses as soon as Jazz was alone.

'Really?' asked Jazz innocently. 'Have you had those glasses tested recently? How many fingers am I holding up?' and she held up her middle finger and walked off before Purple Glasses could comment. She wasn't proud of herself, but there was no denying it felt good.

At the end of the rehearsal, as she was picking up all her things, she could feel Harry approach behind her. As usual he just stopped and stared.

She turned round.

'Do you mean to frighten me by staring all the time?' she asked rudely.

Harry seemed genuinely surprised. 'I only came to ask if you were ready,' he said.

She looked over to Wills who was deep in chitchat with one of Lizzy's pretty younger sisters. She didn't notice Harry follow her gaze. Suddenly, he was spurred into action.

'Right, let's go,' he said and led the way.

Harry's car was not what she had expected. It was messy inside, and because it had been sitting in the sun all day, it was also stiflingly hot and the leather seat was sticky on Jazz's skin.

The journey wasn't long by foot but because of all the one-way streets, it took a while to get there by car. All Jazz could think of was how much she would prefer to be walking. It was the end of a lovely summer's day. Harry took the MG's roof off and they wound down their windows and set off. His driving was forced and awkward, exactly like his manner, thought Jazz. Slowly she began to realise that he was actually self-conscious. She looked out to the left, so as not to put him off and tried not to smile when he stalled while letting a car go past him down a narrow street. She noticed the people in the car stared rudely at him in disbelief as they drove by. The girl shrieked suddenly: 'Oh my God, it's Harry Noble!' How rude, thought Jazz. Harry ignored them completely. As they drove off, the girl shouted out laughingly, 'Wanna shag?' Jazz closed her eyes in embarrassment and disgust.

She had got into his car determined not to be the one to start talking, but when she realised that all Harry's concentration was taken up not driving onto the pavement, she decided it would be fun to engage him in conversation.

'Do you offer people lifts to ignore them in a confined space?' She hadn't meant to make it sound *quite* so hard.

Harry didn't answer.

'I'll take that as a yes, shall I?'

Eventually he answered. 'Do you accept lifts to interrogate people?'

'Of course,' she said with a smile. 'I'm a journalist.'

'And why would you want to interrogate me?'

'To work you out, of course. Anywhere, here will do. That's my block. Number seven. Lucky for some.'

He didn't so much park as stop somewhere near her mansion block.

She was just about to get out when, looking ahead of him, Harry said, 'You enjoy watching people, don't you?'

'As I say, I'm a journalist. Anyway, I could say the same for you,' answered Jazz, squinting in the sun and opening her door.

'Ah yes, but I don't put down my thoughts in a national magazine.'

'That's only fun. No one takes them seriously. And that is my job, remember. The tacky world of women's magazines.'

'I do remember,' he said gravely. He looked at her. 'You write well.'

Jazz was so surprised that she had no answer. If he'd been reading her columns, he'd have seen the few comments she'd made about everyone in the cast, including him. She had written some lovely, warm things about Wills but everyone else had got fairly sharp shrift.

'Thank you.' The vision of him reading *Hoorah!* brought a smile to her lips.

He was still looking at her. 'Are you never worried that your criticisms – witty and urbane though they may be – might sometimes be wrong?'

Riled, Jazz knew she might have guessed there would be an insult behind his compliment.

'No,' she said shortly. 'I'm not. And I can assure you I don't put all my thoughts down. Only the ones I won't get sued for.'

'You seem to have a lot of confidence in your opinions.'

'Yes, and confidence is so unbecoming in a woman, isn't it?' she said, and continued before he could interrupt: 'Tragically, Mr Noble, I'm usually right. Would that I was wrong more often.'

'Are your opinions always that depressing?'

Jazz shrugged. 'Yes. Most of the time. I find most people unlikeable.'

'Such cynicism in one so young,' he half-smiled.

'Ah well, the more people I meet, the more I like my fridge,' misquoted Jazz.

'I think you like to hate. It makes you feel superior.'

Jazz had had enough of the character assassination. 'Oh? As opposed to actually *being* superior – like yourself, I suppose?' she asked.

Harry shrugged. Amazed, Jazz continued. 'I've met someone through this play who seems to have a very different opinion on the matter of your natural superiority.'

At first Harry looked uncomprehending, then a realisation struck and to Jazz's delight, he started to look profoundly uncomfortable. Jazz was determined not to be intimidated by the silence that followed. When she thought Harry would not reply, she picked up her bag as thought to leave. It worked. Harry coughed.

'William Whitby has a way about him,' he said eventually. 'No woman I have ever met seems able to withstand his charms for very long.'

'You sound jealous,' Jazz said quietly.

Harry seemed angry. 'Then you don't know what jealousy sounds like,' he said with ill-disguised scorn.

Jazz ignored that. 'Since he's so irresistible, it's bizarre, don't you think, that he hasn't made it in Hollywood? After all, he has the right connections and the right talent.' Harry seemed to be making an effort to control himself. Thinking she might have gone too far, she changed tack. 'Anyway,' she countered. 'wouldn't you say that you are also pretty confident in your own opinions?'

'Yes, if they're made with sound judgement,' replied Harry.

'Ah. So it's just *women* who make errors of judgement, then?'

111

'Those are your words, not mine. I hope I would never be so sexist.'

'How sweet,' smiled Jazz. 'You'd be the first man I'd ever met who wasn't.'

'Maybe that says more about the men you meet than men in general,' Harry retorted.

Jazz was furious. 'Oh well, of course it would be *my* error and not *men's*. Thank you for putting me right after all these years. It must be ever so nice to be perfect.'

'I never said I was perfect, Ms Field,' said Harry, growing more and more annoyed, 'but I would like to think that perception and judgement are not my faults.'

Jazz refused to give up. 'But tell me, would you confidently say that you've never let professional rivalry influence your opinion-making?'

Harry stared straight ahead. 'I hope I'm bigger than that,' he said shortly.

'Because,' Jazz continued, 'when someone holds as much sway over others' opinions as you do, and someone is as sure of their own opinions as you are, wouldn't you agree that it would be doubly important for your opinions about people to be right?'

Harry frowned at Jazz before answering thoughtfully, 'It's always important for people's opinions about others to be well-founded. The difference with me perhaps is that once founded, my opinions rarely change.'

Wasn't that one of Darcy's lines from the play? thought Jazz. To both of their surprise, they smiled together suddenly. They couldn't avoid the fact that they were starting to think and behave like the characters in their play. Harry was used to this phenomenon – a few years ago, he had actually felt his back ache and one leg feel weaker than the other when playing Richard III – but to Jazz, this was a new sensation, as if her personality was possessed. Even though it was by the personality of Lizzy Bennet, it was still somewhat unnerving.

'The trick,' Harry continued, 'as any good journalist – like yourself – would know, is to go to the right sources instead of – instead of . . .' He broke off, obviously thinking of words to describe Wills.

'Instead of sources which you disapprove of?' helped Jazz.

'Instead of sources that might be misleading,' he finished quietly.

'Well, thanks for the lift,' said Jazz 'it's been most educative.' And she leapt out of the car, slammed the door shut and was gone. If he thought she'd be inviting him in for coffee he was very much mistaken.

She threw shut her front door and, feeling very much like Jasmin Field again and very little like Lizzy Bennet, stomped angrily up the stairs. Dripping with sweat, she jumped straight into the shower where she allowed herself to give vent to her hatred for the man who thought he could criticise her writing just because he had given her a lift home. How dare he? How would he like it if she criticised his acting?

Harry meanwhile, was getting lost down a one-way street. His fury at Jazz was soon taking a different direction. When he got home some forty minutes later, he sat in his car for a while, just thinking. He looked at the seat next to him, noticed some drops of sweat on it and, feeling very much like Harry Noble again and very little like Fitzwilliam Darcy, smiled at how crude he could be sometimes.

Chapter 12

Apart from the unwanted attentions of Harry Noble, Jazz was having to cope with a considerably more annoying pest during rehearsals.

For some reason Gilbert Valentine seemed to think that she and he had something rather special going on. Odd that when they had worked together all those years ago, he had hardly noticed her existence, and now that she saw him for what he really was, he seemed interested. He hardly ever left her side, which was almost more than she could bear at the best of times, but what made it even more infuriating was that it was putting Wills off. He hardly ever came over for a chat any more. She was going to have to do something about it, and tonight was the night. Daniel McArthur – playing Denny, the mutual army friend of Lizzy's sister, Lydia and the wicked Wickham – was giving a party and Jazz was determined that this would be her opportunity to make it bloody obvious that she was not interested in Gilbert.

At the end of the rehearsal, she managed to get five minutes with Wills.

'Are you coming tonight?' she asked.

'I hope so,' he said earnestly, treating her to a long look with those eyes, 'although it might be a bit awkward.'

'Why?'

'Well, rehearsing with the man is one thing, but socialising with him is quite another.'

Jazz was utterly disappointed. She felt pure anger towards Harry.

'You can't let him spoil your life just because he spoiled your career,' she said hotly. 'You *have* to go. Anyway, there's no way he'll be there. He wouldn't lower himself. Believe me,' she tapped her nose, 'inside information,' she said, thinking back to the conversation she'd overheard at the audition, when Harry had insulted his then future cast to Matt and Sara.

Wills looked over at Harry. 'You're right. Why should I let the likes of him spoil my fun?' He grinned broadly at her. 'OK – you're on. If you're going.'

She smiled. 'Of course I am.'

'It's a date,' he beamed.

Later on that evening Mo came into Jazz's room. She had kitted herself out in a new slimline party outfit. It was black. Jazz thought she looked like a slim widow.

'How do I look?'

'With your eyes.'

'Gee thanks. Don't ever become a Samaritan.'

Jazz turned to Mo and gave her a thorough inspection. She smiled. 'You look really gorgeous, Mo.'

Mo brightened. 'Thanks. If I don't get a shag, I'll kill myself.'

Jazz gave a short laugh. 'How post-feminist of you,' she said. 'Emily Pankhurst would be proud.'

Jazz herself was still wearing only a bra and knickers. Outfits were strewn all over the floor.

'Aren't you ready yet?'

'No,' Jazz sighed. 'I'm having a wardrobe crisis.'

'Don't be daft, you've got a lovely wardrobe. Get dressed, we're late.'

'I don't know what to wear,' moaned Jazz and slumped onto the bed.

Mo patiently sat down next to her. 'What do you feel comfortable in?'

'Bed.'

'Hmmm. I've seen you in bed and it's an ugly sight. I don't recommend it.' She looked round the room. 'Hmm. Try that pink top on, by the sofa.'

Jazz got up and put it on.

Mo wished she had Jazz's curves. 'Lovely. Now put on that short floaty fuschia skirt.'

Jazz did.

Mo wished she had Jazz's strong, long legs. 'Perfect. Let's go.'

They were meeting George at the party. It was a regular pattern. Now that George was With Man, she would of course, be going there with him.

They could hear the music as soon as Mo parked her car. As they got to the door, she turned to Jazz and said, 'Knock 'em dead, pal.'

'Or at least knee 'em where it hurts.'

They pushed the door open. Suddenly Jazz shut it again.

'If you see Gilbert Valentine coming anywhere near me,' she hissed, 'save me, for God's sake. Otherwise I won't be held responsible for my actions.'

'OK,' Mo promised.

At first the dark made them both squint; they couldn't see a thing. Gradually everyone became distinct and Jazz realised that the reason it had taken her eyes so long to adjust was because nearly everyone was dressed in black, like Mo. It looked like a wake. Immediately, she became aware of the dark, almost menacing presence of Harry Noble at the back of the room, facing the door. Damn, she thought. What the hell was *he* doing there? Didn't he think everyone here was too far below him to socialise with? And didn't he realise how off-putting it was to have him there? How could people let themselves go when they were in awe? And why was he always looking at her like that? As if he knew something about her that she didn't? A horrid, knowing, half-smile. It infuriated her.

She spotted Gilbert approaching him, so took Mo by the hand and rushed her to the cramped living room where the music was blaring. She and Mo started to dance. Jazz loved dancing. It was the one area of life (that didn't involve manual labour, nudity or pain) where everyone knew that women were superior to men and accorded them the proper respect. As they started to dance, Jazz watched with astonishment as Gilbert started talking to Harry and Harry, totally ignoring him, actually looked over his head and slowly walked away from him, leaving Gilbert standing stupidly on his own, trying to look like he had meant it to work that way. She realised she was laughing. She and Mo boogeyed happily together for about an hour.

Harry honestly hadn't registered Gilbert's presence. He'd been too intent on finding a better position from which to observe Jasmin Field. He had tried not to watch her but couldn't help himself. He had never seen anyone forget themselves so totally. Her eyes were closed and her body moved with such ease and elasticity to the different beats of the music that it was as if the music was going through her body. He couldn't take his eyes off her. Even when she started doing some very stupid-looking steps to a song that would have made Norway proud at the Eurovision Song Contest, he thought she was electric.

A cool voice eventually disturbed his thoughts.

'Still think the Ugly Sister is perfect for Miss Elizabeth Bennet?' It was Sara Hayes. Sara was dressed in the obligatory little black number, which showed off her staggeringly long legs. Jazz was now doing a Mexican wave all by herself, while Mo pogo-ed round her.

Harry found himself in the unusual position of wanting to laugh out loud.

'More than ever.'

'She certainly doesn't care what people think of her,' conceded Sara. 'Just like Lizzy.'

'That's true,' agreed Harry. 'And she's just as fascinating.' And with that he disappeared, leaving Sara feeling sick to her stomach.

Mo started miming having a drink and Jazz nodded. Her hair was starting to stick to her head with sweat. They went to the kitchen, which was packed.

As if from nowhere, Gilbert appeared. 'Well, you two have certainly been enjoying yourselves,' he said in a slightly disapproving tone. He was, as usual, much too close for comfort.

'Yes, well, it's a party, Gilbert,' said Jazz. 'By the way, have you said hello to Mo?'

Gilbert gave Mo a cursory smile.

'Mo's playing Charlotte Lucas to your Mr Collins.'

Gilbert managed to keep his smile going and raise his eyebrows in a show of interest.

'She's my flatmate,' continued Jazz.

Mo smiled at Gilbert and then said to Jazz, 'I'm not that flat, mate.'

Jazz grinned at her. 'Do you know that's funny every time you say it?'

'Thanks,' said Mo with a big smile.

'What drink do you want, Mo?' asked Jazz, desperate to get away from Gilbert. She was damned if Wills would come in to find her talking to *him*. She was hugely disappointed to discover he wasn't there yet.

'Ooh, I'll have a beer please Bob,' said Mo.

Jazz went off and pretended to take ages to get the beers in. She turned round to see if she could spot Wills and gasped in revolted horror. Gilbert was pressing against her in the crowd.

'Hello gorgeous,' he whispered with a big smile. He said it as if it was the concluding sentence to some storyline. Ignoring the significance he'd given his words, Jazz pushed the beers in front of her, forcing a gap between them.

'Gilbert, I'll spill the drinks,' she said, but he put his hands on the sink, cornering her completely. As his mouth approached her ear, Jazz closed her eyes pretending she was somewhere else. Anywhere else. Trapped in a ski-lift with the McGann brothers – anything.

'Come on,' he whispered. 'You know you want to.'

Jazz's body went cold. She hissed back, 'Yes, but I'll be done for GBH.'

'Ooh, sexy,' he laughed as he put one hand on the curve of her waist and rested the other on her hip.

Jazz shrieked at his touch. He seemed a bit surprised and

moved his hands back on to the sink. He raised his eyebrows at her. 'I didn't take you for the shy type,' he said.

'I am not shy,' she spat. 'I'm picky. And you haven't been picked.'

Gilbert didn't seem to hear her. 'I remember you when you were just out of college,' he said huskily, getting nearer again. 'Couldn't take your eyes off me, could you?'

'Yes, but in those days I also liked shoulder pads. We all make mistakes.'

Gilbert chuckled. '*I* made a mistake,' he said. 'I didn't make my move. Go in for the kill.'

'Oh, how *exquisitely* put. Look, Gilbert, how can I say this nicely?' She pretended to give it a second's thought. 'I'm not remotely interested. OK? Is that clear enough? Perhaps you'd like me to show you the hand signals that go with that? And the facial expression? Or I could get someone to come over and translate?' The crowd made it impossible for Jazz to actually move away.

Gilbert smiled. 'Ooh, you've really learned the art of playing hard to get, haven't you?'

Jazz was exasperated. It was impossible trying to get a message across to someone you couldn't bear looking in the eye. 'Look,' she started. 'What can I say? It was a long time ago. My sense of taste wasn't fully developed. Whereas you had peaked in every way. Life's sad but there you go. Face reality, Gilbert. I know it's tough, but it's *ever* so rewarding in the long-term.'

'Mmm,' he whispered, pretending to smell non-existent perfume on her neck.

Desperately, Jazz swiped his head with one of her cans of beer.

'Ow! That bloody hurt!' he said angrily, finally moving away. He looked at her like she was a harpie.

'It was *meant* to!' she shouted. 'Now piss off before I pour the contents down you.'

Gilbert stared at her in disgust. 'Jesus, no wonder you're alone, Jasmin,' he said, eyeing her now as if he wouldn't sell her body to a tramp. 'You always had a foul temper on you.'

And with that he fought his way out of the room towards the door where Mo stood patiently waiting for her drink.

Daniel, the host, appeared at the sink, washing a stain off his shirt. Only slightly shaken, Jazz tried the subtle approach. 'Where's Wills then?' she asked.

'Oh, he's not coming,' Daniel told her. 'Didn't care to share an evening with You Know Who. Actually, he asked me to say sorry to you particularly.'

Jazz was devastated. She tried to smile and started to drink Mo's beer absent-mindedly.

Half an hour later, George came over, grinning like a fool. Jazz had now started to drink her own beer. George looked gorgeous in her little black number. Jack's hand seemed to be glued round her waist and Jazz thought her sister had never looked so happy.

Jack went to get George a drink. Jazz always found it sweet the way men assumed that the second a woman became their girlfriend, she forgot how to do everything for herself – except cook, of course.

'Gilbert's a shit and Wills isn't coming,' she shouted in George's face, not caring who heard. 'But even worse, Wills isn't coming.'

'Oh no,' said George, trying very hard to look sad.

'And it's all because of your – your nice Mr Harry Noble,' said Jazz.

'He's not my Mr Noble.'

121

'No, but you think he's nice. And . . . nice,' she finished weakly.

'I think everyone's nice,' beamed George. 'I'm in love.'

'That's nice,' said Jazz, opening another can that was lying near the sink.

When Jack came over with George's drink, he beamed at Jazz with exactly the same happily dazed expression on his face as George. He whispered something to George and she giggled. Jazz felt lonely in a room full of so many people she couldn't move.

She finished her third beer in no time and decided she was getting drunk. So she had a glass of wine instead and stopped thinking about her own troubles. She began to feel truly happy for George. Her sister had finally found her Mr Right. This was worth celebrating.

Six hours later, she found herself sitting in a small, select group playing Fuzzy Duck, a peurile drinking game, the sole purpose of which was to make people so drunk they couldn't get their words round the title and would end up swearing. It was absolutely hilarious. She thought she'd die laughing. She had even managed to forget that Harry was there, or at least not care less that he was watching, as usual.

'Where's the ashtray?' asked someone suddenly.

Jazz thought this was very funny.

'Where's the ashtray?' she copied and started laughing.

'We've lost the ashtray,' said someone else urgently.

'We've lost the ashtray!' spluttered Jazz. It just got funnier and funnier.

'Spot the ashtray!' commanded someone else, and a few people duly started scanning the furry carpet.

Jazz collapsed in loud hysterics. She thought she might be winded she laughed so much.

'Fido the plant!' she squealed.

There was a pause, while Jazz laughed so much that no noise came out. Then gradually, the others started to join her. Soon everyone was laughing till it hurt.

'Ferdinand the television,' roared Jazz, tears running down her cheeks.

There was an explosion of laughter.

'Digbert the Sofa,' whinnied someone else, and Jazz laughed so much she forgot to breathe in.

As Fuzzy Duck came to a rather unusual end, Harry Noble realised he was in danger of becoming seriously unfocused professionally.

Chapter 13

Jazz woke up feeling very fragile indeed. Somehow, someone had come into her room in the night and placed a throbbing headbrace over her skull and a dead yak in her mouth. She prised her eyes open.

Without moving her head any more than was completely necessary, she managed to heave herself out of bed and into the hall. She had no idea what she was wearing, what the time was or who she was, although the name Tamsin seemed strangely familiar. But when she came face to face with a smirking pyjama-clad Gilbert Valentine in her hall, she knew something was terribly wrong.

'Ooh, nasty,' he beamed when he saw her.

The word 'Likewise' struggled to mind but didn't make it to her mouth. Suddenly, the night before hurtled back to her with some force. Oh God, no. She managed to run into the kitchen.

Mo was sitting at the table with a coffee, toast, the papers and a big grin. Jazz came in, slammed the door shut and leant against it.

'You have to help me,' she whispered, putting her hand to her forehead and starting to whimper.

'Why?' asked Mo.

Jazz started pacing the kitchen, distressed beyond belief. Surely she couldn't have? Not with Gilbert? She could never live with herself again. She was actually wringing her hands.

'For God's sake, Jazz, what's wrong?' asked an increasingly concerned Mo.

'There's been a horrendous – hideous – heinous – *horrendous* mistake,' whispered Jazz dramatically.

'You've been offered a job in the Diplomatic Corps?'

Not hearing, Jazz stopped pacing suddenly and froze on the spot, ashen-faced.

'Jazz, what is it?'

'I think I'm going to be sick,' she mouthed and rushed to the sink.

Mo went straight to her side and started rubbing her back. She was starting to get really worried.

Just then Gilbert's voice came from the hall. 'I'm just having a shower, pussycat!'

Jazz retched. She was ice cold yet covered in sweat.

The retch seemed to do the trick. She didn't think she was going to be sick any more. Slowly she turned away from the sink and walked to the table where she sat down heavily. Mo joined her. They sat there in silence for a while.

'Well?' said Mo gently, her hand stroking Jazz's arm.

Not really, thought Jazz.

'I – I – I –' Jazz didn't think she could form the words out loud. 'I think I,' she whispered, 'may have just . . . just . . . just . . .'

'Yes?'

Jazz was almost inaudible. 'Slept with . . . Gilbert Valentine . . . a bit . . . last night.' And with a gasp at hearing the words out loud, she laid her head on the table

125

and pulled her face into an extremely ugly expression of self-loathing.

'Well now,' said Mo crisply, taking her hand off Jazz's arm. 'That *would* be impressive,' and she stared at her open paper.

'Oh God,' whimpered Jazz, her head still lying next to Mo's paper. 'I'm going to have to commit suicide, it's the only way I can live with myself.'

'Two women in the same night, eh?' said Mo through gritted teeth, pretending to talk to herself.

'I'll leave you all my Boney M records, Mo,' mumbled Jazz pathetically.

'And two women who've been friends since they were four, too,' Mo went on, a bit firmer this time.

'And my papier mâché bin,' continued Jazz.

'Who live in my flat,' finished Mo.

There was a long pause. Slowly Jazz lifted her throbbing head and looked suspiciously at Mo.

'Wha – ?' she interrogated.

'You *didn't* sleep with Gilbert Valentine last night,' Mo told her gently.

'I didn't?' Jazz started to frown and shake her head, but it hurt too much.

'No,' said Mo. 'You slept with a big smile on your face.'

'Oh! Thank *Christ* for that,' said Jazz, emotionally. 'You don't know how happy you've made me, Mo. You're an *angel*.' Grinning, she sat back in her chair. 'I must give something to charity. Have you got any small change?' She padded over to the cupboard where the aspirins were kept.

'*I* slept with Gilbert Valentine,' said Mo calmly.

And Jazz was suddenly stone cold sober.

★　　★　　★

126

'What do you mean, you slept with him?' hissed Jazz.

'I mean I had carnal knowledge of him,' said Mo, straight-faced.

'*What?*'

'I had sexual intercourse with him.'

Jazz felt faint. 'Please. I might want to eat later.'

Mo ignored her and read her paper silently.

Jazz came back to the table and stood by Mo. This was terrible.

'Do you know what you're doing?' she asked eventually. 'He is a lizard of the highest order.'

'I didn't know lizards had orders.'

'He – he – he –'

'He made me scream like a wildcat four times in one night,' said Mo. 'That doesn't happen very often.'

Jazz thanked heaven for small mercies and thought she was going to retch again.

Just when she thought things couldn't get any worse, Gilbert himself came into the kitchen, wearing nothing but her favourite yellow fluffy towel.

'That's my towel,' she croaked.

'Oh, I'll take it off then,' said Gilbert, smiling wickedly at Mo and starting to peel it off.

'No!' screamed Jazz. 'It's fine. You can borrow my robe as well.'

'Hello, pussycat,' Gilbert slimed at Mo.

To Jazz's utter horror, Mo actually purred and Gilbert slid past Jazz to Mo and the two of them started doing some very loud, wet kissing.

Jazz thought she was living in a nightmare. This couldn't possibly be happening. Not in her own home. In her own kitchen. In her own towel. Oh God. She struggled to her room and phoned George. George was out. She paced her room. A whole Sunday to get through and Mo had gone mad in the kitchen and George was in love somewhere. Should she phone Josie? No, Josie had a life, the bitch. Her mother? No, that would only depress her. What to do, what to do, what to do . . .

The phone went. Jazz rushed to answer it.

'Poppet?' It was her mother.

Jazz started crying silently into the phone.

'Hello, Mum,' she sniffed.

'Mo *is* allowed to have boyfriends,' said Jeffrey, sipping tea, while Martha cut Jazz another slice of apple cake and thought her heart would burst.

'Not boyfriends I hate,' sniffed Jazz pathetically.

'You're just jealous, dear.'

'Jealous? Yes, I wish I'd have spent the last month dieting my personality away so I could sleep with Mr Oilslick.'

'Not of her. Of him.'

Jazz paused.

'More apple cake?' asked Martha.

Jazz sat silent.

'Jealous?' she finally repeated.

'Yes,' said Jeffrey. 'You've lost Mo, your soulmate. But don't worry, you'll soon get over it – when you find a true soulmate. Your own longterm partner.' Jeffrey felt proud that he'd managed not to say husband – that was very old-fashioned nowadays.

Martha and Jazz both looked at him in dismay.

'You were doing so well, dear,' said Martha, disappointed. 'For a man.'

Chapter 14

Jazz got into work early on Monday morning. She had woken up at six and after twenty minutes of lying in her bed, fast awake, decided she couldn't get back to sleep. The thought of bumping into Gilbert in the hall again had actually invaded her dreams and roused her before the alarm went off. When she got there, she had only been slightly surprised to find Mark already there, tapping away furiously at his computer. She knew he was hungry, but hadn't realised how hungry. Another one on his way to the tabloids. Alison the secretary had put the coffee on and was already replying to readers' letters, while humming a Tammy Wynette number. Two years previously, when Jazz had started at *Hoorah!* she had been horrified to discover that Alison was only three years older than her. It was enough to make her want to cry. Alison wore little knitted cardis and put her long hair in a bun. Her stockings were never laddered and her eyeshadow was always blue.

'Good weekend?' Mark asked Jazz before she'd even taken her coat off.

'Oh, you know,' said Jazz, pouring herself a coffee. 'Shite.'

She sensed Alison bristle in the corner. Tammy Wynette took a pause.

'Mine was amazing,' said Mark, leaning back from the desk and stretching out as if yawning. Jazz noticed he always did this when he was trying to hide the fact that he was feeling self-conscious. She cupped her coffee and watched him do his act.

'Got laid,' he smiled, and stopped suddenly when he realised he was starting to blush.

He looked at Jazz for a reaction. Jazz looked back at him for signs of a brain. Eventually, they both looked away, feeling lonely. Mark started typing again. God, he wished he worked at *Loaded*.

Jazz closed her eyes and started taking slow sips of her coffee. Suddenly, a voice interrupted her messy thoughts.

'Jasmin?'

Jazz opened her eyes to find Paul, the Art Editor, standing so near to her, he was actually blowing on her coffee. How did he always do that? She checked his feet for wheels.

'Hi,' she smiled, taking a small step back. Coffee was always better hot. And without an Art Editor's saliva in it.

'How's it going?' He cocked a lazy smile at her. He was feeling good today. He was wearing a new taupe shirt.

God help me, thought Jazz. One day I'm going to kill him.

'It's your *My Breast Enlargements Didn't Work!* piece. Um . . .'

Ah yes, my finest hour, thought Jazz. She raised her eyebrows encouragingly.

'Agatha wants to add a column of copy, so I'm afraid you're going to have to cut five hundred words.'

'OK,' she said. She didn't bother asking what the column was. She'd find out soon enough.

'I've got a purple head this week.'

'Beg your pardon?'

'A purple headline. Well, mauve actually.'

'Good.'

'Make a bit of a change. Wake the readers up.'

'Mm.'

'You know me, I like my colour.'

'Mm.'

'And if the head brings them in, they'll read your brilliant words.'

Jazz smiled weakly.

'Right,' said Paul, and then vanished as quietly as he had come in. Jazz looked at Mark and Alison to see if they'd also seen him. They didn't seem to have.

Half an hour later, Maddie, their boss, came in.

'Hi guys!' she said. 'Good weekends?'

Mark sighed loudly. 'Well, if getting laid counts in this *crèche* of a features department, then yes, I had a good weekend.'

Maddie looked at him in surprise. 'How lovely,' she said in a strained voice. 'I went to IKEA. It was marvellous.'

It didn't happen often, but when Maddie was annoyed, you knew it. Her rosy red lips pursed together and she frowned very determinedly. Jazz was always surprised at how much Maddie hated it when anyone got too personal in the office.

'Jazz, can you come into the Editor's office, please?' The Editor's secretary bobbed up over the partition.

Jazz looked at Maddie questioningly but Maddie just shrugged. Jazz knocked on the Editor's door.

'Come in!'

Jazz always wondered what it was about the Editor's office

131

that made her so nervous. Maybe it was the hundreds of vapidly smiling faces on the magazine covers spread all over the wall that made her feel ugly. Or depressed. Or invisible. Or something.

'Sit down Jasmin, we have some very nice news,' smiled Agatha.

Jazz sat down.

'You will be delighted to learn that your column has been shortlisted for the Columnist Personality of the Year Award,' announced Agatha. 'We're all very proud.'

Jazz frowned. 'Columnist Personality of the Year? I've never heard of that.'

'It's a new award, sponsored by the *Evening Herald*. Would you like to hear what they say about your column?'

The *Evening Herald* was massive and its assessment of Jazz was flattering. But she was confused.

'I didn't even know I'd been put forward for it,' she said.

'Well, I didn't want you to be upset if you weren't shortlisted,' said Agatha. 'But you have been − so well done!'

'But I'm not a personality.'

Agatha smiled her fresh, immaculate smile. 'No, but Josie − the character who's your sister in it − is hugely popular,' she said, picking up the readers' survey. 'It appears Josie is our readers' all-time favourite part of the magazine. Seventy-five per cent of the readers want to know about her happy, uncomplicated, family-based life. That's more than any other page, even cookery. Josie fits in with our readers' idea of the young, modern mother. She's got it all. Husband, sisters, parents, child, work, sex and happiness. She is the epitome of what our readers aspire to. In fact,' said Agatha suddenly, scribbling something illegible down on a scrap of paper, 'we

132

might make it *her* diary,' — as if Josie was a features idea that had come out of her head instead of Jazz's very real kid sister.

'No, I think we'll stick with it being by you,' Agatha argued with herself, 'but we'd like a bit more of Josie in the column. Married life, the baby — are any more on the way? Her relationship with her mother, Martha.' Agatha laughed at a memory. 'Martha's a wonderful character, by the way. Wonderful.' She continued with her list. 'Josie's lovely husband. What it's like to be her unmarried, slightly unhinged older sister. That kind of thing.'

Jazz smiled weakly at her boss.

Suddenly Agatha had an idea.

'*Josie's Choice*!' she yelled, her eyes sparkling. 'That's what we'll call it! Perfect! We're always on about women not being able to have it all and here's one who has made her choice! Home-maker, wife, mother! I *love* it!' She smiled at Jazz, ignoring her horrified expression.

It had hardly been a choice, Jazz wanted to say. Michael had only been able to get two days' paternity leave, so Ben never got a chance to bond with him as a baby. So right from the start, Josie had been the only one who could stop him crying at night. She'd been getting two hours' stressful sleep a night at the same time as trying to prove herself a serious employee at the large international firm where she was a lowly auditor. After six months of hell, feeling she was doing neither job well, and wracked with guilt at leaving her new baby with an exhausted Martha or with extortionately paid young women who didn't seem to love Ben like she did, it finally all got too much for Josie. She had given up her job. The job for which she had spent more than three years training. The job she had won after revising non-stop for what seemed like years.

133

The job that meant she could buy her own clothes, her own holidays and her own food. The job she loved. Some choice, thought Jazz.

'The awards are next month,' continued Agatha, standing up and starting to pace with excitement. 'So go out and buy your little black dress now! And make it a sexy one, because the awards are being televised. Well done, you deserve it. Oh, by the way, there is one tiny weeny stipulation.'

Oh dear. Agatha's tiny weeny stipulations included changing entire features minutes before going to press.

'Nothing serious,' she continued. 'You'll have to do an itsy bitsy interview for the *Herald*. You know, *Bright Young Thing on Her Way to the Top*, that kind of thing. Just don't say anything stupid, dangerous or libellous, there's a good girl. Be careful – you know what journalists are like.'

Agatha looked at her watch, which meant Jazz was dismissed. Jazz thanked her boss and walked back to her desk, numbed.

'That's amazing!' said Maddie. 'Well done, darling.' She hugged her. 'Now all you have to do is that wretched feature I told you about – phone that woman whose sister tried to shoot her – and then you can celebrate.'

Jazz moaned. 'What do I do if she's changed her mind about talking to us?' The last time she had spoken to the woman, she sounded petrified.

Maddie looked at her as if the answer was obvious.

'You tell her not to worry. And we'll send her the number of Victim Support, all the charities for depression and an update on the stalking laws. We're not hacks here,' she said snootily, before adding quietly, 'Well, we *weren't*.'

It was the first time Maddie had ever openly betrayed her feelings about the new regime. She was fiercely loyal to her Editor, but Jazz had always known the new *Hoorah!* was as little Maddie as it was her.

Mark snorted very loudly, muttered something about the lunatics taking over the asylum and then left the room in disgust. Jazz knew better than to expect him to run over and congratulate her, but even she was a little hurt by him this time. She noticed that whenever Maddie praised her, he couldn't take it. Maddie chose to ignore him. Instead, she asked Jazz why she wasn't bouncing on her chair in delight.

'It wasn't meant to be about Josie, it was meant to be about me,' said Jazz in a small voice.

'Honeybun, if you win this, you'll be on the tabloids in no time and we can become drinking buddies instead of colleagues,' said Maddie kindly.

Jazz gave a small smile and wished that Mo would send her an e-mail.

'I'm the perfect woman?' snorted Josie. 'Do they know I have piles?'

'I must have forgotten to mention it,' said Jazz.

Ben started wailing at the top of his lungs.

'I have to go and wipe my son's bottom,' said Josie. 'Put that in your magazine.'

'It's not really our market,' said Jazz into an empty receiver.

Jazz dreaded going home now. She knew that even midweek, Mo would either be out at the gym or worse still in with Gilbert. She put the key in the lock and was pleased to find the door locked. She made herself a pasta dinner and was just about to sit down to watch *Emmerdale* when the door opened. Shit.

135

'Hiya!' bellowed Mo, as she rushed up the stairs.

'Friend or foe?' bellowed Jazz back.

'Ha ha, very funny,' said Mo, taking her coat off as she came into the lounge.

'Have you chucked Lizard Man?'

'Why would I chuck someone who makes me happy?' asked Mo angrily.

'For me?' said Jazz innocently.

Mo sighed and looked pointedly at Jazz. Jazz took the point.

'So are you home tonight then or are you off to spend the night at his place?'

'I'm home.'

Jazz felt happy like she hadn't in days.

'Can we have chocolate?' she asked like a child would ask its mother.

'I've got to go to the gym,' said Mo sadly. 'I haven't been for ages. I've put on loads of weight.'

Jazz could only see the thinnest Mo she'd ever seen. She said nothing.

It worked. Mo grinned at her. 'But sod that for a laugh,' she said and rushed to the fridge to get the Giant Galaxy bar.

They watched an evening of crappy TV together and ate chocolate till they felt sick. But somehow it wasn't special like it used to be. Jazz knew Mo's heart wasn't in it and yet at the same time, she noticed that Mo ate much more than usual.

'You know I dreamt of you last night,' said Jazz slowly. 'I kept calling out your name but you couldn't hear me. It was horrid.'

Mo was very interested. 'Did I look fat?'

Jazz stared at her old friend. 'I'm not answering that, Mo.'

136

Mo took another bite of chocolate. Her very, very last.

When she was in bed, Jazz managed to pinpoint what it was that had spoilt an otherwise perfect evening. She had felt as though Gilbert was with them the whole time. Shit, she thought as she drifted off to sleep. Thank God she hadn't based her column on her best friend.

Chapter 15

Jazz had only changed her outfit four times, which was not bad going, considering. Would the *Evening Herald* like her Smart and Understated, Humble and Alluring or Intimidatingly Sophisticated? She had briefly considered Intimidatingly Humble before wearing her favourite chic, smart suit. She walked into the hotel foyer and stopped still. Now what?

'Ay saiy, hailo,' called a voice from her side. She turned to face an amazing body. Long muscular legs, a bust that strained at the tight halter-neck over it and strong round shoulders. It was the body of a strong, glossy colt. Unfortunately, on top of it was the face of one. Jazz took one quick up-and-down glance and knew instantly that she'd seen the type before. High heels, high cheekbones, high bustline, low morals. They always went far. 'Candida Butterworth, *Evening Herald*, we spoke on the phone.' Candida stretched out a long arm and they shook hands.

Impossibly, Jazz felt she was shrinking.

'Hello,' she said quietly.

They perched on a sofa, ordered coffees and Candida got out her dictaphone. 'Can't do shorthand, takes longer than my bloody longhand,' she said and laughed like a braying donkey. Her teeth were enormous. How did they all fit in her mouth? Didn't she have problems getting food in? Maybe that was why she was so skinny. And how did she breathe? Was that why her nostrils had to be so flared?

Jazz had been worried enough about what to say before meeting Candida. Now that she had met her in the flesh she was terrified. There was no way Jazz could take her seriously. The *Evening Herald* had a massive circulation and she knew that this interview could make or break her. Her career was in Candida's hands. And Candida's hands were now in Candida's Wonderbra, hoisting herself up to newer, even better, heights.

Jazz stayed calm. She was not going to be duped into thinking Candida was dumb just because she looked like a horse. She was as determined not to babble and make a fool of herself as she had been before she met her. She would make sure she understood any complex questions before answering them. She was not going to be frightened of pauses. She was not going to be fooled. This was going to be fine.

'Now,' said Candida, getting out sheets of questions, which were written in large round letters. 'Where were you born?'

Oh shit.

Two hours later, Jazz had a headache from talking so much. She hadn't let Candida ask any more questions after her astounding, 'Do you think lady journalists are as good as real journalists?' So she'd talked nonstop, without a pause, about herself. That was always dangerous, because usually when that happened Jazz's brain couldn't keep up with her tongue. This was no exception. Candida sat and nodded silently for two hours. Jazz hoped to God her dictaphone was bust and she'd have to re-interview.

It wasn't.

George and Jazz were nattering during a particularly boring part of the rehearsal. This part was meant to be the complicated dance scene between Darcy and Lizzy where he actually asks her to dance and she forces him to talk about his relationship with Wickham. As usual, Brian needed some extra attention and everything else was being put on hold while Harry fought to control his temper. The choreographer was eating a Mars Bar while reading the gloriously tacky women's magazine *Would You Believe It!* After an hour, Brian was finally mastering his imperious frown, but so fiercely that his face reminded Jazz of a bad Picasso painting.

'Jack wants to be a great actor more than anything,' whispered George to Jazz, as Brian knocked a chair over and Harry started making strange, choking noises.

'Well,' she smiled, 'apart from settling down and having a family.'

Jazz grinned at her affectionately. God, she hoped George was right. She didn't know anyone who deserved to be happier.

'I hope Mum and Dad like him,' said George wistfully.

Jazz was brought out of her thoughts. 'My God, George,' she said. 'This sounds serious.'

George looked at her. 'I know Jazz.' She half-smiled. 'This is IT.'

Matt Jenkins was making his way over to them both and they stopped happily to talk to their producer. By now, Matt was everybody's friend, from the junior props assistant to the great Harry Noble. When he wasn't on stage, twitching with terror, Matt was a supremely organised, efficient man, who had a wonderfully calming, balming effect on the entire proceedings.

As Matt asked the sisters how they were, Harry started bellowing insults at poor Brian so loudly they could no longer hear themselves talk.

Jazz turned to Matt, who, like most people in the room, was now watching Harry and Brian.

'Is there no end to Mr Noble's professionalism?' she asked loudly, as for the first time, Brian was actually bellowing back.

Matt tried to smile and give Jazz his full attention. 'He's under a hell of a lot of pressure,' he replied equally loudly. 'He's all right when you get to know him.'

Jazz smiled ruefully. 'And why would anyone want to do that then?' she asked.

She assumed Matt didn't hear her over the furious row now going on between Brian and Harry.

George was trying to avert her eyes from the embarrassing fight. 'You've worked with him before, haven't you?' she asked, as Brian stumbled off the stage and Harry stood silently, in a world of his own.

Matt nodded briefly, his eyes back on Brian. 'Years ago now. It was just a small production. We were both a lot younger. Harry doesn't let a lot of people get close to him.'

Tragic loss for mankind, thought Jazz as Matt quickly gave them both some rehearsal dates.

Just then a flushed Harry came over and loitered uncertainly near them, giving Matt a short, defensive glance.

Jazz looked up at Harry. 'Nice to see you have the full vocal range,' she said, referring to the row. 'You never know when that might come in handy.'

Harry almost grimaced and ruffled his hair distractedly.

141

Jazz decided to make the most of his unusual reticence.

'Are you sure you're allowed to come over and talk to the plebeians, Hazza?' she asked in a tone that was so rarely used on him that even Matt seemed a bit surprised.

'Meaning?' Harry answered shortly.

'Well,' said Jazz, 'I'm so honoured that you've actually graced our humble company, instead of merely beckoning us to come to you, that I think I may have to lie down with the shock of it.'

Matt gave a warning smile. 'I think you've met your match, Harry,' he said, before realising to his horror that Brian was slowly packing up his belongings.

Jazz turned to Matt with a big smile. 'Do you know that Harry never so much as deigns to talk to us during any breaks? He only ever shouts at us and orders us about? It's fearsome.'

Harry was so determined to defend himself that he was distracted from what was happening behind him.

'It's the only way to get anything done around here,' he snapped. 'And when we're not rehearsing, I don't mingle well. I leave that to other people who seem to have a knack for it.' The words 'mingle' and 'knack' were said like they were well beneath him.

Jazz looked him steadily in the eye. He held her intense gaze with a look of defiance that concealed how much he was enjoying the experience.

'I don't find it as easy as some to act, Mr Noble, but I'm trying my hardest.' With a wide smile, she finished, 'I see it as *my* limitation, not other people's.'

Harry simply nodded his head. 'Well, perhaps you'd like to do some of that now,' he said. 'We have work to do.'

Jazz turned to Matt. 'Wish me luck,' and he smiled at her.

'I don't think you need any,' he said. Unlike himself, he thought sadly, as he wondered how on earth he was going to placate Brian.

Jazz got up slowly, just as the costume girl approached George with a nervous smile and a large sketch pad. The truth was, Jazz was bored by this. Brian was hopeless on stage. She was no actress, but even she could tell. But when she took her place for her scene with him she realised Brian was putting on his coat and picking up his bag. Was he going out for chocolate supplies?

'Where's Darcy going? Was it something I said?' she asked Harry.

Brian started to walk majestically to the door.

'We've – um, we've . . . come to an agreement,' said Harry, taking off his jumper and revealing for a moment a smooth, broad chest before his thin white cotton shirt fell back down again.

'What agreement?' asked Jazz, her attention caught for a split second by the sight of Harry's chest, so that she was completely unaware of Matt flat-footing it after Brian.

'He's leaving.' Harry was now rolling his arms around from the shoulders in odd circular movements while walking towards Jazz.

Jazz couldn't take it in. 'He's not playing Darcy any more?'

'Well done, Ms Field, your mental agility is most encouraging,' he said.

'So who's playing Darcy now?' said Jazz stupidly.

Harry coughed. 'I will be playing the part of Darcy from now on,' he announced loudly, so that the entire cast could hear. 'Brian has other commitments.'

At this, Matt stopped doing his rather feeble impression

of someone running and turned round to Harry with a big, satisfied grin on his face. The door slammed and Brian was gone.

'Right,' said Harry decisively. 'Where were we?'

As he walked towards a shocked Jazz, he glanced over to the side of the hall and did a sudden double-take. Jack was standing very close to George and, what was more, George was letting him. Worse than that, Jack's mouth was inches away from hers and her eyes were half-closed. Jazz watched Harry stare at them, frowning. Eventually he turned away from them and apologised to her. He seemed very preoccupied.

He came and stood by her side, facing the front of the stage. Then he stretched his arm out towards her, palm-up, as in a dance. The choreographer came over with her copy of the script and Harry, never taking his eyes off Jazz, said: 'The dance has to be constrained, correct and elegant, yet at the same time full of chemistry. Darcy and Elizabeth have never touched before and he's already in too deep. She, of course, still thinks he's an arrogant prig.'

Jazz stared at him in astonishment. Was he really asking her to act with him? He eyed her and started flicking his hand up and down impatiently, as if to make her take it.

'You could just *tell* me what you want me to do, you know,' said Jazz, recovering. 'Instead of performing your own rather poor version of the *Birdie Song*.'

Harry sighed. 'We really don't have time for this, Ms Field,' he said.

They locked eyes. She wouldn't touch him until he asked.

Harry sighed again. 'Take my hand, please,' he said impatiently.

Reluctantly, Jazz did so.

Acting with Harry was an amazing experience. Jazz entirely forgot herself. Because he was so utterly convincing as Darcy, her reactions, which had been so tame with Brian, were now highly charged. The rest of the cast stopped talking and started silently watching what was going on. Whenever Harry gave Jazz an idea or suggested trying her delivery a different way, she knew instinctively what he was getting at and what he was trying to get out of her. And they were always both delighted with the result. She was buzzing with excitement. This was thrilling! Jazz loved the way Harry was making Lizzy stronger by the minute. And after a while, he even started accepting her ideas. She managed to convince him to make his Darcy more pained.

'The man's in love, for goodness' sake,' she said at one point.

'Why should that pain him?' asked Harry. 'He still thinks he's superior to her. And is still arrogant enough to assume she would accept his hand.'

Jazz answered as if he was an idiot. 'Because he still thinks he can't marry her – it would go against every one of his principles. And his principles are his whole identity. He's going through constant inner turmoil every time he sees her. He's fighting himself whenever she's there. This is the only woman he has ever felt so powerfully attracted to. Physically as well as emotionally. He's never even *fancied* a woman before. Darcy has never been out of control before – it's terrifying, confusing and amazing all at the same time. Lizzy makes all the other women he can get – and let's face it, he can get all of them – pale into insignificance. She's the only woman who has ever answered him back, who has ever made him think twice about what he says, who has ever made him reconsider his lifelong principles. And yet she's from repulsive lower-class stock. It's like a terrible awakening for him. And every time he sees her he is more aware of the increasingly agonising dilemma he is in. He's getting more hopelessly devoted and yet more aware of the impossibility of marriage to her at the same time. It's – it's living hell.

'And,' Jazz got more and more excited, unaware that Harry was watching her with a new look in his eyes, 'at this point, he realises the worst thing yet – that his biggest enemy in the whole wide world has made an impression on her. Maybe already has planned to elope with her – he knows the depths of Wickham's character enough to fear the worst. Yes,' she finished triumphantly, 'he's a man in great pain. You're doing him too one-dimensional.'

Harry thought about this and nodded slowly.

From that moment on, Jazz was moved by the intensity of his performance. When he looked at her now, there was so much repressed emotion in his dark eyes that she felt slightly embarrassed.

At the end of the rehearsal, everyone else had gone and it was just her and Harry. She was knackered but looking forward to a walk home to blow out the cobwebs in her head. She wanted to put off going home as long as possible. It would either be empty or full of Gilbert. Just thinking about it spiralled her down into a deep depression.

'Want a lift?' asked Harry.

'No,' said Jazz miserably.

'Are you all right?'

She shrugged her shoulders.

'Want to talk about it?'

'Nope.'

146

'Coming to the party on Friday?'

Jazz thought of Wills. 'Yes,' she said, and put her Walkman on.

On her way home, Jazz popped into the newsagent and bought a copy of the *Evening Herald*. There she was on the middle pages. Where had they got that awful photo from? Agatha must have had it in stock. It made her look like a warthog. But that was nothing. The headline said it all: JUST CALL ME 'HONEST JAZZ'! it screamed. The introduction ran:

Thanks to her perfect little sister, journalist Jasmin Field knows she's gonna make it big. She tells Candida Butterworth why her honesty will win her this year's Columnist Personality of the Year *competition.*

Jazz stood stock still in the street, re-reading the headline and introduction three times.

Hell, damnation and buggery bollocks, she thought.

Chapter 16

When Jazz turned up at the party, which was held con-
veniently four roads away from her flat, she was already
drunk.

Only the thought that Wills might be there had made her
come. Now that Mo would be glued to Gilbert's hip and
George to Jack's, there was little else for her to look forward
to at this party.

But as she went up the stairs to the flat entrance, she
was surprised by the sight of Jack rushing down the stairs
and almost colliding with her. He didn't even say hello.

A horrid thought occurred to her and she started running
up the stairs.

It didn't take her long to find George. She was sitting,
crying, amidst a hundred coats on the bed in the boxroom.
Jazz ran to her and George started weeping inconsolably. Jazz
shut the door and sat on the bed with her, stroking her hair.
George was limp.

'What's happened? Shhh, it's OK now,' Jazz whispered
helplessly.

Eventually George wiped her eyes and nose and said weakly, 'It's over.'

'I don't understand,' Jazz said. 'He was utterly besotted.'

'*Was*,' said George and started weeping again.

She calmed down in a while.

'He said he's got to take his career seriously. He can't be unfocused. I was bringing him down—' here she broke down again into quieter sobs.

'What sort of crap is that?' asked Jazz.

'It's not crap, it's what Harry says,' George explained tearfully. 'Harry told Jack that to be a great actor you have to be focused. And since he's been going out with me, he's failed four auditions. If he fails another one, his agent has started making noises about him trying another career. She suggested teaching,' and at this George started wailing.

'Perhaps he's just not as good an actor as he thinks,' said Jazz furiously, but George shook her head.

'No, he's right. My work hasn't been great since I've been with him,' she sniffed. 'But I didn't mind because I thought he was worth it.' She was sobbing silently now.

Jazz started pacing. 'Harry Noble,' she whispered, shaking her head. 'I'll bloody kill him.'

'No,' George shook her head. 'If Jack loved me enough, he wouldn't listen to him. He just didn't love me.'

'That's bollocks and you know it,' said Jazz hotly. 'Jack would do anything Harry tells him to. And unfortunately for him – and for you, sweetheart, Harry is a fuckwit. Of the highest order.'

She hugged George. 'Come on, let's get you home.'

'No, I can't go out there looking like this.'

'Georgie, sweetie, you still look ten times better than anyone else in there. And they're all too stoned or drunk to notice anyway. Come on, we'll go back to my flat and have a hot milky drink and lots of hugs and a long talk.'

They stood up and pushed their way through the crowds. It was only when they got home that George realised she'd forgotten her handbag.

'I'll go back,' said Jazz immediately.

'But you'll have to walk on your own,' said George. 'I don't need it.'

'I'll run,' said Jazz. 'I could do with the exercise.'

George was more than happy to be left on her own for a while. She turned on the telly and watched it, her mind on pause.

The party was much more crowded now. By the time Jazz managed to find George's handbag she was hot and sweaty and in a foul mood. There was no way she was fighting her way through the labrynthine flat full of hot, sweaty people just to see if Wills was there. With a Herculean effort, she forced a passage to the door, only to find herself face to face with Harry.

'Leaving already?' he asked.

Jazz stopped and stared at him. There were so many things she wanted to say to him she didn't know where to start first. So she just stood and stared, wide-eyed and furious. He stared back.

'Want a lift?' he asked quietly.

She didn't notice that he hadn't even come into the party yet. She just thought how much she would rather be driven home than have to run all that way again.

'Yes,' she said curtly, and the two of them went downstairs.

She wasn't going to say a word to him this time. The bastard. First he ruined Wills' chances of a career made in heaven, and then he ruined her sister's life. No wonder he made such a perfect Darcy.

After a silent journey, Harry parked outside the flat.

'See you at the next rehearsal,' said Jazz, and started undoing her seat belt. Before Harry knew what had happened, Jazz was out of the car. He got out too and followed her. He reached her at the door.

'Aren't you even going to say thank you?' he asked angrily.

'Thank you,' said Jazz without looking at him and got her keys out of her pocket. She was so pissed off she didn't notice Harry shift awkwardly, not knowing what to say next.

'Happy with the way the play's going?' he asked quickly.

'What's it to you?'

'I care, actually,' said Harry, surprised at how much emotion was in his voice.

'Not enough, smartarse,' said Jazz, thinking of her distraught sister upstairs and blinking back frustrating tears that were stopping her getting her key in the lock.

To her astonishment, Harry prised her hand off her door handle, held both her shoulders and turned her towards him.

'You're wrong,' he said softly. Jazz stared up at him in shock. She was so surprised, she forgot she was angry. Harry seemed to be having considerable difficulty with his words. For the first time, he was actually tongue-tied.

'I think you're the most amazing woman I've ever met,' he said in a low voice. Jazz couldn't believe her ears. She thought he must be joking. 'I know the press will have a field day that Harry Noble has fallen for the charms of an unknown hack, but the truth is I've never felt this way about anyone before.' And with that he gently cupped her face and moved slowly towards her.

151

Staggered, Jazz pushed him away just in time. She hadn't realised quite how strong – or furious – she was, and he hurtled very inelegantly into the rose bush, where he lay startled. The front security light came on due to the movement, shining on Harry's face.

'What the HELL do you think you're doing?' Jazz managed to scream and whisper at the same time.

'I'd have thought that was perfectly obvious,' said Harry, nursing a bruised elbow and a thoroughly bruised ego.

'Who the FUCK do you think you are?' She sounded like a cross between an angry Alsation and Mickey Mouse. The forecourt light went out but when Jazz started pacing it came on again. 'You are the most astoundingly arrogant shit I have ever had the displeasure of meeting,' she ranted. 'You – you – you – honestly think that I would want to kiss YOU?'

Harry was quick to answer.

'Your biggest worry a moment ago was that I didn't care enough for you,' he said, sitting up. 'You seem to have changed your mind very quickly. Perhaps your ego's a teensy bit hurt. Perhaps you'd have preferred it if I'd told you I was in awe of you because you were the great renowned Jasmin Field, Columnist?'

Jazz was screaming now. 'I couldn't give a gnat's bollock if you thought I was the Queen of England,' she yelled. 'Being famous doesn't stop you being a total fuckwit. OF THE HIGHEST ORDER.'

'That's just hurt pride talking,' said Harry furiously, starting to get up.

'STAY THERE!' shrieked Jazz. 'I HAVEN'T FINISHED!'

Harry did as he was told.

Jazz stared at him until he looked away, embarrassed. 'What is it about you actors that makes you think that fame counts for anything?' demanded Jazz. 'Michael Bloody Fish is famous, for Christ's sake! You're living in another world, you people. I thought journalists were shallow but you lot – well, you take the biscuit.'

She bent down so that she was looking eye-to-eye at Harry. 'Since working with you and your cronies, Mr Noble, I can honestly say that my opinion of actors has sunk so low that I'm seriously considering becoming a theatre critic.'

Harry tried not to wince or smile. Jazz noticed for the first time his features looked distorted and ugly.

'You're all the same,' she went on. 'Your values stink, your judgement is warped and your egos are bigger than solar systems.'

Harry tried to stand up again.

'I take your point, Ms Field,' he said. 'Accept my apolog—'

'I haven't finished,' she said icily. The security light went out leaving them in pitch darkness again.

'And as for you, Mr Noble . . .' words failed her for a moment. She started pacing again and the light flashed back on. 'You are the most repellent of them all. First I find out that you are the kind of mean-spirited oik who would push another man down out of pure ambition—'

'What?' said Harry. He was on his feet again.

'William Whitby,' she hissed dramatically.

Harry looked away, hiding his face.

'Can you deny that you lied to a powerful Hollywood casting agent to halt his career while yours has soared into the stratosphere?' She hadn't mean to spit at him, but now that she had, she was glad.

Harry tried hard to control the emotion he felt. 'You seem a bit obsessed with that man,' he said finally.

Jazz was shouting very loud now. 'He's an innocent man

153

who's suffered at your hands through no fault of his own! You've probably ruined his whole career, his life, through pure malice and self-obsession.'

Harry began to move away. 'I can now see how repulsive you find me. I'm sorry that I tried—'

'I HAVEN'T FINISHED!' shouted Jazz.

Harry stood motionless, staring furiously at her.

'But worse than all of that,' she continued, 'you've broken my adored sister's heart, you – you – you odious little man.'

'What? I don't understand what you're talking about.'

'Don't patronise me,' warned Jazz.

Harry sighed.

'She is upstairs in my flat now, crying her decent, big heart out because you told her idiot boyfriend that if he wanted his career to go anywhere, he had to chuck her. Can you deny it?'

Harry looked straight at her. 'No. Why should I?' he said. 'I'd do the same again. Actors need to be focused – especially actors like Jack. He had lost his focus and was about to lose his agent.' He laughed bitterly to himself. 'I only wish I'd been as tough on myself.'

Jazz stared at him in disbelief. How could he be so cold-hearted about George?

Harry took advantage of the pause and drew himself up before speaking. 'Perhaps though, *Ms* Field, none of these petty excuses would have come out if I had professed myself under the spell of your precious name – your brilliant by-line? If I had pretended you were in the same league as me and had people flocking to see you so much as break wind on stage?'

Jazz spoke clearly and with fire in her belly. 'The words don't exist in the English vocabulary that could have tempted me to fancy you,' she said, desperately trying to hide the hurt in her voice. 'I knew all I needed to know about you before you even deigned to look in my direction. You are the most repulsively arrogant and solipsistic man I have ever had to spend my precious time with. And I've met a lot of actors. You are unattractive to me in every way.' For good measure she added the lie as she turned away, 'And for your information, I prefer blonds.'

The forecourt light went out again just then so Jazz never saw the skin around Harry's eyes blanch at her words. She just heard his car door slam and the engine start up as the tears she'd managed to quell for her sister now started running down her cheeks.

'Harry Noble tried to snog *you*?' George had stopped crying suddenly.

'There's no need to sound quite so surprised,' sniffed Jazz.

'But Jazz, this is *Harry Noble*, Hollywood icon. He could get anyone. I'm staggered.'

Jazz blew her nose and started laughing angrily at the ridiculous situation. 'Yes, so was he. A fact he felt he needed to remind me of frequently.'

She decided she wasn't going to explain that Harry had confessed quite so readily to being responsible for Jack's chucking her. After all, it would only hurt George to know people like him really did exist. It would be like telling a child there was no Santa Claus.

George slept in Mo's bed that night and both sisters had a fitful, unhappy night.

Jazz's weekend was spent trying to cheer George up, which was fine by her. She needed something to take her mind off the ridiculous episode, which was becoming more and more laughable to her. It was such a bizarre experience – she was both hugely insulted and flattered at the same time. But of course, the insults were what stung the most. Unknown hack! How dare he! Eight hundred thousand readers a week was hardly unknown. Bastard.

Jazz knew that if they stayed in, George would practically sit on the phone, willing it to ring. She had to keep her busy. They went shopping, to the cinema and out for dinner. George tried to talk of other things, but couldn't help returning to Jack. Jazz felt overwhelmed with sadness for her sister. Why couldn't she find love? She was so achingly lovable. What was wrong with the men out there?

George had always managed to look on the bright side before. This time, however, there was no bright side. Her voice seemed an octave lower than before and she spoke slower as if the very effort of thinking was too much for her.

Jazz was so worried, that as the weekend progressed, she found she didn't have the mental space to think about the amazing Harry Noble incident. It was only when she was in the shower – practically the only time she was without George all weekend – that the enormity of Saturday night's compliment finally hit home. Wow. Bloody wow, she thought. It was a big compliment. Such a star – such a famous name – such a – such a . . . She thought hard. Such a wanker.

Men, she thought as she dried herself off. However you look at it, they're all wankers. Of the highest order.

Chapter 17

First thing the next day, Jazz clicked into her e-mails as usual to see if there were any messages. Oh goodie, she thought. There was only one but it had a very intriguing title. It said simply **SORRY**. Maybe Mo had written to tell her she was chucking Gilbert and coming home with a truck-load of Mars Bars.

Eagerly she double-clicked it. She gasped when she realised it was a massively long letter from Harry Noble. She scrolled down all of it, her eyes frantically scanning odd phrases here and there. *We got on well at first. You are terrifying. Matt Jenkins knows . . .*

She didn't know what to read first. With a supreme effort of self-control, she scrolled to the beginning and began to read.

To: Jasminfield@hoorah.co.uk
From: HarryNoble@Yahoo.com
Subject: Sorry

Jasmin
Don't panic. This is not a begging letter. I can't quite

157

believe I tried what I tried on Saturday and I'm really sorry for both of us that I did it.

Excuse the e-mail, but I just felt I had to have my say and I couldn't think of a better way to talk to you without risking a broken jaw. I actually got this idea from Darcy, when he wrote a letter to Elizabeth. Remember? (Some say I take on the roles I play too wholeheartedly. But I don't think Darcy's such a bad example to follow, do you?)

The truth is, Jasmin, you laid some rather serious accusations at my door and I can't help but want to put the record straight. I hope none of what I tell you hurts you but I'm sorry if it does.

First things first, your accusation that I lied out of pure malice and ruined William Whitby's Hollywood career. If it were true, that would have been a completely outrageous thing to do. But I didn't lie. I hate to be the one to break the bad news to you, but William Whitby is not what he appears to be. And I should know.

A long time ago now, I was in a production of *Waiting for Godot* with William. We got on well at first. He's a good actor and – as I'm sure you know – he has a very endearing way with him. My younger sister agreed with me. You probably know Carrie, she's the costume designer with us and she's been to a couple of rehearsals. Long red hair? Very quiet? Well anyway, within a few weeks they were going out together and she was completely besotted with him. I was really happy for her, as she's shy and a lot of men don't even notice she's there.

For a while everything was fine. Then at one rehearsal I noticed she was wearing shades. When

I asked her why, she acted really suspiciously. I knew something was up but didn't want to pursue it. Carrie can be very stubborn. It wasn't until two months later – when I was giving her a lift back from a family do – that I found out. She told me that whenever William got drunk – which was pretty often – he became violent. He had hit her several times. I couldn't believe it. He seemed so genuinely kind. When I expressed doubt at her word, she almost got hysterical. If I didn't believe her, how would anyone else? I tried to convince her to stop going out with him but she wouldn't. She told me he was always so sorry afterwards and so gentle and loving. It actually seemed to make her feel more special and between you and me, I think it made her feel she was involved in a very passionate affair. She'd always wanted passion in her life and now she was getting it.

I was distraught. They kept going out with each other all the way through the rehearsals and even the production. I detested him by now but he was always a real pro with me. I assumed he had no idea she'd told me. But not so. When I alluded to it once in conversation – sick to the pit of my stomach at his chummy act with me – he actually winked at me and said (I'll never forget it): 'Sometimes it's the only way to get some peace and quiet.'

He seemed to take offence when I stopped going to the pub with him, but apart from that you'd never have guessed from him that there was any tension between us. I watched him with my sister and I could see that he fed off her insecurity. Carrie's never been hugely secure – I guess it's part of being from a largely acting family and choosing not to be an actress. She thinks everyone's disappointed in her – which couldn't be further from the truth. But her weakness was his strength.

Even worse, whenever Carrie wasn't needed at rehearsal, William would flirt outrageously with the props woman, who obviously had a crush on him. I think they even went out a couple of times – who knows what went on? By now I thoroughly despised the man. I didn't know what to do. Should I tell Carrie that he might be having a fling with someone else – which would break her heart, and anyway she probably wouldn't believe me – or should I watch him going on abusing my sister?

The problem was solved when I got a phone call from her in the middle of the night. She was almost hysterical; I could hardly understand what she was saying. I went round there immediately and discovered her lying in a pool of blood. I phoned for an ambulance and she was rushed into an emergency operation. Four hours later, a doctor came out and told me the baby had died and Carrie would probably never be able to have any more children. You can imagine how I felt. I'd had no idea she was even pregnant. I was by her bed when she woke up and she immediately broke down and confessed everything to me. When she'd told William that she was pregnant, he'd gone out, got drunk, come home and, in a drunken rage – during which he accused her of trying to trap him – he punched her in the stomach and then walked out on her. Even then she needed some persuading to break it off with him.

I had to enlist the help of Matt Jenkins. He was working as producer on the play and I ended up turning to him for some support. It was he who convinced me to talk to the director, Alan Mellis, who got rid of William as soon as he had found a replacement. And it was Matt who finally convinced Carrie to finish with William. Maybe she found him more neutral than me. Matt was wonderful – he still is. He visited Carrie in hospital and saw everything. If you think I would – or could – make up a story like this, please talk to him. He knows that I've told you this. We're very close and I'd trust him with my life.

When the Hollywood agent Howard Fleaback asked me what I thought of William, I told him the truth. What William doesn't know is that I also told him that he's a fine actor. And I really believe that. He is acting all the time.

It might seem odd to you that I would give him a part in another play. It *is* odd. I regret it bitterly, but Carrie convinced me to do it. She has undergone lengthy therapy since finishing with William and for some strange reason she now feels she needs to see him to get him out of her system. Otherwise she's always hearing about him through other actors and it makes her feel he's somehow got a hold over her. At first I was very dubious about this, but it seems to be working. She told me last week that she can't now understand what she saw in him, which as you can imagine, was a massive relief to me.

I've been watching him too, and saw with no great surprise that he immediately picked you out as a favourite. I desperately wanted to warn you – not just for my own selfish reasons but for your own safety. However, it soon became obvious to me that you wouldn't be such an easy target as my sister was. And I think it soon became obvious to William too. Maybe you've noticed that he hasn't been troubling himself to get seriously involved with you, despite the meaningless flirting. I think it's because he can see that you've got too big a personality to be controlled like Carrie and so I suppose you've lost much of your appeal for him. Thank God! And he's right – you would never let yourself be beaten by a man. I now know from personal experience that in a one-to-one, you can be terrifying.

And now for your second accusation – that I have single-handedly broken your sister's heart.

How can I put this without hurting you? I'm not sure I can. Anyway, here goes.

Before I met your sister, I had heard about her. I know lots of actors and – how can I put this delicately? – your sister had, at one time or another, known most of them too.

In fact, I don't know of any play she's ever been in when she's not got involved with a fellow actor. I'm not judging or blaming, it's just a fact. There are actors who are just like that. And in all fairness, exactly the same can be said of Jack. He can't go to an audition without falling passionately in love with whoever's playing opposite him. I suppose you could say they're two of a kind. Jack is always on at me to guide him and show him how to focus himself in his work – he's much more ambitious than he appears – and I want to help him. I love Jack like a brother. So

I told him: Stop the womanising. His career could be fantastic if he would only apply himself. There will be lots of important casting agents in the audience for this production. If Jack is emotionally or physically drained and totally unfocused (like he is in most of his performances), he will get overlooked yet again. Believe me, he has the potential to be great and I find it bloody frustrating that he wastes his time on one-minute wonders. And from watching your sister with him, that is all I thought she was.

And, in fairness, that's all I thought *he* was to *her*. You've got to admit, she's hardly been swooning hopelessly around him, has she?

I suppose you know your sister better than I do so I can only say I'm sorry if I've been instrumental in hurting her. But if she's anything like Jack, she'll be up and bouncing again in no time. You know what actors are like. The minute they are cast to fall in love with someone else, they just can't help themselves. Maybe they just love having a script to work to. Believe me, I've seen it many times before.

So that's it. I just wanted to set the record straight. I would appreciate it if you delete this message. Some of your less principled colleagues might find some value in what I've written.

Oh, I suppose that brings me on to another point. That actors' values are warped, etc. Well, I can only say that reading the front page of any tabloid, the phrase 'the pot calling the kettle black' springs to mind. After all, we're all in the entertainment business, aren't we? It may seem to someone who is not trained as an actor that we are self-obsessed and vain but I hope we are not evil, as I think many journalists are. You see, it's not nice to be tarnished with the same brush as all your profession, is it?

As it happens, I respect your work immensely, although you've got to admit your colleague Gilbert Valentine is a complete dickhead. I believe you trained with him on the same paper under the same man and I can only say that it's a credit to you that you and he have gone on to have such different attitudes and careers.

Well, I think that's it. Sorry if it's been inconvenient for you to get this at work. I just had to get all this off my chest.

I won't be seeing you at rehearsals for a week or two because I'm busy with work, but until I see you again,

Take care,

Harry.

Jazz was thunderstruck. She didn't know what to think. She printed out the missive, put it in her bag for later perusal and deleted it on screen. The first time she read it she was so ready to hate Harry that she kept breaking off with very unpleasant expletives for him. How dare he say such libellous things about Wills? Everyone knew he was lovely. He was famous for playing a priest, for Christ's sake! And how dare he call what had been going on between her and Wills 'meaningless flirting'? That really hurt.

But later, when she read his e-mail on the tube, she was surprised to find that its tone seemed less harsh and she was not insensitive to the occasional compliment that came her way. Later still, when she read it in the flat while waiting for the kettle to boil, she found she was beginning to experience very unpleasant twinges of panic at the possibility of it being true about William. She thought back to his lovely open face, his large, warm eyes. Then she remembered how he'd told her that he and Harry had been in a play before and that Harry had hated him after that. That would fit in with Harry's story. She wracked her brains to remember Harry's sister. She was dimly aware of a quiet presence who had been going round everyone asking them for their dress sizes. Eventually, she confessed to herself that she had been somewhat biased in Wills's favour because she had fancied him so much. Was she really that superficial?

Now she came to think of it, Jazz remembered how Wills had professed himself to not give a damn about the 'likes of' Harry Noble the day of the party and yet he'd given it a miss. It also dawned on her that it was a bit unfair of Wills to badmouth Harry to her when Harry had given him this chance to play against type. But then, Wills had received every sign that she would be only too eager to join him in badmouthing his enemy. God, he must have seen her coming. Finally she realised she knew nothing about William Whitby that he hadn't told her himself and yet she'd believed every single word of it because of his big brown eyes, winning smile and ability to act the part of a kind priest. Her fondness for him was quickly being overtaken by anger.

She was thoroughly ashamed of herself. The more she thought about it, the more obvious it became. Her opinion of William Whitby had been based on her own physical attraction to him, nothing more, nothing less. He was far more like wicked Wickham and far less like Father Simon than Jazz had ever imagined. At first she thought she would take up Harry's suggestion and ask Matt Jenkins the truth about his past. But by the fourth reading of the letter, she realised there was no way this story could be a lie. And somehow, from the manner in which Matt Jenkins had always talked about Harry, she now realised that he loved him in a way that could only have come from seeing him suffer.

She imagined a drunk William beating up a woman. She felt sick that she had spent so much time with him, had shared jokes with him – had even shared *Hobnobs* with him. The man was utterly repulsive – more so because he appeared to be so appealing.

And then she became mortified for another reason. *Jazz Judges* – now to become *Josie's Choice* – a popular column in a national magazine, based on how sharply perceptive and discerning its writer was, was actually based on a lie. It was written by someone who *thought* they could read everyone like a book, but actually got it wrong. She wished, not for the first time in her life, that she was more like her big sister, more generous of spirit, more forgiving. There was nowhere to run, she'd always been so ready to trip others up over their foolish mistakes and here she was, well and truly tripped up by her own. And unlike everyone else, she had always believed herself untrip-upable. She felt bitterly ashamed. Every time she pictured either Harry or William, she had the strangest sensation of a cement-mixer being switched on inside her stomach.

It took longer for her to forgive Harry for his description of George. How dare he call her sister a slut! And how dare he insinuate that George and Jack were a one-minute wonder! It just showed what Harry knew about relationships. But after the sixth reading, when she had finally taken the leap of imagination to realise that she wasn't always right about everyone, Jazz remembered a telling conversation she'd had with Mo. 'Harder to read than a Thomas Hardy novel', was how Mo described George. Maybe – just *maybe* – George was a bit cautious about showing her true feelings. Begrudgingly, she began to see Harry's point. She admitted that she had had nearly thirty years' head start when it came to reading George right.

When she re-read the letter in the bath, her feelings towards its writer were totally different from those she had experienced on first reading it. She found herself agreeing with him about some of her work colleagues – and wincing when she remembered how she had self-righteously ridiculed actors in front of a whole room of them.

Now that her confidence in her own opinion was so utterly shattered – a feeling wholly new to her – she was far more sensitive to the compliments Harry had thrown into the e-mail. And for some reason, she got a not-unpleasant thrill when she re-read his allusion to copying the character of Darcy. Did he see her, then, as his Lizzy?

She found herself reflecting that these compliments, written by Harry in haste after their ridiculous row, probably wouldn't trip so lightly off his tongue now, in the light of day. For some reason, that thought didn't satisfy her like it should have.

As she lay in bed staring up at the ceiling and seeing nothing, she remembered she'd forgotten to make a vital phone call to some B-list actor's agent for an important interview. Drifting off into a fitful sleep, she realised she hadn't been able to think of anything all day apart from her e-mail.

Chapter 18

Work had become impossible. It had never occurred to Jazz before how important self-belief was. It helped you get up in the morning and helped you do your job well. Without it, the smallest task seemed enormous. Why *was* this stupid e-mail upsetting her so much? After about a week, Jazz had worked out the answer. It wasn't just the fact that she had got Harry and William so wrong: it was also the fact that she had behaved as if she was infallible. She had always acted as if no one else's opinion or perception was ever as sharp and accurate as hers. If Mo disagreed with her about George's behaviour, that had to mean that Mo was thick – not that George was unreadable. She had detested her fellow cast members for being biased in favour of Harry despite his behaviour, yet she had been prejudiced against him for little more. Yes, she *had* overheard him say unpleasant things about her . . . but how often had she said horrid things about people in the past? She dreaded to think what Simon might have thought of her if he had ever overheard her belittle him to George, the way she always had. She had said far worse things about him than Harry had said about her. And who knew? Perhaps Harry had been trying to impress Sara? Jazz knew she said stupid things when she was with someone who was easy to impress.

What a know-all she'd been! She was just as arrogant as the great Harry Noble, just as guilty in that department. Yet she had no Oscar, no public adoration, no extraordinary beauty to give her any reason to be so full of herself. Oh God! She had utterly humiliated herself in front of the great Harry Noble, and that's what hurt.

It was only at work that Jazz was able to take her mind off the wretched e-mail. It really didn't help, of course, when her interviewees turned out to have brains made of blancmange. Today she was trying to get a decent article out of a woman who had finally given birth to a baby girl after ten boys. They'd been on the phone for one and a half hours so far and Jazz's neck was killing her. She only had three good quotes.

'How did you feel when you held her in your arms for the first time?' Jazz asked.

There was a long pause.

'Nice.'

Jazz started scribbling as she wrote.

'Gosh, you must have felt wonderful. Ecstatic? Elated? Over the moon? Did you come over all tearful? Were you just relieved? Did you feel special? Like your dream had finally come true?'

There was a longer pause.

'Very very nice, yes.'

Jazz rubbed her neck and stretched her back in the chair.

'Who does Tiffany Kylie-Danii take after most?' she asked, trying to inject the question with as much affection as she possibly could.

There was a big pause.

169

'Her father's a wonderfully gentle man. And so is she.'

Jazz thought she was going to start weeping.

'And how is she different from all your boys?'

'Well,' said the woman, 'she goes through clothes like they're going out of fashion.'

Sheer fatigue made Jazz start giggling.

'I'll have to go now,' said the woman. 'She'll be wanting another feed. Can you phone me back the same time tomorrow?'

If my brain hasn't melted by then, thought Jazz. She put the phone down and let out a heartfelt scream and dropped her head onto her desk.

Mark looked up. 'What do you get if you cross a woman's magazine and a cat's arse?' he asked through his bacon buttie.

Jazz shrugged without moving her head. She was utterly exhausted.

'Fucking expensive cat litter,' he grinned.

Jazz looked up and frowned at him. 'Mark,' she managed, 'have you ever thought of becoming an after-dinner speaker?'

He beamed.

The phone went. Jazz hated answering the phone at work.

'Hello, *Hoorah!*' she said as gravely as she possibly could.

'Jasmin Field please,' said a highly efficient voice.

'Speaking.'

'Oh hello, this is Sharon Westfield at the *Daily Echo*,' said a person for whom this information was most impressive. 'We're looking for a new columnist for our woman's page and read the piece about you in the *Evening Herald*. I'll be completely honest with you – always am. Loved your attitude.

Loved your sister *Josie*. How different she is from you – married, a young mum with a good sex-life, happy family.'

Jazz mumbled a sort of yes sound. She'd always detested the *Daily Echo*; it was a shabby tabloid full of horror stories and scantily clad 'girls' who wore 'panties'. But there was no denying that it had the second largest circulation of all the daily papers, and once you've written for the *Daily Echo*, all sorts of doors start opening for you. Weirdly though, Jazz didn't feel as impressed today as she might have done a week earlier.

'You see,' Sharon Westfield continued, 'that's just the sort of new angle we're looking for. Sort of post-Bridget Jones, post-ironic, post-modern, post-*post*-feminist sort of thing. D'you see? Women being content *and* capable. It's so new. Very exciting.'

'Ye-es,' said Jazz dubiously.

'We'd like you to write us three provisional columns of twelve hundred words each. And remember, our readers are right-wing bordering on fascist, chauvinistic bordering on misogynistic – especially the women – and, of course, thick as pigshit. These are people who *record* Jeremy Beadle. Try and remember all that while you write, it'll save you having to do a re-write. That will be, what? Five thousand pounds?'

Jazz couldn't speak.

'OK – call it seven and a half. Fax it to me by Monday. Triple four, double five, double three. For the attention of Sharon Westfield. Ciao.'

Jazz put the phone down, bubbling with anger and excitement in equal proportions – a reaction that was becoming strangely familiar.

'What was that?' asked Mark, intrigued. Jazz rarely remained monosyllabic on the phone.

Jazz told him.

'Jeez, some people have all the luck,' he said.

'You think I should go for it?'

'Are you stark-bollocking mad? Of course you should go for it! A column at the *Daily Wacko*? You'd be set up for life.'

'Even if it means selling out bigtime?'

Mark frowned. 'What do you mean?'

'Never mind.'

Jazz had the rest of the week to consult George and Mo. And, of course Josie. But there were other things on her mind that she had to sort out first.

Jazz sat on the sofa in her room, the soft sound of monks chanting from her stereo speakers rocking her into a calm state. Now that she had sorted out in her mind why the e-mail had distressed her so much, she realised there was information in it that she should act on. Maybe. She decided she had to speak to George. She needed some advice from someone with strong moral fibre and a heart of gold. She stretched out to the phone behind her.

'Are you going to tell me you can't babysit for Josie tomorrow?' asked George.

In her bewildered state, Jazz had completely forgotten about that. George and she now took it in turns every Thursday night to babysit Ben while Josie and Michael went out together. Jazz was constantly impressed by their marriage. Josie deserved to win an award, whether or not it was under Jazz's name.

'No, that's fine, I can still do tomorrow,' she answered.

'Oh, OK,' said George disappointedly. Then: 'Can I come too?'

Oh poor heart, thought Jazz. 'Of course,' she said in a jolly voice. 'It'll be much nicer with you there.'

'Do you still want to talk tonight?' asked George hopefully.

'Yes, come round,' said Jazz. 'I'll make pasta.'

It was a date.

When George turned up, Jazz had to hide her shock at her sister's appearance. She looked almost emaciated, although she was smiling more than she had been for a while.

'I feel fine,' assured George. 'I just don't seem to want any food.'

'Well, you'll eat everything I serve you tonight,' said Jazz firmly.

'Yes, Mum,' said George.

George picked at the pasta, but managed nearly all of her salad. Jazz watched her in near despair. She had always thought being single would be good for George but now she wasn't so sure. Her sister was practically wilting away before her eyes. Jazz waited until they were drinking coffee and George could concentrate on the matter in hand completely. Maybe it would do her good to think of something else; be made aware that her brain had to go on for others, if not for herself. Slowly and clearly Jazz told George about Harry's e-mail and, more relevantly, the true story about William Whitby. The shock registering on her sister's wan face made it look more animated than it had in days, but she said nothing.

'What should I do?' asked Jazz at last.

'What do you mean?' asked George back. 'Do you want to apologise to Harry?'

'No,' said Jazz, pained. 'I mean, what should I do as a journalist? Wills – William – is adored by the public because they think he's like the priest he plays. And I'm a journalist

173

who knows the truth about him. George, he's an alcoholic woman-beater. What the hell should I do?'

George looked dumbfounded. 'We-ell,' she started.

'I mean, there's legitimate public interest here,' rushed Jazz. 'Should I shop him now and watch his career die – when he's never done anything to me except be positively charming – or do I wait silently, knowing that while the world thinks he's a really nice guy, he's probably beating up his make-up woman?'

George frowned deeply. Jazz continued regardless.

'All I have to do is phone any features desk and William Whitby's career is over. And by sick coincidence, mine is made. What the hell do I do?' Jazz was pacing now.

George was beginning to look a little bit more certain. 'You sit pretty,' she said fixedly.

'I let him go on beating other women?'

'No, I didn't say that. You don't know what went on behind closed doors between him and Carrie.'

'You mean she might have been asking for it?' asked Jazz crossly.

'No, I didn't say that,' repeated George calmly. 'I mean he may never do it with anyone else. Or he may have stopped drinking.'

'But surely it's my duty as a journalist to inform—'

'No, it's *not* your duty,' George interrupted. 'First of all, press coverage – even about something as sordid as this – might give him more fame than he deserves. Secondly, Harry told you in confidence. And thirdly, it's not even Harry's secret to tell, it's his sister's. And it sounds as if she would hate to have her name brought into anything.'

Jazz was convinced.

'Of course,' she said finally. 'You're right – it would kill her. Who am I to do that to her?' She plonked herself down at the table. 'Thanks George,' she said wearily.

They sat in glum silence.

'Of course,' said George quietly, 'you could always let William know that you know about him and Carrie. Keep him on his toes a bit.'

Jazz looked at her sister in a new light. 'You clever, conniving thing. Of course! What's happened to you? Am I slowly having a wicked effect on you?'

George tutted loudly. 'Just because I'm not a cynical hard bitch, there's no need to treat me like I'm Beth from *Little* Bloody *Women*!'

Jazz smiled thoughtfully and wondered if that's who she should try emulating from now on.

'I'm afraid there's something else I need your advice on,' she said softly.

George listened to her career dilemma. Should Jazz start writing for the *Daily Echo*? Could she do that and keep a part-time job at *Hoorah!* just in case the column wasn't successful? At the end, George asked one simple question: 'How will you feel about yourself if you write for the *Daily Echo*?'

Jazz thought hard. 'I suppose I'll feel wretched in one way, but then this is my career. This is everything I've worked for. This is my life, it's who I am. It's *me*.'

'Then do it.'

'But I hate everything this rag stands for.'

'Then don't do it.'

Jazz looked at George. Her eyes seemed dead.

By a fluke, Mo was in the flat the next night. And of course, Gilbert was there too. Although Jazz didn't want to talk in front of him, she knew she probably wouldn't get Mo alone for months – if ever again, she thought sourly. Gilbert lived on his own half an hour away and Mo had practically moved in with him. She hardly lived in her own flat any more. For weeks now, there had been none of her underwear airing in the bathroom, none of her mugs left unwashed on the sideboard and none of her shoes lying scattered in the hall. Jazz missed her terribly, especially during this period of monumental self-doubt and depression. Her father had been right. She *was* desperately jealous of Gilbert.

She didn't suppose it made much difference if Gilbert knew about her work dilemma. He was hardly a rival – being strictly a theatre writer. She just hated having to talk about herself in front of him. Still, it would have to be done. She waited until they were having dinner and joined them for coffee.

Gilbert was still super-smooth with Jazz, but it now took the form of patronising, pitying patter, as if he had done the rejecting and not her.

'Jazzy, sweetie,' he welcomed her into the kitchen. 'Join us, we're just having coffee.'

Jasmin wanted to tell him that she didn't need to be invited to join Mo anywhere. Mo smiled pleasantly at her as she sat down.

'How's it going?' said Mo quietly.

'Fine. The bathroom's been clean without you.'

'Only because you don't use it.'

They grinned at each other. Gilbert sat unsmiling.

'You never laugh at my jokes like Jazz does,' Mo said squarely.

Gilbert put his hands up in the air. 'Sorry, pussycat, I guess I'm not with you for your jokes.' He tried to make that sound sexy, but Mo just looked at him hard. Jazz could have punched him right there and then.

'It's nothing to get het up about,' he continued with an explanatory shrug. 'Everyone knows men are funnier than women.'

'Only to look at,' said Jazz grumpily, an eye on his paunch.

Mo sniggered and Gilbert smiled pityingly.

'You see?' he said to Mo. 'That's just not very funny.' He decided to change the subject. 'Jazzy, me and Mo wondered if you would like to come to the flicks with us one evening, and maybe for a meal afterwards. What d'you say? Make a night of it?'

Jesus, thought Jazz, he actually thinks I'd rather go out with them than stay in all evening counting my nasal hairs.

'Maybe a nice soppy romantic film,' he was saying, in a voice he thought was endearing.

Jazz looked him in the eye, something she hadn't done since the auditions.

'You mean a film where the man gets to make all the sacrifices, deliver all the funny lines, drive all the cars and go on top?' she asked.

He stared at her.

'No thanks, all the same,' she said with a tight smile. 'I've got to stay in. I'm growing my hair.'

She could practically see Gilbert's mind working. Finally, he asked, 'You mean you like to go on top?'

Jazz decided it was time to take control of the conversation before she got suicidal. She told Mo her news. Her column's new angle. The call from Sharon Westfield at the *Daily Echo*.

'That's fantastic!' squeaked Mo. 'Well done! I'm so proud! I always knew—'

'But I don't know if I should do it,' interrupted Jazz.

'Why?' asked Gilbert. 'Sharon's a bitch, but she's a good boss – as long as you don't annoy her, of course. Do that and you can say goodbye to a career in the popular press. Keep on her right side and you have a very powerful friend.'

'When did you ever work for her?' asked Jazz, intrigued.

'Oh, I've done bits and pieces for her over the years,' he said airily. 'She used to be Commissioning Editor on *Your Monthly* periodical.'

Jazz and Mo tried to be mature and not smirk.

'Not a great Commissioning Editor, to be honest,' continued Gilbert authoritatively. 'Waffles in her briefs.'

His perplexed expression at Jazz and Mo's sudden convulsion of laughter grew into a look of repulsion as Mo started snorting. His face only made Jazz laugh more heartily. Perhaps Gilbert wasn't so bad after all, she thought eventually, wiping her eyes.

Feeling happier than she had in ages, Jazz explained her predicament.

'Yes,' nodded Gilbert. 'One's self-respect is paramount in these things.'

Jazz and Mo just gawped at him and Jazz wondered if it would be acceptable to start laughing again.

She chose instead to ignore him.

'So what do you reckon?' she asked Mo as if Gilbert hadn't spoken. 'You think I shouldn't take it?'

Mo looked doubtful.

'I think you should do what you would be happy with,' said Gilbert.

Mo looked on, almost impressed.

'What sort of an answer is that?' asked Jazz tetchily. 'If I knew that one, I wouldn't be asking Mo, would I?' Damn.

They sat there in silence for a while, until Jazz eventually left them to their own company and went to bed. She decided she'd have to talk to Josie. At the *Evening Herald* Columnist Personality of the Year award ceremony.

Chapter 19

The day of the award ceremony, two days before she was supposed to fax her column to Sharon Westfield, Jazz's nerves were stretched to breaking point. She was daunted by the prospect of winning an award for which her boss had nominated her, for a column she was contemplating selling to a different publication. And she was daunted by the prospect of having to wait weeks before seeing Harry. Every time she thought of him, she felt a deep sense of shame. Seeing his proud, haughty face might just be the perfect antidote to that. And she could do with an antidote to the after-effects of that e-mail.

Josie was to be her guest at the awards. Jazz had wangled it with Michael that if she won the award, Josie deserved a night off from Ben and would go with her sister to the next cast party that weekend and stay the night in Mo's bed. Josie was going to leave Michael the number of the local casualty department if anything went wrong, instead of Jazz's mobile. A girl deserved a night off once in a while. Jazz was praying she'd win, just for Josie's sake.

Then on Saturday there would be the first of several

rehearsals without Harry; he was doing a three-week stint at The Pemberton in a one-man play written specially for him by hot new playwright Patrick Clifton. It was already sold out, of course.

Jazz sat in her office frowning at the dailies. The tabloids were full of vitriolic, un-newsworthy gossip and the qualities were so dry she actually fell asleep reading one. Harry was right. What had possessed her to be proud of her career? Things couldn't get much worse, she thought morosely.

She was wrong.

The next morning she had to carry her new little black number in on the tube.

'Ooh, let me see it,' said Maddie excitedly, as Jazz walked into the office. Jazz could hardly look at Maddie any more for guilt about her conversation with Sharon Westfield.

When she showed her the dress, Maddie's grin froze on her pretty little face.

'OhmyGod,' she whispered.

'What?' said Jazz. 'What could possibly be wrong with that? It's just a mangy little black dress.'

'It's exactly the same *mangy* little black dress that I've got,' said Maddie.

Jazz looked at her, bemused. 'All little black dresses look the same, Maddie.'

'This is a catastrophe,' said Maddie, not hearing her. 'One of us is going to have to go and buy another one.'

'Are you joking?' She could hardly believe that Maddie, who coped daily with mad readers, hopeless writers, insane deadlines and a tempestuous Editor, was actually panicking. A line of sweat was breaking out on her upper lip.

'No, I'm not. Where did you buy yours?'

'Paris,' lied Jazz. It was worth a try. 'Years ago.'

'Well then, it'll have to be me – I got mine in Covent Garden. I'll be back in an hour. Take my calls, Alison.' And she was gone.

Jazz looked over to Mark and awaited a smart reply, but he was actually looking concerned. Of course, thought Jazz. Women worrying about dresses made sense in his world.

Three hours later, a radiant Maddie wandered in. She showed her dress off proudly and Jazz was amazed. It was stunning. A miniscule red number with, in certain key areas, sequins where there should have been fabric. If Jazz was the kind of woman who hated being outdone by another woman, she'd have been very unhappy. Instead she just marvelled at the dress. As did Mark.

He gave a very long wolf whistle, which delighted Maddie.

'You may be my boss,' he said approvingly, 'but you know your clothes.'

Maddie was now in a good mood. Alison made her a cup of tea and Maddie sat down to read the papers. Today had been exhausting.

'Ooh,' she suddenly piped up. 'You didn't tell me Harry Noble was on at the Pemberton!' The theatre was a five-minute walk from their offices.

Jazz said nothing.

'Oooh,' swooned Maddie with a silly grin on her face. 'He's fabulous. I could watch him in anything.'

'Yes, I bet,' said Jazz. 'Particularly the shower.'

Maddie gasped at Jazz's comment and then giggled at the truth of it. Then she made a boss's decision. 'We *have* to go,' she commanded.

The sound of a newspaper being furiously rustled came from Mark's corner.

'No way,' said Jazz, before thinking.

'Why not?' asked Maddie. 'He'll never know you're there.'

'He might,' said Jazz. 'I'd kill myself if he ever knew.'

'Why? It would be research. Oh, I've *got* to see him,' and with that, Maddie phoned the box office, told them she was from the press and was immediately promised two tickets. Jazz watched her, frozen. She knew she would be fascinated to see Harry on stage yet mortified if he discovered she'd been there. Maddie put the phone down with a flourish and let out a little yippee.

'Research, darling!' she exclaimed.

Mark tutted from behind a paper. 'Research, bollocks!' he said. 'You're there to watch the man's crotch so you've got something to think about when you jerk off tonight.'

Maddie and Jazz both turned to him in disgust as he twitched his paper violently. Infuriatingly, Jazz couldn't think of anything to say to him that would crush him enough.

Maddie spoke instead.

'You know, Marcus,' she said archly. 'You are *such* a typical Gemini.'

Jazz smiled. She couldn't have done better herself.

With all the stress that was going on in Jazz's life at the moment, she had actually managed to forget that tonight was being televised. It was like a mini-Oscars, full of cameras, bright white lights and big names. The *Evening Herald* obviously knew a thing or two about putting on a spread. A couple of the women's magazines were there and all the dailies plus their Sunday counterparts. In the world of journalists, columns were the new black. Hell, they were so hot, they were the new *grey*.

Jazz looked at the table plan and saw that Sharon Westfield

from the *Daily Echo* was on table five. She scanned the enormous hall and spotted her table. There was only one woman on it. She was sandwiched between two typical elder statesmen of the press, both balding, fat and with very red noses. One was the Patron of the rag, the other his Editor. From their body language, it looked like Sharon was on rather intimate terms with at least one of them. There was no way Sharon would be concerned about finding Jazz with such pressing engagements nearer home, so she relaxed a bit and started to work at enjoying herself. Some of the awards were even more ridiculous than hers.

Rosie Smith and Robyn Anderson had been neck and neck for the Columnist's Most Moving Personal Trauma of the Year Award. Tragically, both were now in hospices, but their colleagues were there to take their places. There was a phone call during dinner to announce that Robyn had in fact died earlier this evening, so it came as no surprise when she won the award posthumously. Seems fair, thought Jazz. First past the posthumous, and all that.

Alastair Gibbon won the Columnist's Most Revealing Intimate Secret of the Year, and as he walked up to the podium to collect his four-inch-high Nelson's Column, the entire audience tried not to think of his anal fissures.

But the rest of the categories were intimidating enough and Jazz was truly humbled to see herself in such company as John Pilkin, whose column had alerted worldwide support for some very worthy charities, and Suzanne Edwards, whose column had reminded everyone that feminism could be trendy once more.

When the Columnist Personality of the Year award was being read out, Jazz's whole body went into fight or flight mode. Great, she thought to herself as her shins started to sweat. At least I know that if I ever get trapped in a dark alleyway, my body will react properly. So tonight won't have been a complete loss. It didn't help that Josie was holding her hand, but Jazz was too nervous to pull it away.

When she heard her name read out over the microphone and her entire table start to whoop, Jazz thought she must be dreaming. She couldn't remember walking up to the front of the room nor thanking everyone nor walking back to her seat. She just knew she felt overwhelmed with a sense of other-worldliness. Josie was ecstatic, and Jazz was too, for *her*.

But she also knew that she was made. This was it, the big time. She was an award-winning columnist. She was on TV. She put on a big smile and tried to stop thinking of that wretched e-mail and how it proved she didn't know what the hell she was talking about.

Immediately after the awards, she and Josie were interviewed live on TV. The young male interviewer had introduced them to camera as 'the acerbically judgemental Jasmin Field and her happily-married sister Josie'. He'd even asked if their parents would be proud, at which point Josie had waved to the camera and said, 'Hello, Mum.' Jazz knew both her parents would probably be weeping with pride.

As the interview ended, Sharon Westfield came over. Thrusting her hand into Jazz's and shaking it vigorously, she said, 'Many congrats, no one deserved it more, absolutely delighted.' She was smoking a cigar.

Jazz mumbled her thanks, hoping to God Maddie wasn't watching.

'We'd love to do a follow-up,' continued Sharon, still shaking Jazz's hand. 'Love to. *Perfect Family* — that sort of thing, right up our street.' She dropped Jazz's hand to place

imaginary words in the sky: "The Field Family – The Last
Happy Family in the Country". *Perfect*.'

Jazz smiled weakly.

Sharon winked at her, tapped her nose with her finger
and whispered loudly, 'Then when you start the column,
our readers will know who you are, eh? Looking forward
to your fax.' And she was gone.

Jazz pulled Josie away from the scene and when her
younger sister asked what all that was about, she said she'd
explain later. She wasn't going to let politics spoil her night.

Later, Jazz and Josie danced the night away with Maddie,
while Mark watched them morosely, slowly getting drunk.
Various tabloid Editors were making fools of themselves over
Maddie and she was in her element. It wouldn't be long
before she'd be leaving *Hoorah!* Jazz thought contentedly.

Yep, it was a good night, she decided, although neither
Maddie nor Josie could pogo quite like Mo.

Hours later, Jazz and Josie sat in Mo's empty flat, tired,
drenched in their own cold sweat and with the music's
pumping beat still slightly deafening them.

It was then that Jazz told Josie her dilemma.

She was a hypocrite. She had danced the night away with
the people who had helped make her career, and all the time
she had been secretly selling her soul to a higher bidder.

As Josie answered her questions, all became clear to Jazz.
Of course. It would be Josie, the one who had been her
inspiration so far, Josie, who had provided her with her biggest
career success so far, Josie, her sister who had it all, who would
go on to show her exactly and precisely what to do.

'*You're* the one who made your career, not them,' she
said simply. 'And you've got them free publicity by winning

186

the award. Agatha didn't nominate you for altruistic reasons, did she?'

Jazz's sense of guilt evaporated instantly. When had Josie become so mature? Was that what motherhood did to you?

'Anyway,' her younger sister continued, 'why can't my story be in a *quality* paper instead? Aren't I interesting enough?'

Jazz sat up. 'You know, I never even thought of that,' she said, suddenly perky.

'Well ring them, idiot,' grinned Josie. 'You're famous now. Wait until later though, it's four in the morning.'

Jazz stood in the phone box, pushing coins into the slot. It took an aeon for someone to answer.

'Features,' said a bored, busy voice at the *News*, one of the more stuffy quality papers.

'Oh hello, my name's Jasmin Field, I'm a columnist for *Hoorah!* magazine and have just won the *Evening Herald*'s Columnist's Personality of the Year Award. You may have caught me on TV last night.' She winced at how that sounded, but kept going. You couldn't sell hard enough in this game. 'Here's the story. I've been poached by the *Daily Echo* but would love to write for you.'

There was silence at the other end. Jazz ignored her dry throat and the countdown on the phone's meter. She put some more coins in. There was silence at the other end.

'My column is all about my sister Josie,' Jazz continued. 'She's a confident, intelligent, happily-married young full-time mum who has all sorts of *hysterical* incidents happen to her.'

Silence.

'It's a sort of modern, post-erm – post . . .' Post-traumatic stress syndrome? Poster Paint? Postman Pat? Bugger. 'She's my sister,' she gabbled.

Silence.

'I'm a bloody fast writer and don't mind re-writing.'

She put some more money in the slot.

'I worked with your Assistant Editor, Jackie Summers, years ago at *Bonkers!*. She might remember me.'

Silence. She'd run out of coins.

'Shall I send you some of my work?'

Silence. Had someone shot him, perhaps?

'Hello?' she said, irritated.

'I know your work. Fax over two new columns written to our style for the attention of Brigit Kennedy, Commissioning Editor.'

And then the pips went.

Jazz put the phone down in a bit of a daze.

Even if the *News* said no, Jazz had already decided that if she worked for the *Daily Echo*, she'd never be able to live with herself. And although she didn't much like herself at the moment, she had decided she didn't want to live with anyone else.

Back in the office, she finished her current feature and then, when everyone had gone home, she bashed out two new columns – one about how her family had reacted to her winning the award, the other about how she was happy being single until the right man came along – a man who would treat her like her brother-in-law treated her sister. Then she faxed them to the *News* and went home.

She'd worry about the *Daily Echo* another day.

Chapter 20

'You're leaving me?' said Maddie, her eyes wide with disappointment.

'Oh, please don't make me feel guilty,' said Jazz keenly. 'You'll be snapped up within weeks. I saw how the Editor of the *Reactor* was looking at you at the awards.'

She knew that would work. Maddie's little mouth turned up slightly at the edges. They were sitting on the table in the tiny area next to the coffee machine. Since they'd gone open-plan, private spaces were a thing of the past. They had to be quick.

To Jazz's amazement, Brigit Kennedy, Commissioning Editor of the *News*, had phoned her first thing the morning after she'd sent in her columns. She hadn't heard anything from the *Daily Echo* and hoped Sharon Westfield had forgotten her.

'Love your style,' Brigit had said. 'It's so rare to get a column that's about a marriage that's working nowadays. Of course, it's a risk because today's readers only want to read about others' troubles, but we think you're a risk worth taking. We'd be delighted to have you on board.'

Jazz was over the moon. 'Thank you,' she breathed. 'You won't regret it.'

'I'm afraid we can only offer you five hundred pounds a column—'

'I'll take it,' Jazz said quickly, and the two women laughed. Contracts were faxed over to her and she'd signed that afternoon. She'd been absolutely staggered at how fast newspapers can move if they really want you.

After the call, Jazz had felt wonderful, ecstatic, elated, over the moon, tearful, relieved and special. Her dream had finally come true. Until she remembered she'd have to break the news to Maddie.

'You're leaving me alone with Mark?' repeated Maddie.

'Oh, you know how to deal with him,' said Jazz sympathetically. 'Anyway, you might find he really lightens up once I've gone.'

'And Angry Alison?'

'I thought you liked Alison.'

'And Mad Miranda?'

'Yes, I'm beginning to see your point,' said Jazz. She hadn't realised Maddie would take it quite so badly. So she explained that she still wanted to do work for *Hoorah!* either on a freelance basis or possibly as a part-timer.

'I'll tell Agatha,' said Maddie. 'Let's hope I come out alive.'

They both smiled weakly.

'I can't believe you're leaving me,' Maddie said once more, her little red lips starting to tremble slightly. They walked back to the office and Maddie told everyone Jazz's news. She'd have to tell Agatha tomorrow; she was in meetings all day.

Mark came over immediately. Miranda continued tapping.

'Say congratulations to our columnist for the *News*, Mark,' said Maddie, as sternly as Jazz had ever heard her speak.

'So are you fucking off then?' he asked instead, leaning back against the empty desk and crossing his arms. His shirtsleeves were rolled up to his elbows and Jazz noticed that the sun had brought out the fine auburn hairs on his forearms.

'Yup. You can talk about shagging now as much as you like in the office,' said Jazz. 'As long as you mention IKEA a few times.'

Mark stared hard at Maddie.

'Don't think this means we won't still come and see you in your play,' said Maddie, veering off on another subject. 'We'll be there with the banners.' Oh God, the play, thought Jazz. She'd actually managed to forget about it.

The next morning, Jazz was staggered to open the *Daily Echo* and see a double-page spread headed IS THIS THE LAST HAPPY FAMILY IN THE COUNTRY? above a massive picture of her smiling family. Quickly scanning the piece, she could see that it was mostly hearsay and speculation with one or two quotes from Martha, whom they had obviously spoken to for two minutes on the phone. At the bottom, in bold, were the words **You can read award-winning Jasmin Field's regular column starting next month. Only in the *Daily Echo*.** Weren't they at all concerned that she hadn't even sent them her first column yet? Maybe they expected columnists to miss deadlines.

Jesus Christ. She hadn't even sent them her fax yet. And Maddie hadn't told the news to Agatha yet. She certainly hadn't signed anything with them yet. What's more, she *wasn't* going to write for them, she was going to write for the *News*.

191

She phoned her mother straight away. 'Have you read the *Daily Echo*?' she asked.

'Yes,' said Martha.

'When did you speak to them, Mum?'

'I hadn't realised I had, dear,' answered Martha, mildly flustered. 'Someone phoned me to ask how I felt about you winning the award and how I felt about having three famous daughters. They said they were the award organisers and this was for their internal journal. Anyway,' she scoffed, 'I didn't say I was "over the moon". I never talk in such ridiculous clichés. Perish the thought.'

Jazz was furious. She had half a mind to phone Sharon Westfield and complain. But what was the point? It was much more important for her to phone Brigit Kennedy and explain that it was all a horrible mistake and then apologise to Agatha before she was sacked.

Brigit Kennedy was surprisingly phlegmatic about it. She knew Sharon Westfield of old – 'She was my Deputy at *Smile!*' she told Jazz. 'Morals of a dog on heat. Knows her stuff though. Don't give it a moment's thought.'

Brigit gave Jazz her first commission there and then. If anything, Jazz felt it had worked in her favour.

Then it was off to Agatha's office. The door was open and Jazz could see Agatha at her desk, reading the *Daily Echo*. Smiling out at her was Jazz's entire family.

She knocked feebly on the door.

Agatha looked up at her. She said nothing.

'I can explain,' said Jazz.

Agatha crossed her arms and waited.

'I'm not going to write for them. They asked me to and I hadn't even sent them my provisional fax yet. It's a horrible mistake.'

192

Agatha started to look slightly more human again.

'That's all right then,' she said. 'Otherwise I'd have had to fire you.' And she turned the page over and ignored Jazz.

Jazz didn't think it was the right time to mention the *News*.

She started her first column for them at midnight when she couldn't sleep. It was full of bile. At 1.30 am she e-mailed it and made herself a Horlicks. She slept very peacefully until 6.30 am.

The next morning she got a call from Brigit.

'Thanks for the column. Really nice. Loved the nostalgic bit about you and Josie arguing about Euro '96. You telling her that football had nothing to do with reality and her pointing out that it had become political because even John Major had told Gareth Southgate he had nothing to be ashamed of when he missed the penalty.'

Jazz smiled over the phone. This was a good start. But Brigit went on. 'And then you saying that Gareth Southgate had never returned the compliment,' she finished, as though Jazz didn't remember the cadence and rhythm of every single one of her beloved jokes. The Commissioning Editor laughed loudly. 'Politics, humour and sport. Keep it coming, gal.'

Brigit told her it would go in as soon as possible, and gave her her direct line. That meant Jazz had to pluck up the courage to tell Agatha very soon. She tried not to think of Sharon Westfield.

Chapter 21

It was a Saturday night and Jazz, Josie and George turned up to the latest cast party together, just like when they were teenagers, hundreds of years ago. Jazz was on a high for the first time in a very long fortnight. George circulated easily among the crowd. Jazz saw that Jack was staying put in the kitchen, nursing a beer and a forced smile and William was flitting. Of course William was at the party, thought Jazz. He could be safe tonight because he knew that Harry would be on stage most of the evening.

Jazz introduced Josie to all and waited patiently for William to flit round to them. She was going to test him.

She didn't have to wait long.

'Hello,' he grinned, eyeing Josie up. Josie had George's vibrant colouring, and even though a few years of exhaustion had faded it somewhat, Jazz knew her sister still looked good.

At first Jazz tried hard not to notice those crinkly lines at the corner of William's eyes nor his warming smile. But then she realised that looking at them didn't hurt her like she thought it would. She introduced him to Josie, and

William seemed delighted to discover there was another Field sister. She wished she'd warned Josie about William, but she supposed there would always be time. Jazz told him that she had managed to get tickets for Harry's play and waited for his reaction. William looked surprised. After a pause he edged nearer to her.

'I suppose knowing the truth about him, you're doubly intrigued to see the difference between a false act and a genuine one?' he said lightly.

Jazz couldn't help but smile at his words. It helped the hurt a bit.

'Oh, I've got to know him a bit better since we last spoke,' she said. 'And I find Harry's manner – with some people – easier to swallow now.'

Jazz got a sense of deep satisfaction watching the different reactions that fought for control over William's pleasing features.

'You mean,' he began, when he could trust his voice to be indifferent, 'that you've grown used to his manner? Or has he turned into a lovely warm chap who will surprise us all at the next rehearsal?'

'Oh no,' replied Jazz, enjoying the conversation even more than she thought she would. This was probably the only good thing that would come out of the e-mail. 'He's still the same old Harry Noble. I just mean that when you get to know more about the man's past – and the past of those he loves – it's easier to understand the reasons behind his actions.'

To her delight, William actually coloured.

'I'm surprised to see that Carrie isn't here,' she said, looking round.

There was now no doubt that they both knew what Jazz was talking about.

'Harry's sister?' he asked evenly, though it was obvious to Jazz he wished he were no longer talking to her. 'She rarely comes to parties.'

Jazz nodded slowly. 'Maybe she doesn't like what drink does to some people,' she said quietly and then with one last look at him, she turned and walked away, leaving him, not without some regret, to talk to Josie. The fact that he looked annoyed instead of embarrassed put a final end to her crush on him.

She was stopped on her way towards the kitchen by Mo. 'Be nice,' Mo said urgently, before Gilbert approached. Jazz realised pretty quickly that he was very drunk.

'Jazzy Jazzy Jazzy,' he slurred and then slumped untidily against the wall. Jazz took advantage of the situation and started talking to Mo as if he wasn't there.

'You'll never guess,' she said. 'I'm going to see Harry in his play tomorrow.'

'What?' said Gilbert, his eyes glazed over. 'Famous Harry Famous Noble's famous play? If you see his bitch of an aunt there – can't miss her, face like a baboon's arse – would you kindly spit in her eye for me?' He took a swig from a bottle of red wine.

Jazz looked at Mo.

'She's stopped sponsoring his magazine. She found out he was in the play with Harry and completely went over the top. Didn't just fire him, she pulled all her money out of the whole magazine,' said Mo.

They both looked dismayed at Gilbert. Gilbert belched. They all knew that without his specialist mag – which was respected by those in the business, even if it was seen as pretentious – Gilbert was as good as on the scrapheap. Without his regular contact with the theatre world, his part-time career would grind to a halt, too. There were always others only too happy to sell sordid little secrets to the tabloids. Respected theatre journalism was notoriously difficult to get into and on the nationals – which would be all Gilbert would be able to tolerate moving to – they were heavily over-subscribed with clever, experienced writers who were far more arrogant than Gilbert could ever aspire to be. Gilbert's only choice would be to end up on some provincial paper, which would lower his profile, ego and reputation beyond repair. A future of bitterness beckoned.

'In fact, you can tell her from me that her acting stinks,' Gilbert was slurring. 'Just like her nephew's.'

When she realised that Mo wasn't going to leave Gilbert's side all evening, Jazz eventually extricated herself from them and watched from a safe distance as Mo tried to pull the bottle out of her boyfriend's weakening grip.

She noticed that Sara Hayes was absent from the party. Of course, she thought. Why would she waste her evening with the likes of us if Harry Noble wasn't going to be there? And then she checked herself glumly. Maybe Sara had a hospital appointment or something, who was she to know? She wasn't always right.

As for the cast, the only people she could be bothered to talk to were Matt, who was always lovely, and Jack, who was now out of bounds. She suddenly found the rest of the cast oppressively wearisome. And even though she had just won a prestigious award, achieved her professional goal and had got tickets for Harry's show that no one else there had managed to get, she was vaguely aware that there was something lacking in the evening's entertainment. Her bubble had silently burst. With growing horror, she realised why. The truth was she'd become very used to being watched

197

by a certain Harry Noble. Hell, damnation and buggery bollocks.

She managed to make dull social chitchat until midnight, when she decided to call it a day. She couldn't find Josie anywhere. Maybe she was already back at the flat, she thought. She'd given her a spare key. When Jazz finally got home, the flat was silent but she assumed that Josie was in Mo's room and went straight to bed.

The next morning, she found Josie dressed and up in the kitchen.

'Nice evening?' she asked, pouring herself a coffee.

Josie grinned sheepishly. 'Fabulous. You didn't tell me what a dish William Whitby was.'

'There's a good reason for that,' said Jazz. 'He's a shit. Of the highest order.'

Josie's face fell. Then she looked sheepish again. 'Who cares?' she said, and was off home.

Chapter 22

Jazz was very, very happy. Her first column had appeared in the *News*, lots of her friends and family had phoned to tell her they loved it and there had been no come-back from Agatha since Maddie had convinced their boss that it would help their circulation having the *News*'s top columnist as their exclusive celebrity interviewer. Maddie had decided, since her interview with Jazz, that Jazz should still work for them on a freelance basis.

When her phone went for the umpteenth time, she picked it up happily. 'Hello, *Hoorah!*'

'I thought we had a deal!' barked a terrifying voice at the other end of the phone.

'S-sorry?'

'What the fuck do you mean giving the *News* your column when I was there first?' It was Sharon Westfield and she was spitting blood.

Although taken aback, Jazz was firm. She knew she hadn't promised them anything.

'I'm sorry Sharon, but—'

'SORRY? I'll show you sorry, young lady. Think you can

do the dirty on me, do you? After we ran a spread on your cosy family picture—'

Jazz didn't think now was the time to mention that her family hadn't enjoyed being duped and misquoted.

'Who do you think you are?' the woman ranted on. 'You wouldn't have got that stupid award if I hadn't tipped the wink. Believe me, young lady, if there's dirt to be had on you, I'll find it. Consider yourself dropped.' And she hung up.

Jazz was mind-blown. She had done nothing wrong. She could go to whatever paper she wanted. Sharon Westfield was quite obviously barking mad.

And she was now Jazz's enemy.

When she told Maddie about her call, Maddie was philosophical. A friend of hers worked with Sharon so she knew all there was to know about her.

'Forget it,' she said simply. 'Sharon won't remember your name next week. Apparently she's going through a really difficult divorce at the moment – it was just bad timing. Anyway, you're not allowed to be worried tonight, we're going to see Harry Noble act. So cheer up and that's an order.'

By the time Maddie and Jazz walked into the foyer of the Pemberton Theatre that evening, Jazz was in a bad way. There were so many knots in her stomach, she could have joined a Boy Scout group. The theatre was packed with beautiful, famous people. Jazz didn't know where to look first. She and Maddie squeezed their way through the crowd and up the staircase to their seats in the front row of the dress circle. Jazz knew this theatre well and it looked as stunning as ever. But never before had she felt so in awe of the stage. It was enormous, and Jazz suddenly felt terrified for Harry. How could he put himself on the line like this? Regularly?

All these people waiting for him to make their evening go with a bang. All these people expecting him to give them their money's worth. If he fluffed even one line, hundreds of people would be disappointed. For the first time, Jazz grew numb with terror at the prospect of acting. In only one month's time, she would be doing the same thing as Harry, albeit in a smaller, less grandiose theatre.

She looked up at the ornate plasterwork and painting on the ceiling above her. The workmanship was breathtaking: it must have taken years to complete – decades even. But no one would be looking at that tonight. She stared hard at the red velvet curtain on the stage. What would Harry be doing now? She knew that he would have no problem focusing himself; unlike her, who was always so easily distracted. God, he must have been frustrated by her in rehearsals. She forced herself to think of something else before the familiar depression took hold.

Maddie was beside herself with excitement. 'Ohmygod, there's whatsisname,' she squeaked. Jazz followed the direction of Maddie's indiscreetly pointed finger with her eyes. So it was. The place was full of actors and directors, critics and celebs. She spotted Brian Peters who, to her enormous surprise, gave her a big smile from his circle seat. And a hush came over all of them when the Noble family entered their box. Jazz saw that Harry had his mother's colouring and his father's strong features. They smiled at everyone regally.

Then the lights dimmed, and Jazz was overwhelmed by excitement, terror and an incongruous sense of empathy with Harry.

The set was the interior of a 1950s house, complete with kitchenette and plastic covers on the couch. The detail was amazing. She could see the gold lettering on the book spine by the drinks cabinet. A door slammed in the distance and in walked Harry. Or rather, in slouched Harry. At first Jazz didn't recognise him and wondered if there was some mistake. He was wearing the unflattering trousers of the day, which belted high in the waist, making his legs look shorter and his stomach look larger. His shoulders were rounded with fatigue, his neck was tense and his head hung as if bowed by misery. His hair was Brylcreemed into an unattractive, slick style. He called out a woman's name and when he got no reply, he went to the fridge, took out a bottle of beer and slumped down on the couch.

Jazz was transfixed. With supreme confidence, Harry flipped the lid off his drink and slowly drank half the bottle. He even belched, which got a snigger from the audience. Then he pushed his hand through his hair – a gesture that brought a confusing squirm to Jazz's stomach – and looked wistfully into the auditorium. She could have sworn he was looking right at her. She blushed in the dark.

He spoke in a Texan drawl, but his voice was the same. It had such depth, such quality. For two and a half hours, he spoke of his life, his desires, his sacrifices. Every little movement he made was entrancing. He could transform his entire audience's emotions with the smallest change of expression, make them laugh with the slightest shift of his eye. He had such control over them, such power. He turned them into one conscious being, instead of hundreds of separate people. When Harry cried, unmanly sobs that came from the pit of his stomach, Jazz thought her heart would break. He was intoxicating.

There was only one moment when she allowed her mind to meander from the play. It was when Harry took his shirt off. That beautiful smooth, olive-brown torso, those gently curved shoulders, the width of his forearms and the vulnerability of the back of his neck ... His body was probably the most beautiful one she had ever seen and its natural grace made her think for the first time how nice it would have been to have walked into a party with him by her side. She had never looked at him *properly* before, and now that she was safely in the dark, she drank him in. And she was in awe. I could have had that, she found herself thinking in wonder. I could have been mistress of that. And she made herself smile and find it funny.

When the play finished, and Harry bowed fully and slowly, as if trying to take in each and every member of the audience, Jazz stayed in her seat, clapping. She wanted everyone else to disappear, she wanted it to be just him and her. She wanted to be up there on stage with him. She wished the spotlight would fall on her now, and reveal her sitting in the audience. She felt a sudden, intense jealousy of everyone whose eye Harry caught as he bowed. She wanted to own him. And, as she glanced quickly at the rapt faces of the audience – not taking her eyes off him for too long – she experienced, for the first time, a deep sense of gratitude for the attraction he'd once felt for her.

She had told Maddie beforehand that they were to leave before the curtain went down, but there was no way she'd do that now. She just sat there, soaking in the atmosphere. When had he found time to learn his lines, to rehearse, focus? And he'd done all this while keeping *P&P* going. She was staggered.

Eventually, the heavy curtain dropped to the floor and wasn't going to go up again. People reluctantly began to leave and she heard snippets of their conversations:

203

'This generation's Olivier' ... 'mesmeric' ... 'hypnotising' ...

She and Maddie took ages to get through the crush. They seemed to get caught behind everyone and, of course, they both had to queue to use the Ladies. Maddie re-did her make-up, but when Jazz looked in the mirror and saw her puffy eyes and red nose, ravaged by forty minutes of intermittent crying, she knew she was past helping. It always took a day or two for her face to recover from sobbing. By the time they left the theatre, only a few people were still around.

When they finally got to the door, Jazz stopped and closed her eyes at the delicious night breeze on her hot and sticky body.

'Jasmin!' called a shocked voice.

She opened her eyes. To her horror, there stood Harry, dressed in a crisp white shirt and narrow-legged, flat-fronted dark trousers, his jacket slung over his shoulders, about to enter the foyer. It was only a fortnight since she had last seen him, but so much had happened since then that it felt like months ago. At first they were both so astonished and uncomfortable, neither could think of anything to say. Jazz's awareness of their shared awkwardness kept overcoming her in waves. Why had she let Maddie force her to come. What would Harry think of her? It was unbearable.

Harry wasn't coping too well with the situation either.

'Congratulations on your award,' he said eventually.

How did he know about that?

'Congratulations on your performance,' managed Jazz back. She was suddenly feeling so shy that she hardly noticed he was even more tongue-tied than her.

There was a painful pause.

'How are you?' asked Harry eventually.

'Fine, thanks. You?' replied Jazz.

'I – I didn't know you were coming,' he continued. 'You could have had drinks in the interval backstage.'

'Oh,' said Jazz intelligently, forcing herself to look him in the eye, like an adult. She noticed for the first time that his upper lip was probably his nicest feature. And his cheekbones were amazing.

'How is George? And Mo?' he asked, as if he hadn't seen them for years.

Jazz couldn't find a suitable reply. George is catatonic? Mo is moronic? Her brain seemed to have stopped working.

Maddie interrupted. 'Mr Noble, my name is Maddie Allbrook. I'm Jazz's boss. We were very lucky to get tickets.'

Harry looked at Maddie and stunned Jazz by giving her a big smile and putting his hand out to shake hers.

'Any friend of Jasmin's is a friend of mine,' he said simply. 'Did you enjoy the show?'

Maddie let out a very unfeminine noise that expressed yes. 'You were – you were ay-mazing,' she finally managed to say.

Harry grinned at her warmly. 'It's very kind of you to say so. Thank you very much, it means a lot.' Then he looked back to Jazz, who was having considerable difficulty believing her eyes or ears. This was a completely different Harry from the one she knew. This must be his post-performance persona. It was the only possible explanation.

Suddenly she remembered that her nose would still be red and she said accusingly, 'You made me cry.' She wished she could read the expression in his eyes.

But Harry made no comment. He turned to Maddie.

'You're from the press?' he asked her. 'Oh dear – I hope you're not going to be too harsh on me?'

Maddie looked shocked and hurt. 'Not all journalists are out to knock, you know.'

'I think your magazine is splendid,' Harry answered sincerely.

'Well,' said Maddie. 'It was once.' She looked at Jazz. 'Its staff are certainly splendid, it's just the readers who've gone downhill. Present company excluded, of course,' she gushed.

Harry assured her that no offence had been taken.

Then he suddenly remembered something and looked at them both.

'Will you come inside and meet my family?' he invited them.

Jazz didn't know what to say.

'They'd love to meet you,' he went on. 'You already know my sister Carrie, Jasmin. They're inside. It'll only take a minute.'

All helpful information, yet Jazz still didn't know what to say.

Maddie answered for her. 'How wonderful,' she breathed and took Jazz's arm, pushing her back into the foyer.

There stood Carrie and their parents. People were walking round them, transfixed, nodding and smiling as if they were royalty. Jazz was fascinated. From the impression she had always got from the press and indeed from Gilbert, she believed Harry's parents to be highly principled, yet cold people who had never given him any affection. So she was very surprised when Harry's father hugged him and the two of them stood like that for a while. His father didn't say anything – he couldn't, he was too close to tears. When Harry bent down to embrace his mother, her grin almost

206

split her face and tears ran happily down her cheeks. Carrie gave him a big hug and then smiled a shy yet proud smile over at Jazz. Jazz smiled back, ashamed that she'd never given Carrie a moment's thought.

'Mum, Dad, this is Jasmin Field, my Elizabeth Bennet.'

Both his parents pretended to know exactly who she was and smiled at her warmly, shaking her hand. His mother actually took Jazz's hand in both of hers while she shook it. They must have been on an amazing high.

Jazz made some noises to indicate she thought that the fruit of their loins had done them proud and that she really ought to leave them to their evening. With that she said goodbye to Harry and walked Maddie out.

But Harry followed her. 'Are you coming to the next rehearsal?' he asked, leaning against the doorframe and looking at Jazz intently. If there is a noise that accompanies the act of swooning, Maddie made it.

'Well,' said Jazz slowly. 'As long as you don't mind the fact that I can't act.'

Harry's smile was so full of affection that Jazz momentarily missed the fact that he didn't contradict her.

'Now that the previews are over I can start coming back to them,' he said. 'I thought we should concentrate on the last scene when Darcy proposes the second time, so it'll just be you, me and maybe Matt. Oh, and Carrie will come later to discuss costumes with you. She thought it would be a good time to get you alone. Perhaps we could all go for a drink afterwards?'

Jazz didn't think she'd ever heard Harry use such long sentences. She nodded. 'Lovely,' she said softly.

And they both separated.

*   *   *

'So *that's* the "bastard", Harry Noble?' Maddie said dreamily. 'Jasmin, he is *gorgeous*. He is a god. He's *so* tall. And broad. And those *eyes*. The man has teeth that were made in heaven.' She started an impression of The Wicked Witch of the West. 'I'm melting, I'm melting . . .'

Usually Jazz would have found this highly amusing, but tonight she wasn't listening.

'I can't believe you made me go,' she said, almost in tears. 'It's all your fault, Maddie.'

Maddie stopped and frowned. 'What did I do wrong?' she asked incredulously. 'He was delighted to see you.'

Jazz shook her head as if trying to get something out of her brain. 'He's just trying to prove me wrong,' she said despairingly. 'He's laughing on the other side of his face.'

'Well, it's a drop-dead gorgeous face, whatever side it's being laughed on,' said Maddie. She wanted to ask Jazz if she was blind as well as stupid, but realised Jazz was in no mood to be criticised. She decided instead to discuss Harry's merits, rather than Jazz's shortcomings, but stopped after half a minute, when she realised Jazz was not only not listening, but was in some sort of private hell.

Chapter 23

Jazz arrived early at the next rehearsal. She was always early when she was nervous. She paced in the church hall going over her lines. It was going to be excruciating having to say these apologetic, romantic things to Harry – but not as excruciating as hearing his replies. She wanted to apologise about what she'd said that night when he'd tried to . . . and yet now she was so much less rational about it all, so much more hurt by his insults than she had been then. It felt like years ago now. Yet she remembered it as vividly as if it was yesterday.

She jumped when her mobile rang.

'Hello, Jasmin Field,' she answered, her voice echoing in the hall.

It was George.

'Jazz, terrible news,' said George.

'What?' Jazz thought her heart had stopped. She'd always dreaded this. Which parent had had a heart attack?

'Are you sitting down?' asked George.

'No,' said Jazz.

'Well, sit down,' said George firmly.

'JUST TELL ME THE NEWS,' shouted Jazz, terrified.

'Michael and Josie are separating,' George said in a rush.

Jazz gasped. How come? They were happily married! What about Ben? What about the unborn baby? How was Josie?

'It gets worse,' said George.

'Go on,' whispered Jazz.

'Josie shagged William Whitby at the party.'

Jazz gasped and collapsed on the chair. William Whitby! Of all the people to choose. And *she'd* introduced them.

'It gets worse,' said George.

'How?' said Jazz, dizzy with shock.

'Are you sitting dow—'

'YES. Just tell me the news,' shouted Jazz impatiently.

There was a long pause.

'Gilbert Valentine caught them at it – they were in the toilet together, can you believe it? – and is threatening to go to the tabloids with it. It would make him a fortune, Jazz – and put his career back on track. He might even get a regular slot.'

Jazz was in fighting spirit. 'It's not big enough for the tabloids—'

'Yes, it is,' interrupted George evenly. 'Wills is famous, you've made Josie a household name for being so happily married and – and – well . . .'

'What?'

'Well, we shouldn't forget that you've got enemies in high places.'

Oh Christ, Sharon Westfield. That bitch would be only too delighted to shop her whole family. And Gilbert knew all about her involvement with that woman, since she had been foolish enough to discuss it with Mo while he was there. He even knew what she really thought of the *Daily Echo*.

He'd given her advice, for Christ's sake! And all the time he'd probably had Sharon's direct line. The Wacko hacks already knew where her parents and sisters lived and what they looked like. Jazz went numb with horror. A scandal like this would be a dream come true for their circulation.

George took this moment to say: 'I'm afraid it gets even worse.'

Jazz moaned.

'He also shagged Kitty Bennet at the rehearsal. So as far as the *Daily Echo* would be concerned, Josie was officially involved in a sex romp.'

Jazz could hear whistling in her ears.

'I'm on my way to Mum and Dad's now,' said George. 'Do you want me to pick you up?'

Jazz whispered yes and switched off her mobile. She put her script back into her bag and started running towards the door. As she did so, it opened and there stood Harry Noble.

She started so dramatically at his entrance and was so hideously pale that he was shocked. 'Good God, are you all right?' he asked.

Jazz shook her head and decided she would deal with this in as dignified a manner as possible.

'No,' she gulped. 'I don't — I don't think I am.' She didn't seem to be able to move.

She let Harry guide her onto a bench by a table, where she sat staring ahead of her.

'Is there anything I can do?' he asked.

Jazz shook her head. It was beginning to ache. Eventually she spoke.

'I've messed everything up,' she whispered and her eyes welled with tears.

'I'm sure you haven't,' Harry said gently. He couldn't

211

think of anything else to say. He'd never seen her in this state before.

She nodded sadly as a single tear crept down her cheek. 'I have,' she said. More tears started to fall and unblinking, she ignored them. Somehow it felt good confessing all to Harry. 'I've ruined four people's lives and my career in one swift move. And I could have avoided it all.' She fought against a sob that threatened to break into a weep.

'What's happened?' whispered Harry.

Jazz found she couldn't keep it from him if she'd wanted to – which she didn't. She looked down at the table and spoke so quietly that Harry had to lean forward and concentrate hard to hear her properly.

'William Whitby and my sister Josie – the married one – had sex in the loo at the party last week.' It hurt just to say it. 'Josie's husband has found out and they're getting separated. They've got a little boy –' At the thought of Ben she started to sob in earnest. Harry put his hand on her shoulder before thinking better of it. 'I introduced them to each other,' she wept. 'Oh God, I've wrecked their family.' And here she closed her eyes and sobbed silently for a moment.

'I'm sure they'll be fine.'

Jazz shook her head sadly. 'I haven't finished.'

'Sorry.' He took his hand off her shoulder.

'Gilbert Valentine, who is now unemployed since his magazine's sponsor, your aunt Dame Alexandra Marmeduke, pulled her finances, says he's going to sell the story to the tabloids. He knows that the *Daily Echo* would be only too delighted to drag me and my family in the mud because I gave my column to the *News* instead of them.'

Harry frowned intently. 'He won't do that, I'm sure. Your

family will be fine.' His voice was so comforting that she almost felt better.

But she shook her head and smiled the saddest, most poignant smile he'd ever seen off stage.

'Oh, I'm not just thinking of my loved ones,' she said to him. 'I'm a journalist, remember? I've already thought past that to my own sordid little career. You see, Mr Noble,' and here she turned her large, sad eyes to face him, 'I've based my whole career on three simple things that are to be my downfall. My sister Josie's perfect marriage, my infallible opinions of others and – ' she dropped her head down to her chest in shame, ' – my constant censure of those who don't live up to my ideals.' She sniffed loudly. 'The second Gilbert's article rolls off the presses, my career as a serious columnist is over and my family is a laughing stock. And I brought it all on myself.'

When she next lifted her head and peered out of heavy eyes, Harry was up and pacing.

She started talking half to herself. 'I should have told the truth about William Whitby. I shouldn't have kept it quiet. What sort of journalist am I? And now everyone's going to suffer because of my stupid decision.'

She realised Harry wasn't listening. Oh God, she thought. He's worried about the play. He's going to need a new Lizzy Bennet. Oh God. And as she watched him, her head aching, her heart leaden, she knew she would want to kill anyone who played Lizzy opposite his Darcy. And there was only one good reason for that. The truth hit her like a brick: she was besotted with Harry Noble.

For the first time, it also hit home that he was so completely different to her – so unaware of the people around him, treating everyone with the same unjudgemental indifference, so focused. What had he called it? Substance and integrity. And it had taken until now for her to realise this – now, when she could feel what little power she had once had over him slip through her fingers. He'd never risk getting involved with her now. It would have been one thing for him to get mixed up with an unknown, but quite another to get involved with a sordid tabloid scandal.

She looked miserably at her hands. The pull to be home was enormous. She couldn't wait for George to get there.

'I'm afraid I'll have to miss the rehearsal,' she said. 'And going out with Carrie afterwards. Sorry.'

Harry looked up at her as if he'd forgotten she was there.

'Yes, of course,' he said brusquely, in a tone she'd forgotten.

The next moment, a car horn sounded urgently outside the church door. Jazz got up and went towards it. She stopped at the door.

'Bye,' she said.

Harry was following her out. 'Take care,' he said simply and watched her get in the car.

She and George didn't talk on the journey. Jazz spent the entire trip staring miserably out of the window. It was a bright, clear day, but all she could see was how ugly the streets of north-west London were. There was so much rubbish lying in the gutters, so many hideous concrete buildings and so much dirt. Every now and then she'd start weeping quietly.

Jeffrey opened the door to his daughters with his only grandson at his side, and the three of them hugged silently in the hallway. Jazz walked into the large kitchen-diner where Josie and Martha sat silently. They were both looking pale and haggard, though there was an air of comfort about them. Jazz didn't know what to do. What was the protocol for greeting a soon-to-be divorced sister? And a soon-to-be ex-mother-in-law? Would Josie be trying to be cool? Would she be distraught?

She and George stood in the doorway. To her surprise, Josie immediately stood up and came to give them both a hug. Jazz started crying.

'Don't you cry!' laughed Josie. 'You're all as bad as each other.'

'But it's all my fault,' sniffed Jazz.

'Don't be ridiculous!' said Josie briskly, and walked her back to the table and sat her down.

Jeffrey was in the corner, making coffee, Ben at his side. Josie started talking.

'Michael and I have been going through a bad patch for the past year. We've been attending Relate sessions for the last few weeks – every Thursday night when you two have been babysitting.'

Jazz gasped. She couldn't have got it all more wrong. She squirmed when she remembered the smug column she'd written about how clever Josie and Michael were because they still went out every week together.

'And then what with the baby coming, we just weren't ready for it. The fling with William was just a symptom of the cause.'

Jeffrey brought the coffee over and went to play racing cars with Ben.

'Has Michael had affairs?' asked Jazz, ready to hate him.

Josie shook her head. 'Not that I know of. No, it's nothing as interesting as that,' she said sadly. 'I think he just stopped loving me.' It was hurting less every time she said it.

Martha started pouring everyone coffee.

'But you always seemed so happy,' said George.

Josie sighed. 'Marriage . . .' she broke off with a big sigh.

'Marriage takes work,' Martha said fiercely, spilling some coffee. 'And he can't be bothered.'

'No, Mum,' said Josie wearily. 'There's nothing there for him to work on any more.'

'Nonsense,' she said sharply. 'That's *exactly* when it needs the work. Do you think your father and I always loved each other? Or even always *liked* each other? That's exactly when you have to try and force yourself to love that person, even if you feel you couldn't care less if they never walked through the door again. When things are going well, there's no work to do. You young people haven't got a clue. There were at least four times when your father and I could easily have split up.'

Martha's daughters looked at her with startled eyes. They didn't want to know any more.

'Don't look so shocked,' she said angrily. 'That's marriage.'

There was an uncomfortable pause.

'What's happening now?' asked Jazz.

Josie lit a cigarette with a shaking hand. 'Michael's left home for a while.' And then she actually laughed when she caught Jazz's expression. 'Don't worry,' she said. 'I got him to empty the bins first.'

'How can you be so flippant?' asked Jazz.

'To be honest, this is a relief,' she said so quietly it was almost to herself, an incongruous tear rolling slowly down her cheek. 'It's been pure hell to live through, watching him fall out of love with me. It was so much slower than when he fell *in* love with me.' She laughed a short bitter laugh. 'For me, marriage means discovering that men love you most when they know you least. The more they get to know every single part of you, the less passion there is. At the beginning, when they make love to you with their eyes shut, you know it's because they're trying to savour the moment. After a few years of marriage, it means they're trying to pretend it's not you they're screwing.'

Martha's face seemed to go grey.

Jazz couldn't bear it. 'Maybe it's just a bad phase. Maybe he'll come back.'

Josie shook her head. 'No. He's emotionally dead. He's indifferent. This separation is for him to work out whether or not he can live without me. And I have a sneaking feeling he'll be fine. We've practically been living separate lives anyway.'

They all played at drinking their coffee.

Jazz hated to bring the subject up, but knew it had to be discussed.

'What are we going to do about Gilbert Valentine?' she asked with a tremor. 'Once the press finds out – particularly the *Daily Echo* – they'll have a field day with it.' Her voice nearly failed her.

Josie and Martha had already discussed it. Martha explained that they thought it would be worth a try for Jazz to work on Mo. Surely Mo could convince Gilbert not to go to the papers? Jazz wasn't so sure. She was beginning to realise that Mo was the kind to stand by her man, whatever he turned out to be like.

'And what if that doesn't work?' she asked, dreading the answer.

They all looked at each other.

'We gear ourselves up for the bad press,' Martha shrugged. 'Phone the rest of the family, warn them it's going to happen – George, you phone your agent – and prepare ourselves.'

Jazz didn't tell them it was impossible to prepare for something like this. When the press decided a family was worth tearing into, they would stop at nothing. It would be hell. And she only had herself to blame. It was she who had turned her family into a sitting target with her stupid columns about their virtuous lifestyle. It was she who had introduced Josie to that snake William Whitby. And it was she who had made enemies in high places. The thought of her family suffering at the hands of scandal-hungry hacks who weren't fit to lick their boots wore her down with sorrow.

Josie stubbed her cigarette in the ashtray and took a deep sigh.

'Sorry everyone,' she said softly.

Jazz was filled with shame.

'No,' she said clearly. 'It's me who should be sorry.'

Chapter 24

What would life be like without her career, pondered Jazz. She'd never thought of that before. For the first time she realised just how important her career was to her self-identity. Journalist. It was hardly a respected career. It wasn't the same as Doctor or Firefighter. But to her that one word had always meant Intelligent, Inquisitive, Interested in Others as well as Financially Independent. And she was going to lose it all in one moment. What did George think of herself as Actor? And, more importantly, how did Josie feel being labelled Housewife? And how would Josie feel when she lost all that – due to Jazz? Come to think of it, what did Purple Glasses think of her label as Props Person? Suddenly a lot of things became clearer. No wonder Purple Glasses tried to make herself seem more important, thought Jazz. She was surrounded by people who genuinely believed that they were worth more than her. How appalling. And she'd been one of the worst offenders. Still, thought Jazz – not quite ready to relinquish her fighting spirit – Purple Glasses was a twat, and no mistake.

She spent many dark moments over the next few days

wondering why she had chosen to make Josie quite so famous. Was it really because it was what her Editor had told her to do? Had she sold her family for an Editor's brief – for her own meaningless career?

She didn't think so. She had truly believed in Josie. Her younger sister's lifestyle wasn't perfect, but at least Josie seemed to have made sense of the world. She'd made sacrifices but she had seemed happy.

The one thing Jazz did know was that, much as she loved her career, she loved her family more. And she would just have to wait patiently until her career – well, until it careered. And then she would be there for her family while the press hounded them.

She wondered idly what else she'd do with her life. She'd always liked the idea of being a Firefighter.

That night, she phoned Mo and they arranged to meet at the flat. Things weren't looking good.

'You do realise that if he goes to the tabloids, I won't be able to talk to you ever again?' said Jazz, her voice shaking with emotion. If only she'd been nicer about Gilbert, she thought desperately, she'd have held far more sway. But surely Mo would do this for her? And for her family, who had been Mo's surrogate family during her early twenties when her mother had died? They all went back such a long way. Far further than Mo and Gilbert.

'I do,' replied Mo quietly. Her reply stung Jazz. 'But I just don't think he has a choice.'

Jazz exploded. 'Of course he has a choice!'

'He has his career to think of, Jazz. Surely you understand that.'

'He doesn't have to have *that* kind of career,' said Jazz.

'It's all he knows,' said Mo. 'And we need the money now.'

Jazz didn't answer.

Mo was forced to add, 'Now that we're getting married.'

Jazz stared at her.

'Who to?' she asked quietly, allowing herself a mad moment of hope.

'To each other,' said Mo firmly.

They looked at each other for what seemed like ages.

'Aren't you going to wish me congratulations?' asked Mo sadly.

'Congratulations,' said Jazz, and walked out of the kitchen before the tears came.

She lay in the bath, her tears falling into the water. What a mess. Her career was on its last legs, she had constantly hurled abuse at a man for whom she now felt powerful emotion, she had caused her family to disintegrate around her ears, she had seen her beloved elder sister lose faith in love for the first time in her life, and now her best friend was marrying a man whose idea of a joke was pronouncing the word meringue 'meringooey' . . .

When the front door slammed she was rudely awoken out of her trance. She realised the bathwater was cold and her fingers were more furry than their fruit bowl.

Every morning Jazz waited for the proverbial shit to hit the fan. But for some reason, the papers were full of other people's scandals – footballers and politicians made better copy than actors, thank Christ. Every morning, she'd scan them all, her breath bated, and every morning, she'd almost cry with relief that Gilbert's piece wasn't there. It was as if, leafing frantically through the papers, she was constantly facing her demons: her

221

arrogance in her own judgements of others, her shallowness in getting her family involved to further her career, and her sheer professional ineptitude.

To her amazement, life continued as normal. Her family spoke more often on the phone, but that was about the only change. Michael had moved out of the marital home and Jazz's parents were looking after Ben more than usual, but apart from that, life rolled on. Jazz's tube journey into work was still the low point of her day and work was still frustrating and exhilarating in equal portions.

Agatha was playing it tough and wasn't allowing Jazz to work part-time. She wouldn't let her write for both the *News* and *Hoorah!* unless she stayed full-time at *Hoorah!* and did her columns at the weekends. Jazz's byline was now to have a mugshot next to it. Agatha was turning Jazz's personal success into a selling point for the magazine. Jazz had been so scared that she would very soon lose her column at the *News*, that she felt she had no choice but to stay on at *Hoorah!* Perhaps she'd be here for life – if Agatha would let her stay after the scandal broke. And of course, through everything, Jazz still had rehearsals to go to.

But rehearsals were now completely different. And it wasn't just because she was ignoring Gilbert and not talking to Mo – who had moved out of the flat now, leaving Jazz living alone in her home – or because she was being pointedly ignored by William.

It was partly because they had now moved to the theatre, which happened to be free for a whole week before the big night. This lent a new excitement and fear to the proceedings. Mrs Bennet was telling even more anecdotes to anyone who would listen, Mr Bennet was parading his splendid paunch around the auditorium while staring out into the audience wistfully and the rest of the cast were merely talking quicker and louder than they had in the musty church hall.

But the main reason for the change of atmosphere was down to Harry, who was a man transformed. He chatted to everyone in the cast, was informal and accessible, spending the breaks talking to his actors and finding out how they were feeling about their parts. So now, surrounded by rich Victorian splendour, everyone was feeling far more relaxed than they had done while rehearsing in a dirty church hall.

Harry's mood affected his direction. It was less harsh, the actors were much happier and every single performance was better. The only person who didn't seem to approve of Harry's new style was Sara Hayes, and Jazz rediscovered her talent for loathing, which came to the fore every time she saw Sara look meanly at whoever Harry was chatting to. To her shame though, Jazz was now aware that her loathing of Sara was due in no small part to an overwhelming fear that Sara might actually win Harry over one day. There was no doubting that the woman was beautiful – in a stick-insect sort of a way. And Harry didn't seem to mind when she needed yet another director's tip on her delivery. He was either extremely patient with her or enjoying her wily ways. Surely he must be able to see through her. Jazz trusted her observations weren't being clouded by her hopes.

But her hopes couldn't hide from her the fact that she was the one person with whom Harry now no longer made an effort. She once or twice caught him looking at her, but the look had changed. It was a far more thoughtful look, almost nostalgic, and it dawned on her that he could well be thinking that he had had a lucky escape. And he always looked away as soon as she caught his eye.

The scenes between the two of them had a new poignancy

for her that she found almost unbearable. Harry seemed to be getting more calm the nearer they got to the big night, while Jazz was feeling more and more exposed – and utterly terrified. It was stupid, she knew, but when she stood on the stage she felt as if she was a hundred feet high and suffering from vertigo. She felt naked. The prospect of remembering her lines and moving all her limbs at the same time in front of a paying audience was looming over her like a big black cloud. And there was only a week to go.

'No, no. You can do better than that. What is Lizzy *thinking*?' Harry asked her at the end of one of their last scenes. Jazz's lines had ground to a stumbling halt.

'She's thinking that . . .' Jazz started to blush '. . . she loves him but he's out of her league.'

Harry nodded. 'Which, of course,' he said, 'we all know is ridiculous. And what we also know and she doesn't is that he reciprocates her love. So there's a nice piece of dramatic irony there, isn't there?'

Jazz nodded.

'Unless, of course,' he continued patiently, 'you're not concentrating. In which case, it's a waste of time. Isn't it?'

Jazz nodded, humiliated.

'As well as a waste of talent,' he continued.

She put her hands on her hips and looked at the stage floor. It had lots of marks on it and bits of luminous sticky tape stuck to it to show the production team where to place various bits of scenery in the dark. The rest of the cast was silent, except for a loud, affected cough from Sara that made Jazz want to throttle her.

'Remember Jazz,' Harry said kindly, 'this is the worst week. Next week will probably be the best week of your life. Believe me.'

224

He tried not to look at her for too long. She'd really changed since that business with her sister and William Whitby. It was as if her central nervous system, which had until now been protected by a thick coating of brash one-liners, had been turned completely inside out, leaving each nerve-ending exposed to the wind. Every now and then he caught the fear in her eyes. Her family tragedy had had exactly the effect he had tried to get from her with his stupid Truth Games.

He felt torn. Should he do all he could to help her overcome her fears? Or should he marvel as her acting suddenly found new depths?

Tomorrow was the first run through of the whole play; the night after that, the technical rehearsal; and two nights after that, the dress rehearsal. Then there was one night off before the big night. Jazz could hardly believe it. She had a horrid feeling that Gilbert was going to publish his piece just before the play or even on the day of the production, which would make it much more newsworthy and would mean she'd have to face a double public humiliation in one day. It was too horrid to contemplate.

After Harry had finished working through her scene, she sat down at the back of the auditorium and watched him direct a scene between Jack and George. Was it his strong, Roman nose that lent his face its power, or his granite-hewn cheekbones? She couldn't decide. Then she decided she didn't need to. She could just watch.

Jack and George hardly needed any help any more, they'd done this scene so many times now. It was the scene in which the young lovers, Jane Bennet and Mr Bingley, first meet. They were both sharing a joke and Jazz was astonished to see that Harry was joining in. She could tell from George's body language that she was much more relaxed with Jack than she had been since they had finished, and more importantly, she could tell that Jack could hardly stop himself from touching her – not the sort of touch that a confident lover gives, but the short, sharp touches that a man gives when he thinks it's all he's ever going to get.

Had he changed his mind about George? Surely not? How the hell did that happen? How did she miss it? And how was Harry letting it happen?

She decided to cadge a lift off George after the rehearsal – if she was going home, that was – and find out what was going on.

Just then Carrie came over. She was carrying two beautiful dresses and looked beside herself with excitement.

'I think you're going to love these,' she said to Jazz in her small, girlish voice.

Jazz gasped as she took them from her hands and found tears coming to her eyes. Jesus, this was getting ridiculous, she was crying at anything these days.

'Oh, Carrie, they're amazing,' she said in a wobbly voice.

Carrie smiled contentedly. 'They'll suit your colouring fantastically,' she promised.

'What – red and blotchy?' smiled Jazz. 'How perfect.'

Carrie laughed and Jazz started touching the intricate bead work at the bust. She didn't notice Carrie's colour heighten as Matt walked over.

'How's it going, ladies?' he asked.

'Have you seen these beautiful dresses Carrie's made?' Jazz showed them to him.

Matt looked at them and then at Carrie.

'Nothing less than I've come to expect,' he said mildly, smiling a twitch-free smile at Carrie.

Jazz nodded vehemently, while scooping up the layered skirts. Suddenly she hugged Carrie and started crying for the umpteenth time that week. She didn't even notice Harry watching her this time.

'We are just good friends,' said George with great control in the car. 'I'm over him – honest, Jazz.'

Jazz smiled her first proper smile for a while. 'Yes, but he's most certainly not over you.' It was so nice not to be talking about sad things for once.

'Yes, he is,' said George, with an impatience Jazz hadn't heard since they were children. 'He's just being friendly.'

Jazz turned away from her sister and watched the road.

'Right you are,' she said happily.

George was upset. 'That's not good enough, Jazz. You have to believe me. I think he's a great guy, probably one of the nicest I'll ever meet and I really enjoy working with him. But nothing's going to happen. It was nice, but it's over. I'm happy being single for the first time in my life.'

'Right you are,' repeated Jazz, just as smugly.

George sighed and changed the subject.

Chapter 25

The run through of the whole play was a revelation to Jazz. Before, she'd only ever thought of the script as a compilation of separate scenes and had wondered how on earth she could possibly maintain the same level of concentration for two hours, but it proved easy. There was a new electricity running through everyone. It felt as if any of the cast members could electrocute each other simply by touch. It was so amazing it took Jazz's mind off her troubles.

Afterwards, Harry sat everyone down and went through his copious notes on everyone's lines, delivery, speed and focus. He was big on focus. Jazz felt disappointed relief that he didn't have any constructive criticism for her and an hour later, when everyone went to the pub for a well-deserved nightcap, she tried not to dwell too much on the fact that he had disappeared on his own into the night. He'd stopped socialising with everyone, thought Jazz sadly. She and George quietly drowned their sorrows in the corner, while Jack chatted easily to everyone at the bar and William got slowly drunk and flirted happily with all the younger Bennet sisters.

The technical rehearsal was the most boring, frustrating day of Jazz's life. She spent hours at a time standing on the stage reciting one line while the lighting crew got their act together. Purple Glasses, who had shown only glimmers of pomposity up until now, was finally in her element. This was her day to shine. She kept yelling, 'Elizabeth Bennet is requested on stage IMMEDIATELY,' while standing next to Jazz, looking at her. It was only Jazz's determination to impress Harry with her maturity that stopped her from punching the woman in the mouth. Harry was in his old foul mood and seemed preoccupied all day. It was as if the acting was tedious now and he had far more important things to think about.

Afterwards, everyone went to the pub again and Harry was once more conspicuous by his absence. So was Sara, and Jazz started to feel real fear in the pit of her stomach. Mo and Gilbert hadn't bothered to join the rest of the cast tonight either, even though it would be one of their last evenings together as a team. William was getting drunk again, although Jazz had to admit he did even that with a certain boyish charm. Everyone except Matt and Carrie seemed to find him highly amusing. Jazz couldn't concentrate on any of the inane cast gossip and didn't care. They could all go to hell.

She had taken the week off work and used the two days before the play to write a couple more columns for the *News*. It kept her mind off everything. After intense pressure from her family, Jazz had agreed to continue writing her column from the angle of what it's like to see two people you love divorce each other. Martha had been fervent in her belief that readers should read about this sort of thing. And it was also a damage limitation exercise. If Jazz made all those involved sympathetic, it would help them when the scandal broke.

To Jazz's surprise, Brigit had been only too happy to accept this new twist in the subject-matter. 'Of course, I'm sorry for you,' she had said politely over the phone, 'but as far as we're concerned, divorce is always a safe subject, especially if there's a toddler involved. To be honest, it was much more of a risk taking you on when you were talking about their successful marriage than a failed one. Especially as Josie's such a well-loved character. People will be desperate to know how she's coping.' Jazz hoped to God she was doing the right thing.

Of course she wasn't going to write anything about the fling with William Whitby. The readers didn't need to know about it and she couldn't deal with the scandal encroaching into her work just yet. She was hoping against hope that if she won herself a devoted readership at the *News*, they might just keep her on when that sordid detail became common knowledge. Although, deep down, she feared that *Josie's Choice* would be cut immediately. The *News* was a serious paper and didn't like being involved in scandal.

So she just pretended it wasn't going to happen. She'd deal with the play first, then Gilbert's piece second. One trauma at a time. And she'd keep writing her columns until she was told to stop. For some reason, Gilbert was taking his time over publishing his story. Either he was in a price war with the papers – he had so many tabloid contacts he was probably auctioning it – or he was waiting until the morning after the play, so that the piece would be newsworthy. Either way, Jazz was living on borrowed time.

She began to notice over the next few days that her writing style had changed. She was far less brash now. Her columns had a moving humility that she just couldn't shake. And she had to admit, it added resonance to her writing that had never

230

really been there before. Within days, Jazz and Josie started getting fan mail from readers of the *News*.

The dress rehearsal was crap. Jazz was beginning to find everything about the play nightmarish. Everyone had made their own spaces in the changing rooms – narrow rooms with naked bulbs round the vast mirrors – and she had thought it would help if she went in the far corner with George. She couldn't have been more wrong. Everyone was hysterical with nerves and excitement, and she was stifled by it all. She felt suffocated. She could hardly dress herself, her hands were so cold. And the first time she looked at herself in the mirror in her costume, she hardly recognised herself. In the low-cut Empress-style dress she could actually see the palpitations of her heart.

Backstage was suddenly a dark, terrifying place. As were Jazz's bowels. She wondered if she could hide a toilet under her petticoat.

When all the women had finished putting on their beautiful dresses and putting up their hair, they sat on their make-up desks, chewing gum or drinking bottled water and laughing boisterously. Weirdly enough, everyone felt far more comfortable in their soft, easy-flowing costumes than in tight modern dress. And, to Jazz's delight, everyone with tans looked decidedly odd. Her paleness looked most becoming, she thought with a tired smile. Everyone was too impatient and excited to listen to Mrs Bennet's anecdotes any more, but she still insisted on delivering them. Every time she realised no one was listening, she pretended she'd lost a hairclip or something. Jazz found everyone pointless and ridiculous.

There was a knock on the door. Harry's voice sounded from the corridor. 'Are you all decent?'

Jazz and George were the only two who didn't try and say something funny to this. George was sitting staring at herself in the mirror, focusing. Jazz was staring at herself in the mirror, feeling nauseous.

Harry walked in. Everyone hushed.

He was wearing a white shirt tucked into breeches. His black leather boots went up to his knees. He hadn't put his tie or his frockcoat on yet and the loose collar of his shirt revealed a beautiful chest. The words 'gorgeous', 'dead' and 'drop' came to Jazz's mind, but she couldn't for the life of her remember what order they should be in. Her mind was slush. She looked in the mirror to check that it wasn't oozing out of her ears.

Harry spoke quietly and calmly, with warmth in his voice. 'You all look fabulous,' he said. Jazz was overwhelmed with jealousy and stared fixedly at herself in the mirror. Harry coughed.

'Now. They say that dress rehearsals are meant to be atrocious. Otherwise you won't know how to cope when anything goes wrong on the night. But if you all focus and stay calm, I think we could have a hit on our hands.' Everyone looked at each other, grinning like idiots.

'Beginners on in ten minutes,' said Harry. 'Break a leg.' And with that he was gone. Everyone got silly again and Jazz thought she was going to faint.

Then George tapped her on the shoulder and without speaking, the two of them made their way down the narrow corridor to the stage.

Standing in the wings, Jazz found she lost her sense of self. All she could see was the stage. When the music started playing and the lights dimmed, she felt herself walk purposefully into pitch-black darkness, aware that George was with her in the gloom. When the lights came on, she saw that George was perfectly poised. As soon as she had said her first line, Jazz was amazed to feel a sense of supreme serenity overcome her. She enjoyed every inflection, every pause, every movement. Her senses were heightened and her body was powerful. She could do anything.

When she walked off, her nerves returned but were less potent this time. She realised that being on stage was OK, it was being backstage that was terrifying. She wondered if she could manage to stay on stage all night. She started getting a bit high. Everything was very funny. Mrs Bennet was such a poppet. She even gave Harry a big smile when they had to wait backstage together for one of the few scenes they had together. When he gave her a condescending, Darcy-ish smile back, she wanted to prod him like a little sister.

Then in their first long scene together, she botched it all up by confusing two of her similar lines. She kept repeating the first one, forcing them to go round in a big circle of the script. She just couldn't get off the circle. Every time Harry tried to bring her back to the right line, her mind went blank and all she could think of was how thick his eyelashes were and how his eyes were almond-shaped. He looked like a cow. It had helped when he tensed his perfect lips with barely repressed anger. The terror came back and the hysteria stopped. God, she thought helplessly. She was so unfocused.

After they'd come offstage, she apologised. He was already taking his frockcoat off. 'Forget it,' he said curtly. 'Concentrate on your next scene.' And he strode off. Damn, blast and buggery bollocks, Jazz thought as she straightened her petticoat.

After the dress rehearsal, everyone went for their last drink together before the big night. Harry was noticeable by his absence again and Jazz sensed his real character coming back to the fore. How long had she thought he would be able to keep it up? Gilbert wasn't there either and she was positive that he was writing about Josie and William. The latter was drunk again and flirting with Lizzy Bennet's neighbour, Maria Lucas. She looked ecstatic to be the chosen one tonight.

Jazz looked over to see if Carrie was all right, and was pleased to see the shy young woman deep in conversation with Matt. At least she wasn't on her own, thought Jazz, and joined them both. She tried to stand so that Carrie couldn't see William and as she chatted to them, she realised she was with her two favourite people in the cast.

But the highlight of the day was when she and Mo sort of made up. Mo had come up to her at the bar.

'What's a nice girl like you doing in a place like this?' she had asked with a nervy smile that betrayed her. Before Jazz had remembered they weren't talking, she'd answered, 'Thought you'd never ask,' and they'd both grinned foolishly at each other. A great knot of unhappiness in Jazz's stomach slid undone.

Then they'd remembered their loyalties and lapsed into an uncomfortable silence. But it had made Jazz feel far less depressed.

When she went home that night, Jazz tried to dream of nice things, but she couldn't. All she could see every time she closed her eyes was Harry turning scornfully away from her and talking to someone else.

Chapter 26

On the day of the performance, Jazz woke at 5.45 am. She'd been having a hideous nightmare. Just as she'd been about to go on stage, Purple Glasses had told her she had to swap parts with Jack and play Mr Bingley. 'But I don't know the lines,' she'd panicked, to which Purple Glasses had replied, 'No one will notice. Just mumble.' Jazz had missed her cue and after what felt like hours of silence she'd finally wandered on stage, then she'd realised she was wearing Wellington boots and a chicken costume.

Jazz decided that getting up before six was preferable to trying to go back to sleep. She went into the kitchen and made herself a peppermint tea. She didn't want a coffee, it might make her stressed.

She hadn't planned anything very energetic for today. She was going to spend it relaxing – have a hot bath and read a book, maybe watch a video or two. Hopefully George would pop over. Maybe even Mo.

As soon as she was dressed she nipped out and bought every single paper, then she took them home and scoured them for Gilbert's piece about William's sex romp with two-in-a-bed 'happily married' Josie Field. It wasn't there. Feverishly, she read them again. Nope, it *still* wasn't there. Thank God. Now all she had to worry about was the fact that her career was over, her family was about to be slandered by the press, Harry hated her, she'd lost Mo to a moron, George was suicidal and thanks to her, Josie and Michael were separated. Oh yes, and not to forget that she was the lead in a play tonight at which all the country's famous people would be present. Piece o' piss.

She dashed to the bathroom.

Half an hour later, she started going over the play.

By ten o'clock, she'd gone over every line in it. She'd listened to her tape of the play while having her bath and then moved the sofa to the edge of the lounge and gone over every stage direction.

Then she wrote a couple of paragraphs for her column about how nervous she felt. She always wrote well about nerves. A couple of her own jokes actually made her laugh out loud. Brigit had been delighted that Jazz was in the play. It had been in the gossip columns for weeks now. Brigit had commissioned her to write a one-off feature about the day of the performance and cast party as well as her usual column. As she turned off her computer and the screen fizzed to black, Jazz felt a surge of self-pity that this might be her last column. Without it, she didn't know what she'd do with herself.

She got up and lay on the floor in the middle of the lounge and practised her deep breathing. She was beginning to feel much calmer now. She'd start to get ready in a while.

Three loud knocks at the door frightened the life out of her. Someone must have let George in, or better still it was Mo.

She opened the door and was stunned to find Harry standing there.

'Hello,' she said.

'Hello,' he said.

Her mind was blank. She knew nothing – except that she wished she wasn't wearing her Goofy slippers.

'Can I come in?'

'Oh yes, of course,' mumbled Jazz and opened the door. 'Tea? Coffee? Peppermint tea?'

'Coffee would be great,' said Harry. Looking a bit confused, he walked over to the couch that she'd pushed to the back of the room and sat down on it. He looked rather small sitting so far away and was obviously feeling totally uncomfortable. He coughed.

Jazz went into the kitchen and tried to breathe deeply while she watched the kettle. She suddenly found the silence horribly oppressive.

She brought out a tray with a pot and two mugs.

She placed them on the coffee table, which was now a few feet away from Harry. He got up and sat cross-legged by the table. She sat down next to him.

'Shall I be Mother?' she asked for no good reason, and then tried desperately not to think of Freud.

He smiled a nod and they sat there for a while, cupping their mugs with their hands.

'To what do I owe this pleasure?' she finally said, very quietly.

Harry put down the mug. He looked at her intently with his dark eyes.

Jazz stopped breathing.

'I just wanted to see how you were. You seemed very tense at the dress rehearsal.'

237

Jazz started breathing again. Oh wow, how sweet. She'd never seen this side of him. Her heart beat faster and all her movements suddenly felt magnified. She tried to concentrate on slow, deep breaths.

'Sorry about that bit where we went round in a circle,' she managed to say.

Harry smiled. 'It's OK. It won't happen tonight – it's never happened before. But change the line if it'll make you feel better.'

Change the line? This late? Was he mad? She had visions of Elizabeth Bennet suddenly coming out with 'The more my toes, tiddlypom'. It didn't bear thinking about.

'I'll be fine, thanks.'

Harry smiled. 'And everything else – is it OK? Or is it as bad as your column says it is?'

Jesus. He had followed her column into the *News*.

Jazz shrugged. 'We'll cope. Worse things have happened at sea, as they say.' Why was she talking like her mother? Any minute now she'd be telling him that he should take his coat off and feel the benefit.

'I just wanted to say that everything will be OK. I know it will.' Harry seemed to be quite certain of that. He continued, 'Gilbert won't do anything to hurt you or your family, I'm absolutely positive.'

Jazz was incredibly touched. She didn't know what to say. Harry's eyes were focusing on her feet. Dear God, she thought, *why* the Goofy slippers?

'You may not believe it, but I sometimes get nervous. I have panic attacks,' he was saying. 'Not when I'm on stage – that's fine. It's whenever I go on tube trains. I keep trying to overcome my claustrophobia but it happens every time.' He was starting to gabble. 'That's why I finally bought my own car, although I hate driving. The last time I went on the Underground, I fainted in the carriage. It took them ages to wake me and drag me to a side office. Then when they realised who I was, they made me wait until they'd ordered a car to pick me up outside the station. They had to put all the trains on hold before I was able to leave. Otherwise I swear I'd still be there today,' he half-laughed. 'It was the most embarrassing day of my life. The only way I got out of there was by staring straight ahead and reciting "To be or not to be" until I reached daylight.'

Jazz stared at him in amazement.

'It was the day of the auditions, actually,' he continued. 'The day we . . .' A little smile, a little cough. And then he was back to normal.

'You see, I focused, Jazz. And I got out in one piece. Focus is all – I honestly believe that. Just forget everything else that's going on in your life – your writing, Josie's divorce, Gilbert's article – let it all go and *become* Elizabeth Bennet. I know you can do it. It's going to be a spectacular performance – we'll be the best part of the whole week. Especially you. I know you'll do me proud. Just focus, Jazz.'

He looked up, and Jazz's expression had undergone a rapid change. She gave a short, bitter laugh. So *that's* what all this was about. His bloody reputation. She should have known better than to look for a bit of heart beneath that torso. God, he must have so little faith in her, to think she needed a home visit on the day of the play. Or maybe he was doing this to all the cast members he thought needed a personal pep talk. And she'd almost fallen for it. How utterly humiliating. Sara was probably in the car downstairs. With her legs. She felt a sharp stab of hurt in the base of her stomach.

'I'm not going to spoil your precious reputation, Mr

Noble,' she said. 'I promise not to make any mistakes. And I won't be changing any lines.'

Harry pretended to be surprised, but she could see right through him. He may be an actor, she thought hotly, but he can't bluff *me*.

'Oh, come on, Jasmi—'

'Look – I need to get ready.' She stood up and towered over him. 'So I'm afraid you'll have to leave now.'

Harry stood up too.

'Jasmi—'

She turned her head away from him.

He seemed to stay there for ages. She crossed her arms and stared at his untouched mug of coffee.

'Right then, I'll go,' he said, marching towards the door. 'Don't bother to see me out,' and he slammed it behind him. He stormed down the stairs, furious.

George picked her up at 4.30 pm. Jazz checked her bag five times. Yes, she had enough hair slides. And rollers. And tights. And the right shade of lipstick. She put her battered script in her bag just in case. She'd show Harry and Sara. She'd be bloody brilliant.

They went to a local restaurant, picked at their meals and then drove straight to the rehearsal.

Her stomach started to grip tightly as soon as they turned into the road where the theatre was. Jazz went straight to the toilet in the foyer. By the time she walked into the brightly-lit auditorium, George was nowhere to be seen. Harry was there, talking to Matt and the lighting guy, Alec; TV camera operators were already setting up in the audience. No one noticed her as she stood staring up at the stage. The set was all ready for the first scene, which surprisingly made her feel reassured. She walked silently down the auditorium, through the swing doors at the back and into the dressing room.

She didn't notice Jack and George snogging in the corner until she was walking towards them.

'*Waargh!*' she exclaimed maturely, and they both jumped apart. Jack whispered something to George and she giggled coyly; he then walked past Jazz with a big grin on his face.

Jazz's jaw parachuted to the floor.

George was making a high-pitched sound and running on the spot, like an excited child.

'How the hell did that happen?' asked Jazz.

George started mock-swooning and laughing out loud. She was hugging herself. Jazz started joining in the laughing.

Eventually George ran over and hugged Jazz. Thank God, thought Jazz. Something's going right.

'He's in love with me,' she sang, as if this was the most unbelievable thing in the world.

'Of course he is,' smiled Jazz.

George said blissfully, 'I was just standing here, trying to gather my thoughts, pretend I was calm, trying to push him out of my mind for the fortieth time today—'

Jazz felt guilty. Preoccupied with her own misery, she'd forgotten that George would still be at that painful stage.

'—when he just came in, walked over, told me he'd made the biggest mistake of his life and that he was in love with me.'

'And of course you told him that it was too late because you'd changed your mind, and anyway, you'd rather die an old maid than forgive him,' queried Jazz.

George grinned at her. 'I want his babies.'

'Really?' laughed Jazz. 'How many has he got?'

George was beaming at herself in the mirror. 'Oh God, I'm

so happy I think I'm going to burst,' she said to her reflection. 'He told me that these have been the worst weeks of his life and he's never going to put his work before his happiness again. He said we might never be rich but – ' she gasped and put her hand over her mouth as she realised what she'd just said ' – but we'd always have each other.'

Jazz smiled at her sister. Only George could fall for *that* line. She didn't think now was the time to remind her what their mother had said about the realities of marriage.

Other actresses started coming into the room and George and Jazz had no choice but to begin getting undressed. This news had certainly helped to defuse Jazz's nerves. Thankfully Mo was in the other ladies' dressing room with Sara and Maxine, so with any luck, she wouldn't see her until they were in the wings waiting for their cue. She put on her costume quickly and without fuss. Her Regency hairstyle needed to be fixed in place twice, but the second time, she secured it so tightly with hair grips that she thought she might have punctured her brain. Her hair was up there for good now. Probably for ever.

Purple Glasses came in and shouted shrilly, 'Everyone on stage IMMEDIATELY,' and they heard her go into the other dressing rooms shouting the same message.

The curtains were closed and Harry was standing on the stage. The auditorium would start filling up in ten minutes. He smiled at everyone as they came in, but didn't meet Jazz's eyes. Sara stood very near him, laughing at all his jokes as if they were private ones.

There was a controlled excitement in his voice. His eyes were darting round all of them as he spoke. Except for Jazz. 'I think you're all wonderful,' he was saying. Was he going to cry? He looked down as he said the next bit. 'And I want you to know that I've learnt as much from working with you as you may have learnt from me doing this play.'

There were some very happy faces among the cast.

'It's been an honour to work with you,' Harry finished quietly. Then he looked up again and rubbed his hands together. 'Now. There are people out there who are willing us to fall flat on our faces.'

Jazz thought with some shame that he was talking about the hacks and columnists who had been calling him misguided and shallow. Edward Whilber in *This Nation's Voice* had called him a 'shambling, hollow performer' who was trying to recapture his career by jumping on the cancer charity bandwagon and producing a play 'performed by amateurs and sycophants who couldn't help but make him look good'. And this, only days after calling him 'a hero of our times' in Patrick Clifton's play. As for Brian Peters, his review of Clifton's play had gobsmacked even cynical Jazz. Not one of the humiliating experiences he'd undergone while attempting to act had even begun to teach him that Harry Noble was truly gifted at the art. In fact, his hubris was worse than ever. To read his scathing remarks on Harry's acting, you would think that Brian Peters could act him off the stage.

Harry was getting very animated now. 'But there are more people out there willing us to be fantastic. My mother for one.' Everyone laughed. Sara managed to imbue her laugh with such meaning that everyone assumed she knew his mother personally. Scraggy cow, thought Jazz menacingly.

Harry was still talking. 'Now, unlike any other play you or I are likely to act in, we've only got *one night* to wow all our critics. *One night* to prove that we were right all along. And, of course – let's not forget,' he reminded his cast, fully aware that every single one of them had done so, 'only *one night* to dedicate to those who have suffered and are suffering the pain of breast cancer. I don't know about you, but that makes this the hardest play I've ever been in. But I haven't got a single doubt in my mind that it's going to be fabulous. And that *you're* all going to be fabulous. And you shouldn't have any doubts either. You've done me proud.'

Jazz thought back to this afternoon. Yeah, right, she thought.

'Break loads of legs,' he said. 'Beginners in place in fifteen minutes.'

Everyone rushed back to their dressing rooms, talking animatedly. Suddenly, Jazz was aware of someone tugging her arm.

'Quick,' said Mo, pushing her into the corner of the corridor by the stage. It was silent here.

'Gilbert's got his job back!' she announced excitedly.

Jazz stared at Mo. Did she really think she'd be that excited about Gilbert's good fortune?

'Dame Alexandra Marmeduke has changed her mind. His magazine is back in business!'

'And this should affect me how?' asked Jazz crisply.

'Don't be a fuckwit, Jazz. We haven't got time,' said Mo. Jazz tensed.

'Don't you see? It means he won't be writing the piece about your sister. He doesn't need to, now. They've made him Editor and everything! Isn't it wonderful? We're going house-hunting tomorrow!'

Jazz's eyes lit up. 'OhmyGod, that's amazing!' The relief was enormous. She managed to stop herself from sobbing because she wouldn't have time to redo her make-up.

'I know!' squealed Mo back. 'I'm so pleased. Now you'll talk to me again,' she said, before she had time to stop herself.

244

They beamed stupidly at each other.

'I've got to get back,' Jazz heard herself say, and they made their way to their dressing rooms.

Purple Glasses was standing officiously in the corridor looking for Jazz. She pounced as soon as she saw her.

'Elizabeth Bennet on stage NOW,' she hissed.

Mo ignored her. 'I just had to tell you before it began,' she whispered. 'And it's all down to Harry. He was a star – literally.'

'Wha—' started Jazz.

'On stage NOW,' hissed Purple Glasses.

Jazz glared at her, felt guilty for doing so and then ran to the wings.

George was already there, waiting silently. She turned and grinned a massive grin at Jazz, her eyes shining in the dark. What the hell did Mo mean? pondered Jazz, then forced it out of her mind. George held her hand tight and Jazz tried to think of all the people in the audience, in an attempt to steady her nerves and focus herself. All her family would be there. Mark and Maddie, too. Harry's parents, of course. Gilbert's cronies, some of whom she'd worked with in the past. And then there were all the celebs who were filling up the front rows. And the cameras that would be catching every nuance, every mistake, for posterity. Yep, it was working: she was focused. Was there time for a last trip to the loo? She looked behind her and saw Mr and Mrs Bennet, Kitty, Lydia and Mary, all standing silently in a row.

The music started, the lights dimmed and the curtains rose. She walked purposefully on to the stage and began.

The first half was going smoothly. Mrs Bennet's bonnet

had almost fallen off at one point, which had unnerved her slightly, and William had got his cane stuck in a chair. Jazz had been quite impressed at the way he'd slowly and calmly – and completely in character – slid it out, given her a charming smile and exited. He was good. Very good.

The next time she got a chance to talk to Mo was just before the interval. She caught up with her while the last scene was going on.

'What did you mean, Harry's a star?' she said.

'Well, I was sworn to secrecy but bugger that for a bunch of fairies,' said Mo, untwisting her tights and pulling them up to the crotch again.

'sssssHHHHH!' Purple Glasses glared at them. Mo glared back and they went to the side corridor again. No one would hear them here.

'Last week, Harry went to see his aunt – you know, Captain Marmeduke?'

'But I thought they weren't talking?'

'They weren't,' said Mo.

'So how come he went to see her?'

'I know – I've got a brilliant idea!' exclaimed Mo. 'Why don't you shut up while I talk?'

Jazz smiled. God, she'd missed Mo.

'Monday night after the run through, he went down to Devon to see her, broke a twenty-year rift with her, *got on his knees* and apologised for writing some letter or other, told her all his family were devastated by the feud and everything. She fell for it hook, line and stinker. He used all his acting skills – cried, the works. She told him she'd only wanted to help him, had been watching his career all his life, she even showed him all her scrapbooks full of all his reviews.'

'How do you know all this?' Jazz was totally baffled.

'I'm sorry, I thought I was talking,' said Mo impatiently. 'Sorry.'

'They talked all night and eventually – at about three a.m. to be precise – she brought up the fact that she was closing her mag because she'd been so hurt by Gilbert's treachery. And Harry told her that was utter madness – she shouldn't let her feelings rule her life like they had for the past twenty years. And anyway, Gilbert had been the catalyst that had brought them together. He said that it had been Gilbert's stories about his wonderful patron that had made Harry realise how much he was missing, not knowing her. And that was it. She changed her mind. As simple as that! Then Harry told her that he'd been working with Gilbert and thought he'd make a wonderful Editor.' Mo was beaming now. 'He even negotiated an amazing new salary for him.'

Jazz was still looking baffled.

Mo realised she'd need more information. 'Then the next night, after the technical rehearsal, Harry asked to have a word with Gil. I came with. Harry explained everything and told him that if he published his piece – which, I hasten to add, Gilbert had already finished but was waiting until the day after the play so it would be more newsworthy and make him more money – he would lose his new, highly paid Editorship. Gil didn't even have to think about it,' she said proudly. 'He never loved his tabloid work as much as his theatre work. Especially as the tabloids always pay much more for stories about footballers or MPs. It always made Gil feel like a poor relation. He's promised me he'll give up the tabloids for good, now that he can afford to. So this way he gets a good, steady job doing what he does best and we can settle down.'

It was hurting Jazz to frown for so long.

'I don't understand,' she said. 'Why would Harry do all that? He doesn't care about Gilbert. It doesn't make any sense.'

Mo looked at her incredulously. 'Jesus, Jazz, are you really as thick as you look? Anyone with half a brain can see Harry's mad about you.'

Jazz started to feel all fizzy. 'You mean it's just Gilbert who hasn't spotted it?'

Mo snorted. 'Do you mind,' she grinned, delighted. 'That's my fiancé you're talking about.'

Jazz was walking on air. Wasn't everyone lovely? Wasn't life wonderful? She started listening to one of Mrs Bennet's hilarious, pithy anecdotes while taking off her dress and putting on her new one. He still liked her! Was mad about her, Mo had said! After everything she'd said to him that night when she'd shoved him in the bushes! After everything he knew about her! She looked at herself in the mirror with her heaving bosoms and tendrils of dark hair framing her flushed face. Bloody Nora, she grinned at herself. Bloody blinking Nora.

And then she remembered. She'd been foul to him only that day. Absolutely hideously, ground-swallowingly foul. Suddenly the feel-good factor was replaced by a sense of wretchedness, remorse and grief. She'd practically ignored him at his one-night play and then she'd insulted him when he'd come round that afternoon. She gasped. Of course! That was what he'd been trying to say to her this afternoon – that everything would be all right! He knew it would because *he'd* sorted it. He'd sorted out her career, her family's reputation and her relationship with her best friend. Just by swallowing the infamous Noble pride.

248

She had to let him know that she knew what he'd done. She *had* to thank him. Jazz ran out of the dressing room, and saw him striding down towards her. He'd taken his frockcoat off again and was undoing his tie. Jazz wondered what it would be like to take off the rest of his clothes herself. With her teeth.

'Don't go anywhere, I need to talk to everyone,' he said curtly. 'I'll go and get the others.'

'But I want—'

'There isn't time. I have to talk to everyone.' And he was gone.

Buggery bollocks, thought Jazz and went back inside.

She sat in the corner where Jack and George were holding hands and looking dewy-eyed at each other. Everyone was squashing up together and on a communal high. She even smiled at William and then cursed herself.

'Right,' said Harry, running his hand through his hair. His thick, dark, gorgeous hair, thought Jazz. 'Well done, everyone. It wasn't as pacy as I would have liked – '

There were calls of dismay.

' – but that's OK. I don't think anyone would have noticed. They're a very appreciative audience and we're doing very well. I've just heard from my sources that the *Stalwart*'s critic, Sam Gregson, is bloody impressed. And I'm not surprised, quite frankly. You're all stonkingly good. William – well retrieved with the cane, Margaret – it was perfectly in character that Mrs Bennet's bonnet would do that. You coped well and you didn't get flustered.'

Margaret beamed proudly.

'Jasmin, you need to pause a bit more. Beginners on stage in five.' And he was gone.

Jazz was crushed. She started breathing so quickly from her

249

upper chest she thought she was going to fall out of her dress. Oh God, she was going to start crying.

No one had noticed and she tried desperately to get a grip on herself. He hated her. Or worse still, he thought she hadn't paused enough.

'Don't take it too seriously,' said a friendly voice. It was William. 'I thought you were excellent.' He was looking at her without so much as a twinkle in his eye.

She smiled a genuine, grateful smile at him. 'Thanks.'

He put his arm round her in a chummy way and she let him. Together they walked to the wings where they could see Harry on stage, watching all the props people, including Purple Glasses, place everything in its allotted space. Harry wasn't on stage again for ages. Purple Glasses was managing to do a job of very little effort with as much bustle as she could, lots of tutting and an exasperated look at Harry which meant, 'My job is impossible and you actors don't make it any easier.'

'Thanks, Fi,' Harry whispered. 'Don't know what we'd do without you.'

Purple Glasses blushed and came into the wings where she started officiously tidying the props desk. On catching sight of William and Jazz, she gave them both a look of withering scorn. Jazz wished William would take his arm off her shoulder now.

Harry followed Purple Glasses' glance and, on seeing William with Jazz, he instantly looked away again. Then he walked right past them without a word and disappeared round the back to the other side of the stage.

Jazz felt totally disloyal. How could she be seen to be friends with William after Harry had told her what he'd done to his sister? She felt awful. She *had* to talk to him. Maybe she could catch up with him. Just as she turned round, the lights dimmed, the music started and she and William walked on to the stage, where the rest of the cast joined them from the other side.

Jazz tried so desperately hard to focus her thoughts, but was unable to rid herself of an overwhelming sense of wretchedness. Worse still, every time she came off stage, Gilbert started following her. He was only in one scene in the second half and he was now determined to convince Jazz that they were still friends. He kept popping up beside her with some crass joke and a meaningful look, which she knew meant 'Do you forgive me?' The more she tried to shake him off and find Harry, the more he clung to her.

She knew the only time she would have alone with Harry was in the wings just before his second proposal scene when Lizzy finally accepts him. She had to talk to him. And the only way she could get rid of Gilbert was to tell him she forgave him. She would have to lie to the shit, pretend that it was all OK again. With a monumental effort she turned round to him and interrupted him in a story about Dame Alexandra Marmeduke.

'Gilbert,' she said.

'Hmmm?' said Gilbert with a big smile.

'It's all right. I forgive you.' And she started walking towards the wings where she could see Harry waiting. She knew she only had a few minutes.

'Are you sure, Jasmin?' said Gilbert, speeding up beside her. 'Because you don't know how much it means to me and Mo that you're still our friend. Josie's little . . . escapade will go with me to my grave. I promise.'

She stopped walking and clenched her fists. 'I'm sure. I love you both. I have to go on stage now.'

She couldn't make out if Harry was facing them or had his back to them.

'I never *wanted* to write the feature,' gabbled Gilbert. 'I was just desperate.'

'I know. It's OK. I have to go now.'

To her growing frustration, Gilbert started hugging her very slowly. She patted him twice on the back. He started swaying. She tried to move away but he didn't loosen his grip. She could see Harry standing alone in the wings. She had to get to him. Gilbert let out a deep sigh and pulled away, holding her by the shoulders. 'Mo and I love you very much,' he whispered.

'That's nice,' said Jazz and ran away.

She reached Harry's side, hoping Gilbert wasn't following her. Harry was standing with his arms folded, staring out at the actors on stage. Jack and George's physical proximity was horribly anachronistic, and Jazz knew Harry would be upset. He looked down at Jazz and then back at the stage.

'Yo, Fitzwilliam,' she whispered and then cringed inwardly. *Yo Fitzwilliam?*

He smiled briefly. Jack and George were almost half-way through their scene. Once Mrs Bennet went on, Jazz would have a matter of moments. She didn't know where to start.

'I – I just had a word with Mo,' she whispered loudly. Purple Glasses tutted behind her. There was a sign just above her head that said *NO SPEAKING, SMOKING OR SMOOCHING IN THE WINGS*. Purple Glasses obviously saw it as her job to ensure the sign was adhered to. Hah! thought Jazz cruelly. If she couldn't get any fun, why should anyone else? Anyway,

252

she thought huffily, her tut was much louder than my whisper.

Harry glanced down at Jazz and then looked back at the stage. Oh God, he was going to make this difficult.

'She told me about you and your aunt.' Her whispering was getting louder. Purple Glasses tutted again, louder still. Jazz flinched, but tried not to react. Purple Glasses was only doing her job. It wasn't her fault Jazz found her ridiculous.

This time Harry looked at Jazz and held his look. She wished it wasn't so dark, she couldn't make out what his face was doing.

'Oh,' he whispered almost inaudibly, nonplussed.

'Yes. And I wanted to say thank you.' Her voice was hoarse. 'I'm so grateful, I don't know what to say. You've,' here she gave up whispering and started speaking in a hushed, excited voice, 'you've saved my life. And I can only guess how hard it must have been for you to do. And I – I – it's *wonderful*.' The words seemed so insignificant compared to how totally indebted she felt to him.

Purple Glasses tutted once more. Before thinking, Jazz whirled on her and demanded: 'Is there anything wrong? Or have you got food stuck in your brace?' Purple Glasses stalked off, insulted. Jazz was mortified. Where did all her anger come from, for Christ's sake? She'd have to apologise later. Oh God, how hideous. After a moment of valuable time spent feeling guilty, she turned back to Harry; his wide smile was hidden by the darkness.

'And I wanted to tell you how dreadfully sorry I am for acting like a complete twat,' she concluded.

'There's no need to say sorry,' he breathed. 'It was done for purely selfish reasons.' He cleared his throat.

Further down in the wings, Mrs Bennet was adjusting

her bonnet and straightening her cleavage. Jazz seriously contemplated tripping her up.

'What do you mean?' asked Jazz urgently, as Mrs Bennet trotted on stage.

Harry turned to her and she heard him take a deep breath. 'I couldn't very well fall head over heels in love with someone whose family was in a sex scandal, could I? I've got my career to think of too, you know.'

And in the darkness, she could see his eyes were bright with emotion.

'That's your cue, Jazz.'

Jazz almost ran on stage and stood there, blinking in the light.

When Harry joined her on stage five minutes later, looking like a great big solid hunk of loveliness, Jazz felt herself almost burst with emotion. She wanted to laugh out loud, it was killing her not to. She did make a couple of funny sort of gasping noises that Elizabeth Bennet probably wouldn't have made, but she didn't think anyone noticed. And anyway, her performance was set alight by the intensity of her emotions. She *was* Elizabeth Bennet: she felt sure of it. And Harry *was* her adoring Mr Darcy. The chemistry between them would have been embarrassing if it wasn't what was required.

It was wonderful. The scene they were playing now was when Mr Darcy proposed to his Lizzy a second, successful time. In the book, the characters had been walking behind the lovers, Jane Bennet and Mr Bingley. In this adaptation, Lizzy and Darcy had to stop by a make-believe bench while Jack and George were off-stage, supposedly walking up ahead. Or snogging in the toilet, thought Jazz happily.

When Harry said the line, 'My dearest, loveliest Elizabeth,'

254

with such affection in his eyes, Jazz thought she was going to have to sit on her hands to stop her flinging them around his neck.

She didn't, of course, and tragically she was on stage all the way until the end of the play, except for a moment while the set was changed for the joint wedding and then she and Harry came on from opposite entrances.

Harry had worked it that there should be no final snog as such, but that the lights would dim as they all started to go for the clinch. Jazz was suddenly terrified. Should she? Shouldn't she? Would he? Wouldn't he? She searched his eyes for clues and got none. As she felt the lights start to dim, they slowly started to hug. It was a full-bodied, long hug that she never wanted to end. Harry's body was damp with sweat and his heart was pumping.

Before she knew it, the sound of applause started echoing and the rest of the cast came on stage in orderly lines and she, Harry, George and Jack exited sharpish.

They got into the wings where George and Jack started snogging furiously. She watched as Harry observed his cast. She might as well not have been there.

'Right, we're off,' he said and they all went to take their bows.

Jazz had never bowed to an audience before. It was the most exhilarating moment of her life. She decided she'd audition for another play immediately. It made everything worth it. All the nerves, the rehearsals, the boredom. The clapping seemed to go on for ever. Now she could hear whooping. Harry took a step forward and the clapping got even louder. It was almost deafening. She could see that some of the audience at the left of the auditorium were standing up. She realised she was laughing. Then

Harry took her hand and they were bowing together. She couldn't stop laughing, yet she couldn't even hear it over the noise.

Eventually the curtain went down and everyone started hugging everyone. Just as she was about to turn to face Harry, George appeared at her side and hugged the breath out of her. And everyone, she noticed, started hugging Harry. He got further and further away from her as people swarmed round him. He had never looked so dishevelled. As Wills took her in a firm, friendly hug, her eyes caught Harry's. He was being hugged by Sara and was drenched in sweat, his cheeks flushed and his hair messy. Jazz's stomach lurched.

'Right,' said Harry eventually and everyone shushed instantly. 'Everyone in the men's changing rooms.'

There was a charge to the dressing rooms.

Once there, everyone squeezed on top of each others' laps, kissing each other and talking nineteen to the dozen. As soon as Harry spoke though, there was silence.

'What can I say?' he started and they all laughed. He tried to compose himself.

'You have surpassed even my wildest dreams.' Some of the girls started sniffing. 'I can honestly say that I've learnt more from directing and acting in this play than any other piece I've ever worked on.' His voice cracked on the last few words. 'And I think you know I'm not talking about just the acting. Thank you all. I'll never forget this experience and I hope you don't either.'

There was a long pause and then Mrs Bennet started clapping and they all joined in. She gave him a big hug for which he was eternally grateful, because it wouldn't have done for them all to see he was crying. Eventually he pulled himself away and said hoarsely, 'See you at the party.' And everyone started rushing to get ready.

Jazz felt totally lost. She had the party – when he'd be surrounded by his family and friends – and then she'd probably never see him again. She ran to get changed.

The dressing room was abuzz with excitement. People were sharing deodorants and shouting at each other with bright, animated faces. She had to get out of there. She had to get to the party.

George insisted she wait for her, which was so aggravating that she almost lost her high. Maybe Harry falls for all his leading ladies, she thought as she watched George dress. Maybe he'd only said it to shut her up. Oh hell, she had to see him again. But she knew that the chances of getting him alone were now minimal.

Finally George was ready. They almost ran to the audience and saw people clustered round their own family member. Harry's family were sitting high up in the dress circle, now reunited with Dame Alexandra Marmeduke. Famous people were dotted around, but most had already left. George and Jazz spotted their family at the same time. Everyone was there. Even, to Jazz's astonishment, Michael. As they hurried towards them, a few people grinned their congratulations to them both. It was wonderful. Far better than any by-line. Before she reached her family, Jazz noticed Mark and Maddie sitting near the aisle, grinning inanely. They both looked so different out of the office.

She rushed up to them. Maddie gave her a big, warm squeeze and even Mark pecked her cheek. They both seemed very happy.

'You were amazing!' said Maddie.

'Fabulous. You never told us you could act,' said Mark.

'Oh, are you sure you enjoyed it?' asked Jazz, and the question almost echoed round the room, so many people were asking it.

'Loved it,' they said together, and then started laughing. Jazz sensed something a bit strange about them, but was too preoccupied to try and work out what it meant. Outside the office, Mark had shed his bravado completely. He was effusive and charming and Jazz realised how lovely-looking he was.

'By the way,' said Maddie, 'Agatha got a call this afternoon from one of her old journalist cronies – used to work with her on *Gossip!* Well, now she's got three children and she's desperate to come back to writing part-time. I think we may be able to persuade Agatha about you doing a job-share now. Then you can have your weekends back.'

Jazz couldn't believe it. It was all too perfect.

'Excellent!' she squealed. 'You are coming to the party, aren't you? We've taken over Flamenco's in Angel Street.'

'Wouldn't miss it for the world,' said Maddie.

'Strictly as guests – not as press,' said Jazz firmly.

'Yip,' said Mark. 'Scout's honour.'

She gave them the address of Flamenco's. Then she raced over to her family, walloping various people with her bags and baggage and apologising profusely to all of them.

Martha got to her first but it felt like they were all hugging her at once. Jazz pulled Josie aside. 'What's Michael doing here?' she demanded.

Josie grinned. 'Well, he said he wanted to see you in the play as you were still officially a relative of his. Then when he came to pick me up and drop off the sitter, he told me that ever since he'd known about me and William he'd been feeling ill. It had made him realise how much he loved me and how near he'd been to losing me. So you can stop feeling guilty now, honey. It looks like you might have saved my marriage.'

Jazz couldn't believe her ears. She hugged Josie till it hurt. Michael came over to them.

'Hi sis,' he said, a little nervously.

'Come here, you,' she said and gave him a hug that was only slightly less painful.

'I'm sorry,' he whispered.

'Me too,' she whispered back, grinning at Josie over his shoulder.

And then she spotted Harry walking over very slowly. He almost stopped when he saw her hugging Michael, but as soon as their eyes met, she let Michael go. Harry reached them and no one really knew what to do.

George did the introductions. Jazz suddenly felt very guilty, remembering with a stab of horror that the only thing she'd ever told her family about Harry was how rude and arrogant he was, and that he'd called her The Ugly Sister. She wished she'd had a chance to tell them all the latest development . . . then they'd know that it was only thanks to Harry Noble that their family name wasn't mud.

She cringed inwardly when she saw how muted her parents' greeting to him was. It was also very embarrassing to see how much in awe of him they were. He must get this all the time. It was as if they were a lower caste than him or something. No wonder he had become so arrogant. It must be impossible not to. He shook all their hands and then said to her parents, 'You have very talented daughters.' Martha beamed majestically at him. 'Are you all coming to the party?' he asked with a little cough.

Josie and Michael said yes, Martha and Jeffrey laughed at the very idea.

'Well, it's been a pleasure to meet you,' he said, and raised his eyebrows at Jazz. 'See you at the party,' he said to her and wandered off.

Just when George, Josie and Michael were finally ready to go, Jazz suddenly remembered she'd left her make-up bag in her dressing room. While the others went to get the car, she hurtled back through the auditorium, picked it up and whizzed back. As she forced open the doors into the foyer, she saw an old woman sitting on an upright chair against the wall, waiting patiently for someone, her right hand resting on an imposing-looking gilt-edged cane. The woman looked at her and gave her a beautiful smile that lit up her entire face. She must have been a beauty in her day.

'Ravishing, my dear,' she said dramatically. 'Simply ravishing.'

Jazz felt embarrassed.

'Thank you,' she smiled and kept on walking.

'I've seen some chemistry in my time, believe me,' the woman continued in a rich, mellow voice, her dark eyes sparkling, 'and that was *some* chemistry.' Then she stopped smiling and looked intently at Jazz. 'Never lose that spirit, girl,' she said. 'Never lose that fire.'

The old face suddenly saddened, and her eyes looked distant. 'But never let it control you,' she said softly, almost to herself.

Jazz's eyes drifted to a black and white still shot, framed and displayed above the woman's head. Olivier, playing Hamlet, was holding his Ophelia – a radiantly young Dame Alexandra Marmeduke. Jazz's body went cold as she realised that the same face was before her now, in living form.

The woman saw her look and nodded graciously, closing her tired eyes.

Exhilarated, Jazz mumbled something about being ever so grateful and ran out into the cold, night air.

Chapter 27

Five minutes later, George was driving Jazz, Josie and Michael from the centre to the north of London where the nightclub was. The windows were open, the music was blaring and Jazz felt on top of the world. But she wished George would drive faster. Every time they got stuck in traffic, she wanted to hurl abuse at the other drivers.

After an eternity, they arrived at the club. It seemed they were the last there. Suddenly Jazz didn't feel so confident. At first she couldn't see anyone from the cast and went to the bar. Mark was standing there, waiting for a drink.

'Hiya,' shouted Jazz.

He smiled at her, bought her a beer and then motioned for her to move to the door. He wanted to talk to her. Oh no, she thought. He wasn't going to embarrass himself, was he? She realised he was a bit drunk.

'Listen, I'm sorry I've been a bit of a plonker for the past . . .' he paused thoughtfully.

'Year?' said Jazz helpfully, then felt guilty when she saw how taken aback he was. He was obviously more sensitive than she'd thought. She assured him it was a joke.

'I've got a bit of a confession to make,' he said. Oh no – not here, not now. Not when she had to get to Harry.

'I've been hopelessly in love for a whole year,' he said. 'It's been doing my head in.'

'Oh,' said Jazz.

'She just didn't know I existed,' he was going on. 'Bloody IKEA excited her more than Yours bloody truly. It's been hell, Jazz, hell.' He didn't notice that Jazz was staring at him wide-eyed. He was too busy confessing.

'Anyway, I've decided. I'm going to tell her tonight.'

'Tell who?' asked Jazz.

'Maddie, of course. Maddie,' he said, imbuing the name with heartfelt emotion, as he watched her chat to someone.

Blimey, thought Jazz. She'd managed to miss that one completely. Had she ever got anything right at all?

'Perhaps you should slow down a bit,' she said, looking at the bottle in his hand.

'Oh yeah,' he said. 'Thanks, Jazz. You're a pal.' And he actually hugged her. As he did so, she caught Maddie's eye. Her boss stared back with a none too friendly expression and suddenly a year's worth of office politics clicked into place in Jazz's head. Maddie and Mark!

Thinking on her feet, Jazz guided Mark to the dance-floor where he started doing a movement not unlike an epileptic hoeing. She beckoned Josie to join them, introduced them to each other and left them to it. She had to tell Maddie her latest information. Fast.

As she made her way through the bodies on the dance-floor, she saw something that made her heart sink. Sara Hayes was dancing with Harry. They made a very handsome couple. Unlike any man she'd ever seen on a dance floor, Harry didn't dance like a gibbon. He didn't move much, but what he did move looked bloody sexy. Sara kept touching him. She looked amazing. She was wearing platform heels that made her almost the same height as Harry and a mini-skirt so short you could almost see her bottom. Her legs must have reached Jazz's shoulders. The chemistry between herself and Harry felt like years away. The Harry who had stood next to her backstage was so different from the one she was watching now. Jazz almost left the party there and then. How could she have been so stupid? How could she have ever thought that she was in the same league? How could she kill Sara without witnesses?

Someone thwacked her on the shoulder. It was Mo.

'Now that *is* too skinny,' she yelled in Jazz's ear. Damn, had she been that obvious? They started dancing together and Jazz managed to pretend to ignore that Harry was behind her. She loved dancing with Mo, though now her smile was forced and her usual easy movements came hard. Eventually, Mo started miming drinking a beer.

As they pushed their way to the bar, a woman who looked strangely familiar appeared in front of Jazz.

They stared at each other and the woman, who seemed to recognise Jazz, pushed rudely past her. Who the hell was it? Her eyes were a watery pale, mud blue and she'd put heavy mascara on her four eyelashes. It looked like a spider had donated its legs for her vanity. Suddenly Jazz realised who she was. Purple Glasses! Without the glasses! She followed after her, trying to remember her name.

'Fi!' she called out. Purple Glasses looked round and stared a very hostile stare at Jazz. She waited. At first the words just wouldn't come out, but after what felt like an eternity, Jazz managed to blurt out: 'I – I wanted to say sorry for how horrid I've been during this play.' A fraction of her black mood lifted. 'I've been quite stressed over the past few months, but—'

'Well, haven't we all?' said Watery Eyes.

'Yes, well, I was just about to say that that was no excuse.' Jazz tried to keep her tone measured and calm. 'And I'm apologising now, and saying that I think you're marvellous at your job. Which is a brilliant job, by the way. So – sorry. And thank you. But mostly sorry.'

Watery Eyes just stared at her. Then she said slowly and very clearly, 'I've worked with some horrid people in my time, but you, Jasmin Field, were the absolute all-time worst.'

Oh, thought Jazz. Glad we've got that sorted out then.

'Does that mean I get a medal?' she eventually asked in a small voice.

Watery Eyes sighed and then said in a painfully patronising tone, 'Jasmin Field, you're *very* lucky I'm in a good mood. That's all I can say,' and walked off.

What, no hug? thought Jazz with a bitter shake of her head. Standing in the middle of the crowded nightclub, she had a quick word with herself, explaining, not for the first time, that life would never be anything like *Anne of Green Gables*, and she had better get over it once and for all. Then she went to join Mo.

'I have a very important question,' Mo said, as soon as she got there. Was she going to ask her to vacate the flat? She didn't want to hear it. She seriously didn't think she'd be able to cope just now. At that moment she spotted Maddie at the bar.

'Hold on a mo, Mo,' said Jazz, and then sniggered. 'I'll be back in a mo.' Hey – how come she'd never thought of that joke before?

She rushed over to Maddie.

'Hiya,' she said.

'Hi,' said Maddie shortly.

'Mark just made a confession to me,' continued Jazz.

'Mmm?'

'Mmmm. It appears he's been hopelessly in love – that was how he put it – with a certain Features Editor whose spiritual home is IKEA.'

Maddie's face lit up. 'You're kidding.'

'Nope. Did you have any idea you've been putting your junior through living hell? What kind of a boss are you anyway?'

Maddie was grinning from ear to ear. 'A happy one,' she said.

'Well, go and give your employee a full de-briefing. It's way overdue.' Maddie gave her a quick kiss on the cheek and grappled her way to the dance-floor.

Mo came over. 'Finished?' she asked.

'I'm just sorting out everyone's love-life,' Jazz told her. 'Because I'm so good at sorting out my own, ha ha.'

Mo followed her eyes to where Harry was now dancing with Mrs Bennet. The latter was pretending to do a striptease, starting with her scarf, which she had draped over Harry's smiling face. Sara was standing next to him, taking the scarf off and giving it back to its owner, pretending – badly – to find the lark as funny as he did. Harry didn't seem to mind.

'He spent the whole week saving your life,' said Mo.

Jazz sighed. 'Yes, but only because his reputation rested on it,' she said in a hollow voice.

She was so angry with herself she could cry. She'd always scoffed at George for getting so involved in a part that she regularly fell for her co-stars, and yet she had done exactly the same thing. In the past few months, she had felt so empowered by Lizzy, so strengthened by her that she had managed, for a few foolish hours, to get carried away and convince herself that she too could have Lizzy's happy ending. She looked miserably over to Harry as he laughed and joked with Mrs Bennet, and she felt too melancholy to look away when his eyes met hers. Had he said he was in love with her merely to bring out the best in her performance? He was probably that much of a perfectionist – and he was also a convincing actor. If that was the case, had she been *that* easily readable?

She was drowning in self-pity and humiliation. This is real life, she thought unhappily. This is not some stupid play.

'Listen, give the guy a break,' said Mo. 'Remember how terrifying you are. He's probably scared stiff of you.'

'Oh, don't be ridiculous,' said Jazz.

'I am not. You can be truly terrifying. Remember that Scout and Guide camp we went on when we were fourteen? You fancied Jonny Smith.'

Jazz frowned at her. What did that have to do with anything?

'Jazz,' said Mo slowly, 'you set fire to his rucksack. And then wondered why he didn't ask you out.'

Jazz smiled in amazement at the memory. She'd forgotten about that. Had she really done something so dangerous? At the time, she'd thought her heart was going to break.

'Well,' she said stubbornly, 'that certainly taught him to ogle Melanie Margate instead of me during exercise.'

'Yes,' agreed Mo. 'It also taught him how to extinguish a burning T-shirt while still wearing it, and how to sleep on his stomach for the next six months.'

Jazz grimaced and put her head in her hands. It felt

heavy. 'I didn't think it would take so well,' she said in a muffled voice.

'Face it, Jazz,' said Mo kindly but firmly. 'You don't realise how scary you can be sometimes.'

Jazz faced it. 'So what do I do? I've already apologised for being a bitch. If he doesn't want me, he doesn't want me. Fact. I'll just kill myself. It's the simplest thing for all.'

Somehow just saying that out loud made her feel better.

Mo sighed and put her hands on Jazz's burning cheeks.

'I have two things to ask you. One: will you be my Best Woman at my wedding? And Two: when you start going out with Harry Noble, will you still remember me?'

'You're getting married!' Jazz whispered, as though this was the first time she'd been told. 'I haven't even asked about the proposal. Tell me *everything*.'

Mo's face went all dreamy. 'It was wonderful,' she confided. 'He took me to lunch at the Pont de la Tour. And then afterwards, when we were standing by the Thames at dusk, he proposed.'

They both sighed together. 'And what was it like?' asked an enraptured Jazz.

'Well,' started Mo, 'for hors d'oeuvres, we had the most amazing—'

'Not the food, Mo, the proposal.'

'Oh.' Mo went all dreamy again. 'He got down on one knee – I had no idea he was going to—'

As Mo went on, Jazz maintained her smile, while marvelling that at the turn of the new millennium, intelligent, educated, responsible women still relied on men to decide when, where and how the most important decision of both of their lives was to be made.

'You'll have to help me diet for the big day,' said Mo,

when she'd finished her story. She wasn't smiling any more – she had come crashing back to reality.

'Bog off,' retorted Jazz. 'Why would I do that? I love you.'

'I mean it,' said Mo. 'I've put on loads of weight since I started going out with Gil.'

'I mean it too,' said Jazz equally sincerely. 'He doesn't know how lucky he is.' Then she added, as an afterthought, 'I'm so happy that you're happy, Mo.' It was the nearest she would ever be able to get to saying 'I'm happy you're marrying Gilbert.'

Mo looked at her and gave her a long, slow smile. 'Thanks, Jazz,' she said quietly. And then she returned to her diet stories. 'It's not so much a case of how much I eat,' she pondered – convinced, as all dieters are, that other people gave a flying fig-roll about their diet tales – 'but how short a time I do it in. If I only had more *time* to eat what I want to eat, I'd be fantastically slim.'

Fascinated though Jazz was by the conversation, she noticed Harry come over to the bar near where they stood and get himself a drink. Her palms started to sweat. Mo noticed too and without so much as a glance at Jazz, she rushed headlong on to the dance-floor. Jazz almost wished she hadn't gone. Almost.

Harry was standing just too far away for Jazz to be able to speak to him without moving, yet too near for her to pretend she hadn't seen him. He took long, slow gulps of his beer. Jazz watched his Adam's apple as he gulped. She'd never noticed before how masculine an Adam's apple was. She looked at it in the mirror behind the bar for a while and then realised he was watching her. She felt herself go crimson with embarrassment. She forced herself to smile at

269

him. He tried to smile back while still drinking and beer dribbled down the side of his mouth.

'Nice!' mouthed Jazz at him in the mirror. His shoulders started shaking with laughter and he wiped his face with his hand. He looked so much nicer when he smiled.

She picked a napkin off the counter and handed it to him. She was now standing next to him. 'Still a bit of work to do on the old hand-to-mouth co-ordination, eh?' she asked with a grin.

He laughed again. 'And I thought I'd just got that sorted,' he said, using the napkin.

He ran his hand through his hair and coughed. Jazz's insides tried valiantly to steady themselves. She just stood there, leaning against the bar, looking up at him. How long did she have before Bambi-legs appeared by his side? She'd better get her apologies out as fast as possible.

'Listen,' she started, 'I'm really sorry my family weren't very warm to you.'

'You can stop saying sorry any time now,' he said.

'No, I mean it. I must explain. You see, they have no idea how much they owe you. The only thing they know about you is that you once called me The Ugly Sister. Naturally, they feel protective.'

Harry looked at her blankly. 'When did I call you that?'

'At the audition.' She looked a bit sheepish. 'I was standing outside. I overheard you.'

Harry clapped his hand to his head. 'Jesus, no wonder you acted like I'd raped your mother.'

'Well, something like that, yes,' said Jazz, recoiling from the image. Had she been that bad? Was she really as terrifying as Mo had said? She'd had no idea. Perhaps Mo was right. Perhaps Mo should have the column instead of her. It was becoming more and more obvious to her that whereas she thought she knew everything about people, she did in fact know less than nothing.

Harry leant his elbow on the bar, turned to face her and tried not to make too much fuss of sitting down on the stool behind him. It lowered him enough to make their faces almost level. Smooth, thought Jazz, and started playing with the napkin that was now lying between them.

With a look of intense concentration, Harry started speaking.

'I'm sorry I called you an unknown hack,' he said very slowly. 'It was a stupid, insensitive, arrogant thing to say. Will you ever forgive me for being a prize dickhead?'

'Of the highest order,' completed Jazz.

'Of the highest order,' he repeated obediently.

'Well,' she said, heaving her shoulders. 'On one condition.'

'Hmm?' He tried not to smile. He failed.

'You forgive me for all the horrendous things I said to you that night.'

'I deserved every single one.'

'No, you didn't!'

'I did. You were absolutely right – I *was* an obnoxious prat. I deserved all of it. Although perhaps the shoving part was a bit hard. I still have a bruise.'

They grinned briefly at each other then both seemed suddenly fascinated by their footwear. Jazz was about to thank him for saving her career when he started talking.

'You see, even when I was a little boy, my parents were already famous. We'd get stopped in the street by people asking for their autographs,' he said gravely. 'You can't help but think you're superior, and in all honesty, my parents loved

271

the adoration they got and never taught me how to keep it in perspective. I suppose they never really got anything else out of acting – certainly not any money – so they saw it as their payment.' He sighed heavily and shook his head. 'Then at drama college, I was treated like a star in the making, by teachers *and* students, and that did my head in. And if that wasn't enough, the media then put me on a pedestal. By the time I got to Hollywood I didn't stand a chance.'

Jazz was nodding. It was a miracle he remembered how to talk to normal people at all.

He kept going.

'I'm not trying to make excuses – well, I suppose I am – look, all I'm trying to say is,' he paused and looked at her intently. 'I had totally lost my perspective. Until I met you.'

Jazz's body went hot. She stared at the napkin. It was white and square.

'And you taught me in no uncertain terms that I would have to *earn* your friendship. Jazz, this may sound big-headed, but I can honestly say that no one has done that for years. That's why I try to only mix with people I really know well, like Matt, my sister Carrie, and Jack. Anyone else I have always treated with downright suspicion and contempt. Which I'm bloody ashamed of now.'

'What about Sara?' said Jazz.

Harry grinned foolishly. 'Ah, Sara,' he nodded. 'Or Pin-prick as I call her.'

Jazz tried not to grin too widely. Life just got better and better.

'The fact is, you've given me back my faith in human nature,' he went on. 'I really enjoyed directing the play, once I started treating everyone as individuals and not just as hangers on. I came to realise that the more you treat people like equals, the *less* they expect of you, so you can be more fallible – and the more confident they are in themselves, so the more interesting they are. It's so simple really. And,' he gave her a minuscule bow with his head, 'it's all down to you.'

'And all because you called me ugly. Aren't I something?' Jazz smiled.

'No, it's not just because of that. It's because I was such a complete and utter idiot. And I'm truly sorry. You'll probably never know how sorry.'

'Oh, I think I will,' she said, thinking of how crap she'd been feeling for the past month. 'I've learned a lot recently, too,' she told him.

Harry looked at her keenly.

She gave out a long, loud sigh. 'I've spent my life judging everyone. That's a far worse crime than just ignoring them, as you did. You may not have liked people much but you didn't constantly criticise them, as I did. And what's more, I've learned that I'm very often wrong in my judgements, too.' She paused. 'I was wrong about you.'

Harry shook his head. 'No, there you were right. And it's entirely down to what you said to me that we're even having this conversation. What did you call me? "Repulsively arrogant and self-obsessed . . ."'

'Oh no, don't,' cringed Jazz. 'I'm so sorry.'

'Please don't be sorry,' he said, giving her an eloquent look. 'I'm not.'

They were both static, staring at each other, for what seemed like a couple of light years. OK, now this is getting embarrassing, thought Jazz.

Suddenly, a thought occurred to her. 'By the way,' she asked quickly, looking briefly away from him while inching nearer. 'How come Jack has suddenly decided that focus is one thing but George is quite another?'

Harry smiled. 'Well,' he inched closer. 'I – I sort of – reminded him that work is work but love is love,' he said. 'And I've never heard him talk about anyone the way he talks about George. She is definitely The One for him.'

Jazz just raised her eyebrows at him, amazed and rather concerned at how easily influenced Jack could be by Harry.

'We'll see,' she said simply, too scared to hope. 'We'll see.'

Jazz looked round the room as a slow track started. Jack and George were slow dancing, their eyes shut and dreamy smiles on their faces. Maddie was leading Mark confidently by the hand to their first slow dance together. William had cornered Watery Eyes. With one hand leaning against the wall at her back and the other casually on her waist, she was well and truly stuck. He was whispering in her ear and she looked like the cat who'd got the cream. Jazz watched with distaste. She didn't like the woman, but she certainly wouldn't wish *that* on her.

Not far from them, Mo was shouting at Gilbert and he was making a great show of surprise at her anger. Near the door, Josie and Michael were standing motionless, hugging each other. Michael's lips were touching the top of Josie's head and his arms were squeezing her tight. Her face was hidden in his chest, but from the movement of her body, Jazz could tell she was sobbing. And Jazz gasped and prodded Harry as she saw Matt shyly put his arm round a smiling Carrie.

'Excellent!' said Harry. He looked at Jazz with an enormous grin. One of his teeth had a tiny chip in it. 'He's been in love with her for years.'

Jazz raised her eyebrows. Of course he had. That's why she'd missed it.

They smiled happily at each other. They were so close now, she could feel his breath on her cheeks. The sentimental lyrics were beginning to get to her. Oh God, this was excruciating. What to do? What to do?

Jazz put her life in her hands. 'I lied to you actually,' she said quietly.

Harry looked at her questioningly.

'I – I don't prefer blonds.'

He smiled. Please please please, she thought, do something. Anything.

'Thank God for that,' he said, and looked at her seriously.

Tell me I'm beautiful, she thought. You think I'm beautiful.

He spoke so slowly that each word could have had a sentence spoken around it.

'I think you're . . .'

Jazz held her breath. *Beautiful. You think I'm beautiful.*

'. . . beautiful,' he whispered.

TADA! went Jazz's stomach. Open Sesame! went her heart.

She beamed and, unable to stop herself, she leaned over slowly and whispered in his ear: 'You can kiss me now.'

Harry laughed but didn't move away. 'I'm afraid I can't,' he whispered in hers.

Jazz's body locked. Oh God, why? I'm not beautiful enough? I'm not the right kind of beautiful? I'm *too* beautiful? Terror gripped her. I'm not as beautiful as Sara?

'Oh,' she said simply. 'OK.' She wanted to die.

Just before she started to move away, he whispered quickly, 'I'm too scared.' His cheek was now touching hers and his eyes were closed. The faint trembling sensation coming from his legs convinced her he wasn't lying. 'I've tried before, remember?'

Jazz smiled as she felt his soft, uneven breath on her neck.

'Well, we'll have to work at getting over that fear, won't we?' she whispered.

As she edged her body fractionally closer to him, he slowly moved his long legs apart so she could get nearer. His arms tentatively enveloped her as she softly kissed his perfect lips for the first time.

He was delicious.

Remember this feeling, she thought, as her body melted and her stomach fizzed. Remember this feeling. It doesn't get any better than this.

Chapter 28

'So when did you realise just how tasty I really was?' asked Jazz, stretching out, making herself comfortable.

Harry smiled at the memory and leant up on the pillow, his head resting in his hand. He put his other arm round her bare waist.

'I don't know,' he prevaricated.

'I do,' grinned Jazz. 'It was when I was so rude to you all the time. You like a challenge. Otherwise you wouldn't be such a stunningly successful actor.'

He looked into her eyes and kissed her gently on her forehead. She had never noticed that it was an erogenous zone before.

'It wasn't just because of that,' he said. 'It was also your – your . . .' He thought hard, picturing her at rehearsals. Her eyes, her smile, her strength, her vulnerability, her humour, her gravity, her passion, her indifference, her . . . her. Her.

'I think I realised just how tasty you were moments before I realised I was in love with you,' he said as calmly as he could. Could she tell he was trembling?

Jazz was too moved to ask when, exactly, that was. She'd

ask another time. She was too busy adding earlobe, neck, collarbone and shoulder to forehead in a new list she was compiling.

Harry had turned out to be a whizz at cooking. Which made up for his complete lack of ability at DIY. 'It's all right,' Jazz had said. 'We can get a man in.' But it meant that Sunday brunches were a gas.

'Do you need any help in the kitchen?' called Mark from the patio. Mark probably wouldn't have asked anyone else, but seeing as it was Harry Noble, he didn't mind. Kitchens were strictly out of bounds for him, usually. Luckily Maddie loved to cook. Anyway, Jack and Harry were enjoying themselves too much in there together to need any help.

'No thanks, just help yourself to wine,' shouted Harry back.

Maddie, George, Jazz, Mark, Carrie and Matt did as they were told, and enjoyed the last of the summer sun as it nudged behind the growing conifers.

It was perfect. It might have been even more perfect if Mo had been there, thought Jazz, but there was no way she was inviting Gilbert Valentine into their home. She saw less of Mo these days, especially now little Tarquin Valentine was on the scene, but she had finally realised that there had to be a price for happiness, and the loss of Mo was her price. And such a realisation had helped to make that loss more bearable.

Epilogue

The television was on.

'Ooh, look – it's whatsisname'
  'Kevin Atkinson'
  'he's brilliant. Have you ever worked with him?'
  'yup. He's a bit dull actually'
  'really?'
  'yeah. And he's got four children by four different women'
  'you're kidding'
  'and those are contact lenses'
  'bloody Nora. Who'd have guessed it? Kevin Blinking Atkinson.'
  'Kevin Blinking Atkinson'
  'You know everyone, don't you?'
  He smiled and kissed the head of the only person he thought worth knowing.
  'uhhuh'

Acknowledgements

Thank you, Mum and Dad, my meticulous copy-editors through life, for your constant, enthusiastic and totally biased support.

Thank you, Andrew, for being away on business so much that I had time to write a novel. And thank you for coming back, reading my work again and again, laughing at the right bits and making constructive criticism so sweetly that I didn't want to shoot you.

Thank you, Frances Quinn, for your practical and emotional support. It proved invaluable.

On a more general note, thank you, Claude Lum, for being a rock in my life through the hard times.

Without these people this book would not have been written. So if you don't like it, go to them.

The very best of Piatkus fiction is now available in paperback as well as hardcover. Piatkus paperbacks, where *every* book is special.